Builders of our Country II

This edition published 2025
by Living Book Press
Copyright © Living Book Press, 2025

ISBN: 978-1-76153-753-0 (hardcover)
         978-1-76153-764-6 (softcover)

First published in 1910.

All rights reserved. No part of this publication may be reproduced, stored in a
retrieval system, or transmitted in any other form or means – electronic, mechanical, photocopying, recording or otherwise, without the prior permission of the
copyright owner and the publisher or as provided by Australian law.

A catalogue record for this
book is available from the
National Library of Australia

Builders of Our Country II

by

Gertrude van Duyn Southworth

George Washington

Contents

I

Patrick Henry

"GOD SAVE THE KING!"

Quebec fell. The French and Indian War came to an end. And with its close came the last of French power in America. On that September day of 1759 it seemed as if the might of England were established in America forever, and "God save the King" was sung in every village and town of the loyal English colonies.

The long struggle was over. The victory was won. And now the colonists turned to the peaceful duties of home once more. Life was much the same as before the war, and yet in some respects there were marked differences.

To begin with, the English colonists no longer dreaded the French and their cruel Indian friends. Thanks to English courage and perseverance, that fear was gone.

Moreover, the courage and perseverance which had gained this great blessing had not all belonged to the King's red-coated troops. The colonists justly felt that they themselves had done much toward conquering the foe. They had left their homes and families, had made long hard journeys over unbroken lands, and had fought shoulder to shoulder with the English troops on many battlefields. Yes, surely the victory belonged as fully to them as to the King's regulars. Their pride was great.

Before the war each colony had stood alone. But now the settlers from the different colonies had met in a common cause, had fought a common foe, and had come to realize that they dwelt in a common country—one well worth fighting for.

And so, with their enemy beaten, their ability to fight established, and their love for their land increased, these loyal colonists sent up the heartfelt petition, "God save the King!"

Meanwhile, however, in 1760, the King of England, George II, died; and immediately his grandson was proclaimed King in his place. Just as the colonists were settling down to work, and starting to enlarge their already profitable trade, this new king, George III, took a step which threatened trouble for them.

About one hundred years before George III became king, England had passed certain "Navigation Acts." These Acts had declared that the English colonies in America must not carry on trade with any countries other than England and her possessions, must not ship their goods in any but English or colonial ships, and must not manufacture their own products into finished articles. But these laws had not been enforced; and so, in spite of their existence, the colonies had sent their goods to Spain, France, and the West Indies, and had used their lumber, iron, furs, and other products as they saw fit.

All this was now to be changed. George III proposed to put the old Navigation Acts into force and to insist that his American colonies obey them.

This meant nothing short of ruin to colonial commerce.

ARGUING AGAINST THE WRITS OF ASSISTANCE BEFORE THE KING'S COURT IN MASSACHUSETTS.

As the colonists had disobeyed the Navigation Act's for so long, without hindrance, there seemed no reason why they should obey them now. Hence they commenced to smuggle goods and to hide them in their houses.

The King was determined to stop the smuggling, so he issued "Writs of Assistance." These writs gave the King's colonial officers the right to enter any suspected house and search it. It was very easy for an officer who suspected a colonist unjustly to enter his house, and very unpleasant for an innocent colonist to have his house searched from top to bottom at the whim of an officer. Bitter feeling sprang up, and appeal after appeal was sent to the King—but all in vain.

King George had found that, with his throne, he had inherited enormous debts. One of them was the great cost of the French and Indian War. Moreover, he intended to keep

A COLONIAL STAMP.

British soldiers in America, to prevent the French from regaining what they had lost. This standing army would be a further expense. But why should not his prosperous American colonists be made to pay for a war that had been fought chiefly in their behalf? Why should they not also help to support a standing army sent for their protection?

The next question was how best to get some of the colonists' money into the English treasury. The King and his Parliament decided to do this by means of a stamp tax. Stamps of different kinds and values were to be issued and sent to America to be sold. Thereafter, in America, no business paper, such as an insurance agreement, a will, a note, or a deed, would be legal unless it were written on paper that bore one of these stamps—the stamp of right kind and value for that particular purpose. The stamps were to be so varied in their uses that they would cover nearly every line of business. Even each newspaper was to be stamped, so that the man who bought it would pay, not only for the thing itself, but for its stamp as well. All the money received from the sale of the stamps would go to the English Government.

To George III this seemed an excellent plan. Early in 1765 the Stamp Act, as it was called, was passed by Parliament. Word was sent to the American colonists that by November 1st of that same year they might look for their stamps; for on that day the Stamp Act would be put in force.

The First Breach

The news that the Stamp Act had been passed swept from end to end of the colonies. Everywhere men heard it with serious faces and asked each other what it meant. Never before had England tried to tax her American colonies without their consent. Were they to allow it now?

What worried the colonists was not that they must help pay England's war debt, although they had already fully paid their share; or that they were ordered to support in their midst an army of British soldiers, just when they had learned to defend themselves. The trouble was that they had not been consulted in these matters.

Virginia was the first to summon her House of Burgesses, as her legislative assembly was called, in an effort to find an answer to the grave question. Its members met at Williamsburg, on the 30th of May, 1760. The discussion began. All were opposed to the Stamp Act, but the remedies that they suggested for the evil were extremely mild. True Englishmen at heart were the Virginia burgesses, and the lifelong habit of obedience to their King prevented most of them from any thought of radical action. "Let us send the King a statement

PATRICK HENRY ADDRESSING THE HOUSE OF BURGESSES.

of our rights and petition him to consider them," said these conservative members.

For a moment no protest was raised. Then Patrick Henry rose slowly to his feet. All turned toward him wonderingly, and well they might. Only twenty-nine years old, roughly dressed, stoop-shouldered and awkward, surely this new member could have little to say on so great a subject. Quietly glancing from one to another of the dignified bewigged and beruffled older members, Henry began to speak. According to English law, he argued, King George, could place no tax on his subjects at home or abroad without the consent of those subjects or their representatives in Parliament. Had the American colonies been asked their opinion of this Stamp Act? No! Had they any representatives in England's Parliament to give consent to such a measure? No! Then clearly King George had no right to demand that his American colonists pay this tax or buy his stamps. And he, Patrick Henry, had written some resolutions which he respectfully requested the burgesses to hear.

These resolutions he read from the fly leaf of an old book on which he had just jotted them down. They were a clear and concise statement of the rights granted the Virginians by their charter—rights which belonged to each and every subject of the English King, wherever he dwelt in that King's domains. And, concluded the resolutions, His Majesty's liege people, the inhabitants of this colony, are not bound to obey any law which imposes a tax, unless that law is made by the Virginia House of Burgesses. Moreover, any person who denies this exclusive right to the House of Burgesses shows himself an enemy to the colony.

At once all was excitement. On every hand the conservative members were attacking this open defiance of the King—this declared intention to disobey his stamp law.

Again Patrick Henry rose to his feet. This time his head was high, his eyes flashed, and his wonderful voice thrilled every listener. In plain terms he now repeated his views of the Stamp Act, and the King and Parliament who had passed it. "Caesar had his Brutus," he cried, "Charles the First his Cromwell, and George the Third—"

"Treason! Treason!" rose on all sides.

"And George the Third may profit by their example. If this be treason, make the most of it," added Henry; and without another word he took his seat.

Now followed argument after argument for and against Patrick Henry's resolutions. And gradually, one by one, the members of the Virginia House of Burgesses began to see the situation with Henry's eyes.

Finally came the deciding vote. When it was counted,

it was found that Patrick Henry's resolutions, in a slightly modified form, had been adopted.

Henry, content with the result, threw his saddlebags over his arm and set off for home, leading his horse. He had made his fight and won. Compared with this, it mattered little to him that he had been charged with treason. And yet to be charged with treason was no small affair. Treason means an attempt to betray one's country, or one's king. It is still considered the greatest crime that a soldier or a citizen can commit; and in Patrick Henry's day its punishment was death.

Troublous times followed. Into the peaceful relations with England a breach had come. Wider and wider it grew. Still, as at the beginning, the conservatives were in favor of patching up the gap and holding to the mother country. Patrick Henry, on the other hand, felt that only galling chains could now tie the American colonies to England. Hear his words to the members of the House of Burgesses assembled in Richmond, when the crisis came in 1775:

"Gentlemen may cry 'Peace! Peace!' but there is no peace. The war is actually begun. The next gale that sweeps from the north will bring to our ears the clash of resounding arms. Our brethren are already in the field. What is it that gentlemen wish? What would they have? Is life so dear, or peace so sweet, as to be purchased at the price of chains and slavery? Forbid it, Almighty God! I know not what course others may take; but, as for me, give me liberty, or give me death!"

II

Samuel Adams

THE STAMP ACT

Virginia was the first colony to declare her opposition to the Stamp Act after it became a law. Patrick Henry's resolutions against it were printed and scattered broadcast throughout the country. Their sentiments were read with satisfaction from north to south. But nowhere did they find a stronger echo than in the hearts of the Massachusetts colonists.

Here, even before the Stamp Act had been passed, these stanch New Englanders had begun to voice their opinions of old England's doings. No sooner had the mere rumor that such a law might be passed reached America than Samuel Adams made known his views on the matter.

This Samuel Adams was a Harvard graduate, a thinker, a lover of his country. For several years he had served in one office after another, until now, at the age of forty-two, he had come to be as well versed in colonial needs and conditions as any man in Massachusetts.

There was not the slightest question in his mind regarding this proposed Stamp Act. Not only through the common rights of all Englishmen, but also by their charter, the Massachusetts colonists could claim a voice as to the taxes they were to pay. England could not tax her colonies without the consent of their representatives. The American colonies had no representatives in Parliament. Therefore there was but one conclusion: England had no right to pass this law.

So Samuel Adams believed, and so he stoutly declared. And others were so convinced that he was right that a protest based on his views was sent to England, stating how Massachusetts felt.

However, as we have seen, the King and his Parliament passed the Stamp Act and notified the American colonies that it would go into effect on November 1, 1765.

When that day dawned in America, the sun shone on a state of affairs which King George had not foreseen. Flags waved at half mast, shops were closed, and business was at a standstill. The colonists had agreed that, come what might, they would not buy the stamps. Already boxes of them had been seized, and burned or thrown into the sea. And already the men chosen to sell the hated stamps had been pointedly warned not to attempt to carry out their orders.

How was it all to turn out? Surely the time had come for stern measures; and, thanks to Samuel Adams, stern measures were adopted throughout the colonies.

Now it was that his non-importation plan was put into practice. This meant that the American colonists refused to buy goods from England as long as the Stamp Act remained a law. "We will eat nothing; drink nothing, wear nothing coming from England, until this detested law is repealed," they declared.

Such a course was hard on the English merchants. Their large orders from America were canceled, and their goods left on their hands. So they, too, pleaded against the Stamp Act.

Glorious News.

BOSTON, Friday 11 o'Clock, 16th *May* 1766.
THIS Inftant arrived here the Brig Harrifon, belonging
to *John Hancock*, Efq; Captain *Shubael Coffin*, in 6
Weeks and 2 Days from LONDON, with important
News, as follows.

From the LONDON GAZETTE.

Weftminfter, March 18th, 1766.

THIS day his Majefty came to the Houfe of Peers, and being in his royal
robes feated on the throne with the ufual folemnity, Sir Francis Moli-
neux, Gentleman Ufher of the Black Rod, was fent with a Meffage
from his Majefty to the Houfe of Commons, commanding their atten-
dance in the Houfe of Peers. The Commons being come thither accordingly,
his Majefty was pleafed to give his royal affent to

An ACT to REPEAL an Act made in the laft Seffion of Parliament, in-
tituled, an Act for granting and applying certain Stamp-Duties and other Duties
in the Britifh Colonies and Plantations in America, towards further defraying
the expences of defending, protecting and fecuring the fame, and for amending
fuch parts of the feveral Acts of Parliament relating to the trade and revenues
of the faid Colonies and Plantations, as direct the manner of determining and
recovering the penalties and forfeitures therein mentioned.

Alfo ten public bills, and feventeen private ones.

When the KING went to the Houfe of Peers to give the Royal Affent, there
was fuch a vaft Concourfe of People, huzzaing, clapping Hands, &c. that it
was feveral Hours before His Majefty reached the Houfe.

Immediately on His Majefty's Signing the Royal Affent to the Repeal of the
Stamp-Act, the Merchants trading to America difpatched a Veffel which had been
in waiting, to put into the firft Port on the Continent with the Account.

There were the greateft Rejoicings poffible in the City of London, by all Ranks
of People, on the TOTAL Repeal of the Stamp-Act,—the Ships in the River
difplayed all their Colours, Illuminations and Bonfires in many Parts.— In
fhort, the Rejoicings were as great as was ever known on any Occafion.

It is faid the Acts of Trade relating to America would be taken under Con-
fideration, and all Grievances removed. The Friends to America are very powerful, and difpofed to affift us to the utmoft of their Ability.

Capt. Blake failed the fame Day with Capt. Coffin, and Capt. Shand a Fort-
night before him, both bound to this Port.

It is impoffible to exprefs the Joy the Town is now in, on receiving the
above, great, glorious and important NEWS—The Bells in all the Churches
were immediately fet a Ringing, and we hear the Day for a general Rejoicing
will be the beginning of next Week.

PRINTED for the Benefit of the PUBLIC, by
Drapers, Edes & Gill, Green & Ruffell, and *Fleets.*
The Cuftomers to the Bofton Papers may have the above gratis at the refpective
Offices.

HANDBILL ANNOUNCING THE REPEAL OF THE STAMP ACT.

Even stubborn George III could see at last that a mistake had been made, and that he and his Parliament must give in to the colonists. But he would do it in his own way. The Stamp Act was repealed; but, with the repeal, word was sent to America that England declared her right to bind her colonies in all cases whatsoever.

The repeal was received with joy, while the declaration passed unnoticed. Once more flags floated free from the top of mast, tower, and steeple. Bonfires blazed, bells rang, and men shouted from sheer happiness.

But their joy was short-lived. The very next year they came to understand the meaning of England's declaration of her right to bind her colonies. Again the mother country tried to tax them. This time a duty was placed on glass, paper, paints, and tea.

Again the colonists refused to be taxed without their consent. And once more English merchant vessels were obliged to sail home with the same cargoes they had brought. The colonists would buy nothing from England. Bitter indeed was their opposition. Boston especially won the royal displeasure. Her citizens were so hostile to England's demands that the Massachusetts governor finally called for British troops to back him in the doing of his duty.

The Boston Massacre

One day in September, 1765, the troops arrived. There were two regiments. They landed with great pomp and marched to Boston Common. The Governor insisted upon their being quartered in the center of the town, for his better protection.

Naturally the colonists resented such treatment, but what could they do? There the soldiers were, and there they stayed.

To begin with, all went well. But gradually the soldiers grew tired of their quiet life in Boston, and gradually the Boston people came to hate the very sight of these men sent to force them to obedience.

At last the smoldering fire flamed up. It seems that one wintry night in March, 1770, a boy in the street yelled insults at a sentry on duty, until the redcoat, angry beyond control, struck the boy. Slight as was this offense, it was enough. A crowd gathered; the boy pointed out the sentry, and a rush was made at him.

THE BOSTON MASSACRE.

ADAMS BEFORE THE GOVERNOR.

"Help! Corporal of the Guard, help!" shouted the sentry. Immediately the guardhouse gate swung open, and an officer and eight soldiers joined the sentry. Forming themselves in line, the soldiers raised their loaded muskets ready to fire, if necessary.

"Fire if you dare, lobsters, bloody backs! Fire if you dare, cowards!" yelled the crowd.

And fire they did. No one knows whether the officer in charge really gave the signal, or whether his soldiers merely thought he did. The result was the same. A volley rent the air, and three men lay dead on the ice.

The town was wild. No longer should these redcoats be allowed in Boston!

Next day a great meeting was held. The people flocked from far and near. As usual Samuel Adams was there to guide the colonists and urge them to defend their rights. In stirring terms he spoke to them of the happenings of the night before—the Boston Massacre. When he had finished, he was appointed one of a committee to visit Acting-Governor Hutchinson and demand that the British troops be removed.

"I have no authority to remove the troops," replied Hutchinson. This was no answer to carry back to an aroused people. The committee was not satisfied. So it was suggested that one of the regiments might be sent away.

It had been agreed that the committee should report the result of their errand at three in the afternoon. By that time the meeting had grown so large that the building was packed and the crowd overflowed into the street. As the committee made its way through the people, Samuel Adams whispered to right and left, "Both regiments or none. Both regiments or none."

The hint was taken. On hearing the Governor's reply that one regiment should go, a shout of "Both or none!" resounded through the hall.

Back to the Governor went the committee. "If you have the power to remove one regiment, you have the power to remove both....The voice of ten thousand freemen demands that both regiments be forthwith removed. Their voice must be respected, their demands obeyed. Fail not then, at, your peril."

Thus spoke Samuel Adams. And, when in the gathering darkness, the committee for the last time returned to the meeting, they carried with them the Governor's word of honor that both regiments should leave Boston at once. And leave Boston they did.

The Boston Tea Party

Soon the colonists gained another short step in their struggle against oppression. King George agreed to take off the duty on glass, paper, and paints. The one little tax on tea, he positively would not remove; he would assert his right to levy duties. But a tax was a tax; and, were it small or large, the colonists would not pay it. Now the Boston Massacre concerned Massachusetts alone. But the tax on tea concerned the whole thirteen colonies. If they were to work together against this common evil, it followed that they must be kept in touch with one another.

To make this possible, Samuel Adams originated the idea of Committees of Correspondence. The plan was a good one. Soon each colony had appointed a committee whose business it was to send out to the twelve other colonies letters telling of the doings at home, so that every colony might know the exact condition of the whole country.

In 1773 word came that several ships laden with tea were headed for America. "We will not buy it," agreed the colonists everywhere. And they kept their word.

Late in November the first of the ships sent to Boston entered the harbor. The patriots insisted that the tea should not be landed, and placed a guard to watch the ship. The Governor insisted that it should be landed, and would not permit the ship's captain to sail out of the harbor. Thus the matter stood for nineteen days.

Now there was a law that if a ship lying in the harbor was not unloaded by its owner within twenty days, the Custom House officers had the right to unload the cargo. This must not happen. So on the ship's nineteenth day in port the citizens were called together to determine what was to be done. By this time two other tea ships had arrived. Once more Samuel Adams was on hand with a clearly thought-out course of action.

The owner of the first ship was called, and he agreed to clear the harbor if only the Governor would give him the necessary permit. "Then go and ask him for it," directed the crowd.

It was December weather, cold and bleak; nevertheless the poor distressed merchant was obliged to make his way to Milton Hill where stood the Governor's country house.

The short winter day was over when he returned, but the patriots were still waiting, crowded in the gloomy meeting house, which was lighted by only a candle here and there.

THE "BOSTON TEA PARTY".

"What news?" was anxiously asked, as the ship owner entered.

"The Governor refuses to give a pass," came the answer.

"This meeting can do nothing more to save the country," said Samuel Adams, rising.

These words were a signal given by the recognized leader. As if by magic, an Indian war whoop rent the air; and a band of men dressed as Indian warriors, in paint and feathers, appeared at the door for a moment. Then away they went.

With a mighty cheer the crowd followed at their heels. Down the street they dashed, headed for the tea ships. Once on board it was quick work to rip open three hundred and forty-two chests of tea and pour their contents into the sea. Their task finished, the Indians disappeared. But as they went, on many of their faces the watching crowd recognized the familiar smile of old friends.

From the days of the first rumor of the Stamp Act to this December night,—nine anxious years,—Samuel Adams had led the people of Massachusetts. Always upholding colonial rights; always ready with helpful suggestions; always alive to the best interests, not only of his colony, but of the whole country, he richly deserved his title of "The Father of the Revolution."

Lexington and Concord

When King George heard of the Boston Tea Party his anger knew no bounds. This rebellious colony should be punished, and that right soundly.

The Boston port was closed to all trade until the destroyed tea should be paid for. And General Gage, with several regiments, was sent to govern the people of Massachusetts.

"We are outraged," declared the colonists. "Such things are not to be endured."

So they organized a new government quite independent of General Gage, with John Hancock and Samuel Adams at its head.

Nor was this all. Massachusetts decided to have an army of her own to defend her rights. "Minute men," the soldiers were called, because they agreed to be ready to fight at a minute's notice. Arms and ammunition were collected, and stored in Concord.

Before long, news of this hiding place reached General Gage. He determined to send a secret expedition to take

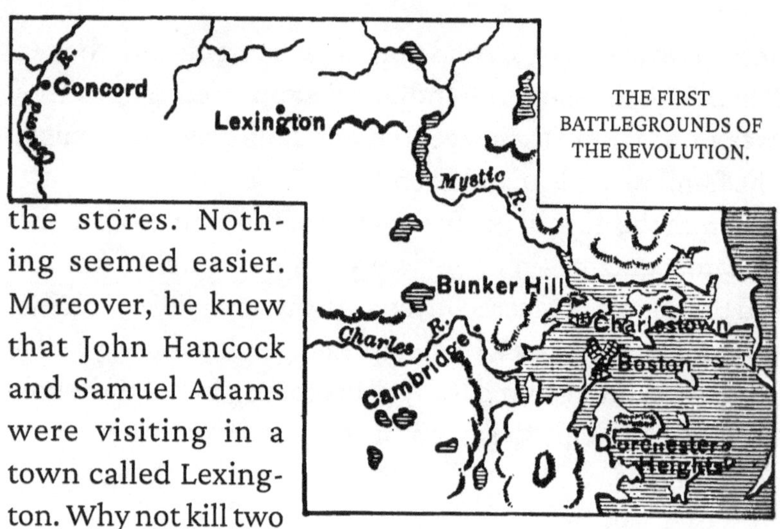

the stores. Nothing seemed easier. Moreover, he knew that John Hancock and Samuel Adams were visiting in a town called Lexington. Why not kill two birds with one stone and direct his soldiers to march to Concord by way of Lexington? Thus they could seize not only the soldiers' arms, but also their rebel leaders.

The plan seemed perfect. So at dead of night on April 18, 1775, General Gage ordered nearly eight hundred redcoats to slip quietly out of Boston and march through the darkness to Lexington. The start was made.

However, there was one thing General Gage did not count upon. He did not know that Paul Revere had already suspected this move, and had stationed a comrade in the steeple of the old North Church to signal the advance of the British. He did not know that Paul Revere himself was even now waiting, bridle in hand, for that signal to tell him to carry a warning to Lexington.

Suddenly two lights flashed out from the old North steeple. In an instant Paul Revere was in the saddle and away. His was a wild night ride. As his horse's hoofs clattered sharply in the stillness, men threw open their windows and

THE BATTLE ON THE VILLAGE GREEN OF LEXINGTON.

were greeted with the cry, "To arms! To arms! The regulars are coming!"

On went the daring rider, until, reaching the house in Lexington, where Hancock and Adams were staying, he warned them of their danger and led them to safety.

Just before daybreak of the 19th the redcoats appeared in Lexington and marched to the village green. Here they found themselves face to face with a band of minute men.

"Disperse, ye rebels!" shouted the British commander.

"Stand your ground!" urged the patriot leader. No one moved.

Then in answer to their commander's order the regulars opened fire. Seven Americans fell. It would have been folly for the handful of minute men to have engaged in battle with so many regulars; so, firing an answering volley, they retreated.

Then on to Concord marched the King's troops. Here too

they came too late. The patriots had already carried off most of their military stores. Two cannon had been left behind. These the British spiked.

By this time four hundred minute men had gathered and were marching against the regulars. At Concord Bridge the two forces met. And here it was that the Americans "fired the shot heard round the world."

Several redcoats fell, and soon the British soldiers gave up the bridge and began to march toward Boston.

But what a march! True to their name the minute men from all about had hurried to their duty. And from behind each wall and tree crouching figures now fired upon the retreating regulars.

All the way the minute men were at their heels "They fairly seemed to drop from the clouds."

To go on was desperate. To stop was certain death. So, weak with hunger and thirst, the King's boasted troops pushed on through the six miles between Concord and Lexington, under an almost constant fire. Nearly three hundred English soldiers fell dead or dying on the road. At Lexington reinforcements joined them; and after a short rest, they went on to Boston.

Bunker Hill

It was certain now that war had begun, and the Americans went into it heart and soul. Collecting a goodly army, they formed a semicircle surrounding Boston on its land side and laid siege to the town.

There was a hill overlooking Boston known as Bunker Hill, and in June the Americans decided to fortify it. One night a detachment made its way up the side of the hill,

THE LAST DEFENSE BEHIND
THE BREASTWORKS
OF BUNKER HILL.

and, working with a will, had dug trenches and thrown up breastworks by daybreak.

With the daylight, the finished fortifications dawned on General Gage's astonished sight. This would never do! From Bunker Hill the Americans could fire into his very camp. His only course was to drive them away at once.

That same day he sent a force of three thousand soldiers against Bunker Hill. Up the hill they marched. Fifteen hundred Americans waited in the trenches. Their supply of powder was pitifully small, but their courage was of the finest. "Don't fire till you see the whites of their eyes," ordered the colonial officer in charge.

On came the British troops, firing as they came. All at once a volley thundered from the breastworks. The front rank fell. There was a second's pause, and then the regulars retreated.

Rallying their men, the British officers urged them to a second attack. The result was the same. Waiting until they came within thirty yards, the Americans again fired a deadly charge; and again the English troops fell back.

But now the Americans' powder was spent. So when a third time the enemy advanced, there was no volley to check them. Still fighting, however—although clubs, the butt ends of their muskets, and stones were their only weapons--the Americans were at last driven from their fortifications.

The battle of Bunker Hill resulted in victory for the English and defeat for the Americans. The effect, however, was just what might have been expected had the reverse been true. England judged General Gage at fault in his methods and recalled him in disgrace. To the colonists one point stood out clear and bright above all others. Their colonial army had twice forced British regulars to retreat. What had been done could be done again. And so with renewed courage and stronger faith in their final victory, the whole country now bent every nerve toward defending their rights—the rights of the thirteen American colonies.

III

George Washington
Before the Revolution

HIS BOYHOOD

Among the builders of our country one man looms up above them all. Thousands have risked their lives in America's battles. Hundreds have given the best of their energy to the building of America's institutions, and many have served as her chief executive. But none of these have needed the steadfast faith and courage to hold together a few crude colonists against a king's disciplined army. None of these have faced the problem of forming a nation out of thirteen impoverished colonies, at the close of a long war. At the very head of America's great men stands George Washington, the father of his country, "first in war, first in peace," and always "first in the hearts of his countrymen."

George Washington was born in Westmoreland County, Virginia, on February 22, 1732. While he was still a little fellow his father, Augustine Washington, moved to a plantation near Fredericksburg. Here the family lived in a frame house with an immense chimney at either end. There were four rooms on the first floor, and above was an attic under the steep sloping roof.

One day during the summer of 1739 all was excitement in the frame house. "Lawrence is coming! Lawrence is coming!" shouted the boys, while their mother completed the last details of the homecoming she had long ago planned for her stepson. Lawrence and his brother Augustine had been in England, being educated; and now Lawrence was coming home to live.

There was no need to go far to meet him. In those days each large river plantation had its private wharf. Slowly the ship sailed up the Rappahannock to Augustine Washington's landing, and Lawrence was home.

And now life had many new interests for George. Lawrence, like all colonial men, was a good shot and a fine horseman, and loved hunting, horse racing, and sports of all kinds. In this older brother George saw what he himself wanted to become; and in George, Lawrence found a straightforward, honest, earnest boy. So, in spite of the fourteen years difference in age, the two became fast friends.

Lawrence had been back barely a year when war broke out between England and Spain, and Lawrence Washington set out to serve under Admiral Vernon.

Soon came reports of the regiment's bravery, which gave George an added pride in his elder brother, and raised in his heart a great and lasting love for a military life. And George too became a soldier.

Mr. Hobby's schoolhouse stood out in a field, and there George was commander-in-chief. With school out and work done, drills, parades, and battles became the order of the day. Although the young commander was quick-tempered

MOUNT VERNON A CENTURY AGO.

and determined, he was generous and willing to play fair; and his companions loyally charged numberless walls and fought countless battles under his command.

In the autumn of 1742 Lawrence came home again; but it is doubtful if George saw quite as much of him as before the war, for the elder brother soon fell in love with Anne Fairfax, and became engaged to her.

The next spring George's father died suddenly. To Lawrence he left his estate on the Potomac, which Lawrence called Mount Vernon in honor of the Admiral under whom he had served. To the second son, Augustine, he gave his old estate on Bridges Creek in Westmoreland County. George was to have the house and lands on the Rappahannock, when he became of age. The other children were all provided for, and they and George were left under the guardianship of their mother.

In July Lawrence Washington and Anne Fairfax were married and went to live at Mount Vernon. Augustine, too, left the family home to take charge of his property on Bridges Creek.

There was no question as to the course these two were to follow. With George it was different. He had learned about all that his old schoolmaster, Mr. Hobby, could teach; and that was little enough. There was no other school near his home, and it was impossible to send him to England as the elder brothers had been sent.

A HOUSE SLAVE OF WASHINGTON'S DAY.

A good school for those days was kept by a Mr. Williams not far from Augustine's home, and at length it was settled that George should live with Augustine and go to this school.

From the accounts of his life at Bridges Creek it is hard to decide whether he worked or played with greater diligence. His copy books still exist, all done with such neatness and care that it would seem as if they could have left no time for play. On the other hand he entered into so many sports, practicing each so thoroughly, that it would seem as if there could have been little time for study. In running he had no equal. Not a boy in the school could throw as he could, and with wrestling it was the same story.

While her son was away at school Mrs. Washington did

not fail to keep in touch with him; and she arranged to have him at home whenever that was possible.

Here, thanks to her untiring efforts, affairs went on much as before her husband's death. She attended to every detail. She was stern and quick-tempered; and when she drove her open gig to any part of the plantation and found that the slaves had failed to carry out her directions to the letter, they had good cause to fear.

She was devoted to her children, but even they stood in awe of her and gave her unquestioning obedience.

There is a tale which shows that, while demanding much, she was just and willing to forgive. Early one vacation morning George and some companions were looking over his mother's splendid Virginia horses. Among them was a sorrel which especially pleased Mrs. Washington. George told how no one had ever been able to ride this horse, so fierce and ungovernable he was. And then because George was young and strong and looking for adventure, he impulsively proposed that if his friends would help him bridle the horse he would ride him. Of course they were ready to help, and somehow the bridle was put on. George sprang to the horse's back. Away they went. The horse reared and plunged. The other boys fairly held their breath expecting each moment to see George thrown. Still he held on. Finally the wild furious animal gave one mighty leap into the air, burst a blood vessel, and fell dead. Just then came the call to breakfast, and the frightened boys walked toward the house asking each other, "What shall we do? Who will tell what we have done?"

As luck would have it, at the table Mrs. Washington asked,

"Have you seen my horses this morning? I am told my favorite is in excellent condition."

The boys exchanged a glance, and then George said, "Your favorite, the sorrel, is dead, madam," and went on to tell the whole story.

First an angry flush came to Mrs. Washington's face; but when George had finished she proudly raised her head and said to her guests, "It is well. While I regret the loss of my favorite horse, I rejoice in my son who speaks the truth."

When George was fourteen he took up the study of surveying, as that seemed to give the best promise for the future. By way of practice, he surveyed the fields around the schoolhouse and on the neighboring plantations, making exact and careful calculations, all of which he neatly put down in notebooks.

In the autumn of 1747, when he was under sixteen years of age, Washington's schooling came to an end, and he went to Mount Vernon to live with Lawrence.

The Surveyor

Lord Fairfax, a relative of Mrs. Lawrence Washington, owned large tracts of land in the beautiful valley of the Shenandoah. All this land had to be surveyed, and to his young friend George Washington, Lord Fairfax gave the work. Of course Washington was delighted with the opportunity; and in March, 1748, when he was sixteen years old, he set out on horseback with a small company of assistants.

A hard month was before him. The rivers were so swollen from the spring thaws that fords were out of the question, and it was necessary to swim the horses across the ugly streams. The weather was cold. Fires were not always to

LORD FAIRFAX ON HIS VIRGINIA ESTATE.

be had. Food was none too plentiful. What there was each man must cook for himself on forked sticks over the fire. Chips were the only plates. Nights in a tent, or more often on the ground, were varied by an occasional night in a settler's cabin.

Such incidents with long hard tramps and constant work made up the story of Washington's first surveying trip. In April he reached Mount Vernon and laid the result of his work before Lord Fairfax. Lord Fairfax went over the carefully prepared maps and was so delighted that he used his influence to have Washington appointed Public Surveyor for Culpeper County. This appointment gave authority to his work, and how well it was deserved may be seen from the fact that his surveys are unquestioned to this day.

Now anxious times came to Mount Vernon. Lawrence became ill with consumption; and in July, 1752, this much loved brother died. When his will was read it was found that he had appointed George guardian of his little daughter, and heir to his estates in case the child herself should not live. And so it was that on her death, not long after, Mount Vernon became the property of George Washington.

Governor Dinwiddie's Messenger

In the early days when the English settlers were founding colonies along the Atlantic, the French were doing the same along the St. Lawrence River. Gradually, as the colonies grew, the settlers turned their attention to the great lands that lay beyond what they had already seen.

This was true especially of the French. First, missionaries worked their way along the northern border of New York, floated in canoes on the Great Lakes and even down the Mississippi River. And later, French explorers followed the missionaries and established forts here and there, as they went along.

The English, too, were attracted by the wild western

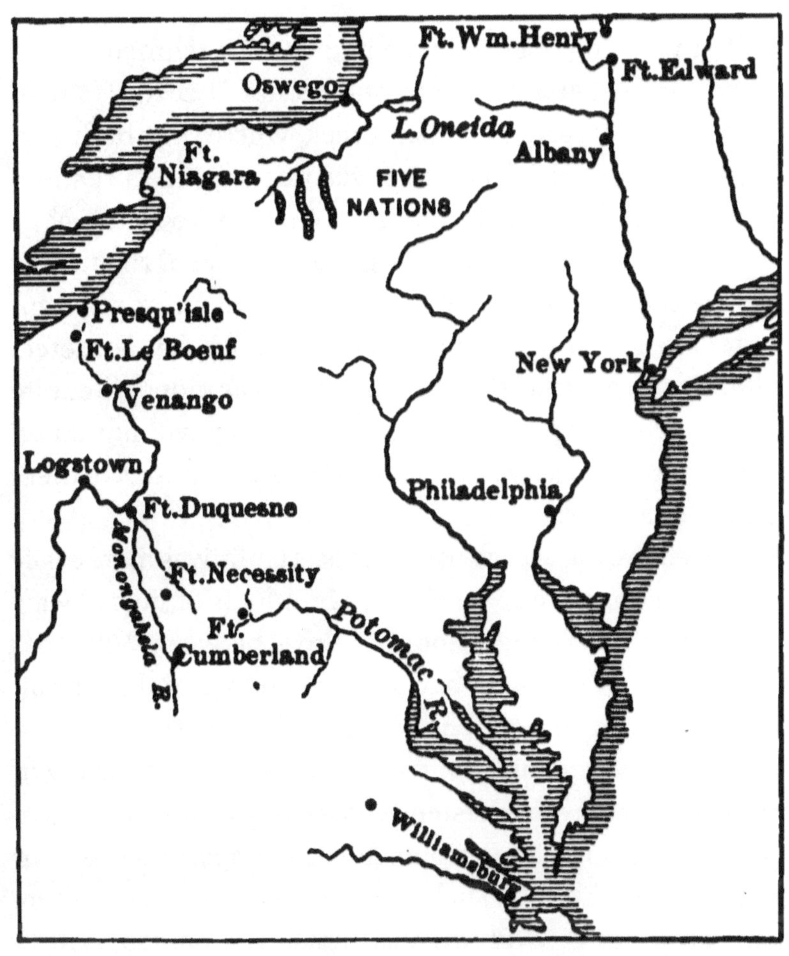

THE FRENCH AND ENGLISH FORTS OF THE WESTERN FRONTIER.

lands and sent fur traders to barter with the Indians there. Both France and England claimed the land.

Rich in game, fertile, covered with fine forests, the beautiful Ohio country seemed especially desirable. So, while the English formed what was known as the Ohio Company, and laid plans for sending out colonists to take possession of the disputed district, the French built forts and stirred up the Indians to attack English settlements.

In the spring of 1753 fifteen hundred Frenchmen landed at Presqu'isle, erected a fort, and set about cutting a road through the forests to French Creek, where they built Fort LeBoeuf. News of this move was not long in spreading throughout the English colonies. What was to be done?

Governor Dinwiddie of Virginia was one of the first to realize the seriousness of the question. He promptly sent letters to England, telling of the danger. England ordered, "Build forts near the Ohio if you can get the money. Require the French to depart peacefully; and if they will not do so, we do hereby strictly charge and demand you to drive them off by force of arms."

To require the French to depart peacefully was more easily said than done. The French were hundreds of miles away; many high and rugged mountains rose between Williamsburg, Virginia's capital, and the French fort; and over half the journey lay through the unbroken forests. The man who should carry England's message must know something of the country, must understand Indian ways, must be used to hardships. He must be strong, full of courage, and ready for whatever might arise. Such a man was George Washington. And Governor Dinwiddie chose him as his messenger.

It was the middle of November when the twenty-one-year-old leader and his party got away from Will's Creek—the end of civilization. Tramping through the forests amid blinding snowstorms, crossing raging creeks, always on the outlook for Indian treachery, slowly they worked their way toward the French fort. On December 4th they came to Venango, a French outpost, and at dusk on the 11th reached Fort LeBoeuf. Early the next morning, Washington presented Governor Dinwiddie's letter to the French commander.

For three days the Commander and his officers discussed the answer which was to be sent to the English Governor. Meanwhile Washington looked over the fort, drew its plan, and learned all he could regarding its strength and the number of soldiers detailed to guard it.

The days of waiting were anxious ones. The snow was falling faster and faster. Finally Washington and his companions got away from the fort, homeward bound.

On the journey home, the party encountered new difficulties. They had canoes that they had borrowed from the French; but in many places the creeks were so low that the men were obliged to get out of the boats and, wading in the icy waters, haul them over the shoals. After nearly a week of such traveling they came to the French outpost. Here Washington proposed to Christopher Gist, one of his men, that they leave the rest of the party and make for Will's Creek on foot; and so it was decided.

They walked eighteen miles the first day. The cold was dreadful. All the streams were so frozen that it was almost impossible to find water to drink. By night Washington was nearly exhausted. The next day they met an Indian who seemed so friendly that Washington asked him to guide them through that part of the forest. For ten miles all went well. Then, as they came to an open space, suddenly the guide, who was only fifteen paces anead, turned and fired.

"Are you shot?" shouted Washington.

"No," answered Gist.

Together they rushed on the Indian before he could reload. Gist wished to kill him, but Washington would not listen to that. "If you will not have him killed, we must get away and then travel all night," urged Gist in low tones. "He will

GIST PULLING WASHINGTON FROM THE FROZEN STREAM.

surely follow our tracks as soon as it is light, and we must have a good start."

So, pretending that they thought the Indian's shot an accident, the two men let him go; and, when sure he was out of hearing, they crept away in the opposite direction. All that night and all the next day they hurried on, with no sleep and with sore and bleeding feet.

At last they came to a place where some Indians had been hunting. Mixing their tracks with those of the savages they separated for a time, in order that their bloodthirsty guide, if he followed them to this point, could find no two trails going on together. When they met again some distance farther on, they felt for the first time that it was safe to sleep.

They had now reached the Allegheny River, which was full of floating ice. A whole day was spent in building a raft on which to cross. They pushed off. The current was very swift, and before the raft was half way across the river it was being jammed on every side by cakes of ice. Every moment they expected that it would be forced under, and that they would perish. Struggling to keep a clear space for the raft with a long pole, Washington was all at once jerked into the water. It was by the merest chance that he was able to catch hold of one of the logs and so pull himself back on the raft.

There seemed no hope of reaching either shore now; so when the current carried them near an island, both Washington and Gist jumped into the freezing water and swam for the land. Gist had all his fingers and some of his toes frozen. By morning the ice in the river was solid, and it was comparatively easy to reach the mainland.

A few days later Washington arrived at Williamsburg and gave to Governor Dinwiddie the letter that he had carried so carefully on his long and dangerous journey.

As usual, Washington had kept a journal of the trip; and this, too, he gave to the Governor, thinking it the simplest way to report all the events of his travels. So straightforward was the journal and so clearly did it set forth the exact conditions on the Ohio, leaving out all complaint of hardship, that Governor Dinwiddie ordered a copy of it sent to each of the colonial governors.

Washington found himself the hero of the hour. Not yet twenty-two, he had faced a great responsibility and had done well all that he had been asked to do. But still, far from being proud and self-satisfied, when he was told that his journal was to be published he modestly wrote in it, "I think I can do no less than apologize for the numberless imperfections of it."

Great Meadows and Fort Necessity

That the French would not depart from the Ohio for the asking, was plainly shown by the French commander's reply to Governor Dinwiddie's letter. Then they must be driven away by force. Governor Dinwiddie determined that Virginia should do her full share, and ordered the enlistment of men at Alexandria. In February, 1754, he sent out a company to build a fort on a site chosen by Washington, where the Allegheny and Monongahela rivers join.

On the 2nd of April Washington set out with a small force to garrison the fort that was being built. Before long discouraging reports reached him. Five hundred French-men had landed and demanded the builders of the fort to surrender. They had surrendered, and their victors were even now building Fort Duquesne on the very site chosen by the English.

Here was a gloomy outlook for Washington. However, it was decided to push on. When the little army had covered about half the distance, an Indian came to Washington bearing word that the French army was coming.

Washington had been expecting as much; so, hurrying

ATTACKING THE FRENCH HIDING PLACE.

his soldiers forward to a place called Great Meadows, he had the bushes cleared away and trenches dug. But no enemy appeared. A few nights later another Indian messenger reported that his chief was in camp six miles off and felt sure that the French were hiding near him.

Prompt to act, Washington took forty of his men and joined the Indians. Scouts tracked the French to a hollow surrounded by rocks and trees; and in single file Washington, his men, and the Indian warriors crept to the French hiding place, and surrounded it. While Washington was moving through the trees, he was seen by the French. They sprang to their arms. In a moment both sides were firing. For fifteen minutes the fighting lasted, and then the French gave up.

This little skirmish proved of much greater importance than could have been foreseen. In it was shed the first blood of the French and Indian War. Moreover, the attack of the English added to the French determination to drive the English away from the Ohio. Washington appreciated the situation; and when he got back to Great Meadows, he began the work of strengthening Fort Necessity, as the encampment was now called.

On the morning of the 3rd of July, the French appeared before the fort, and a battle began. All day it lasted. At eight that night the French asked for a parley, which was granted.

The French proposed that, on condition that the English would surrender, the whole garrison might go back to Virginia. But for a year they must not attempt to build any more forts this side of the mountains.

With almost no provisions, with their powder about gone, with more than fifty of their men dead or wounded, while the French might be reinforced at any moment, Washington and his officers could see no course but to accept the conditions. So in the morning the fort was deserted, and the weary, half-starved soldiers started slowly home. On the way Washington shared their hardships and encouraged them by his cheerful and uncomplaining endurance. And all the time his heart was heavy. He was young; he had set out to win and was going back defeated.

At Williamsburg he reported to Governor Dinwiddie, and then went to Alexandria to recruit new companies to lead against the French.

But England had now decreed that any officer holding a commission from the King should outrank any officer holding a colonial commission. To have commanded an expedition, and then to be outranked by any upstart officer from England, was more than Washington's pride could bear. He therefore resigned from the service.

BRADDOCK'S CAMPAIGN

By his little skirmish with the French in the wilderness hollow, Washington had started a war which was to spread beyond the colonies and become of grave concern abroad.

France sent eighteen war vessels filled with French soldiers to Quebec. And England, not to be outdone, likewise sent troops to her colonies here. Two regiments were assigned to Virginia; and early in 1755 the British ships sailed by Mount Vernon to put the soldiers ashore at Alexandria, only eight miles away.

Whether in the army or out, Washington could not withhold a lively interest in the redcoats. Many an early morning found him on horseback headed for the English camp, hoping to learn from the trained soldiers much that would help him, if ever he had the good fortune to reenter the service of his country.

Knowing of course who he was and his story, the British

officers watched the young Virginian as he went about their camp. He was six feet two inches tall, broad-shouldered, straight as an Indian; and he walked with a strong, swinging gait. His dignified bearing, and his way of looking each man in the face, could not fail to win friends. Soon General Braddock, the English commander, noticed Washington, learned of his desire to serve and the sole reason he was not on duty, and offered him a position on his staff.

Exciting times followed. It was easy to see that the strength of the French lay in their splendid line of forts. Troops, ammunition, and food could be hurriedly sent from one to another. To defeat the French, this line must be broken. Therefore it was agreed that one force should be sent to take the post at Niagara; that one should march against Crown Point, and a third against Acadia; and that General Braddock himself should take Fort Duquesne.

General Braddock was brave, resolute, and energetic. But his bravery was of the sort that made him despise his enemy; and his energy led him to underestimate the task before him. He knew nothing of the Indian way of fighting; nothing of the hardships of the wilderness. He was extreme in his British contempt for colonists.

By the middle of May, General Braddock's troops had arrived at Will's Creek; and on the 10th of June, 1755, the great procession headed for Fort Duquesne.

The 9th of July was chosen for the attack on the French fort, and at sunrise that morning the army was on the move. What a sight it was! With drums beating, fifes playing, flags flying, bayonets flashing in the sun, and redcoats showing bright against the forest green, the army marched to victory. All was in perfect order. Riding with the General's

BRADDOCK'S MARCH.

staff, Washington was thrilled and delighted. Finally the last ford was made, and now Fort Duquesne was only eight miles away.

"Forward! March!" ordered the officers, and the soldiers went briskly along the road that led through the forest to the fort.

Suddenly a French officer was seen rushing down the road, while behind him came swarms of French and Indians. At a signal, they darted into the woods, hid themselves among the trees and in the thickets, and with blood-curdling yells began pouring a deadly fire into the English lines.

"Scatter your men as they have done," Washington, begged the General. But that was not the English way of fighting. The soldiers must stand in ranks to fire. The fearful yells and the smoke from the enemies' rifles were all that told them where to aim.

The officers did everything in their power to keep order and encourage the men. But soldier after soldier fell, picked off by the shots of the hidden foe.

From time to time a savage in war paint and feathers leaped from behind a tree to scalp a victim or seize a horse whose rider had been killed. And he in turn was killed by the sure aim of some Virginian, firing from the shelter of the trees. For the despised Virginians knew the fashion of savage warfare, and, like the French and Indians, had scattered through the forest. By keeping their senses and fighting, every man for himself, they did much to protect the redcoats huddled in the open roadway.

The English troops were fast becoming panic-stricken. All orders were unnoticed. They shot at random. No foe was to be seen, and yet the constant firing from the thickets increased.

Washington was everywhere. With flashing eyes and determined face, he galloped back and forth in the thickest of the fight, repeating the General's orders and shouting to the men to keep up their courage. His horse was shot under him. In a moment he leaped on another. Soon this, too, went down. Four bullets tore through his coat, and still he rushed on unwounded.

At last General Braddock was shot, and fell from his horse. The troops broke and ran wildly. On, on they tore, leaving Washington and a few officers and provincials the task of carrying off the dying General. The defeated army returned to Virginia.

SECOND ATTACK ON FORT DUQUESNE

The next three years Washington spent in protecting the Virginian frontier from Indian raids. He had been offered the command of Virginia's troops, and had gladly accepted.

In the fall of 1758 Washington's troops joined in another attack on Fort Duquesne. But the reception at the fort was very unlike the one given General Braddock. Scouts had reported to the French commander the English approach. Winter was coming on, and the French line of forts had been broken in the North. There was no hope of reinforcement or supplies from that direction. The whole garrison at the fort was not over five hundred. To wait for the English would mean certain surrender. So, when the British troops were within a day's march, the French commander blew up his magazine, burned the fort, and retreated with his men.

Imagine the astonishment of the English. A stout defense and a brisk battle was what they had expected, not an empty fort. On the 25th of November, Washington and the advance guard marched in and raised the British flag over the smoking ruins of Fort Duquesne.

Now, finally, the Ohio country was secured to the English. And no longer responsible for the safety of the Virginia frontier, Colonel Washington could honorably resign his commission.

The war was not yet ended. Fighting continued in the North. It was not until September of the next year that Quebec—the last great stronghold of the French—fell, and not until 1763 that the treaty was signed which put an end to French power in America.

IV

George Washington, Commander and President

LIFE IN VIRGINIA

Just back from the road in New Kent County, Virginia, stood the little church of St. Peter. It was the 6th of January, 1759,

MARTHA CUSTIS, WASHINGTON'S BRIDE.

and the usual quiet of the countryside was broken. One after another great colonial coaches rumbled along the road and stopped before the church to set down the colonial dames in their richest London gowns. British officers in scarlet and provincial officers in buff and blue rode up, dismounted, and went into the little church. Planters from far and near, and even the new Governor himself, came to do honor to Colonel Washington and Martha Custis on their wedding day.

Washington took his wife to Mount Vernon. To the best of his knowledge, his military duties were at an end and before him stretched only peaceful years of plantation life. These years held no prospect of idleness, however; for, with Mrs. Washington's lands added to his own, Washington was now one of the wealthiest men in Virginia, and it would be no small matter to manage so great a property.

Each morning he got up early. After breakfast he rode out to inspect the work that was going on; and it was no unusual sight to see him throw off his coat and go to work with the laborers, putting up a fence or some sort of building on the new lands he was continually buying.

By a little after nine at night all were in bed, and the house was still. On Sundays, regularly, a ride of seven miles brought the family to church, excepting when the weather was unendurable or the roads impassable.

The Virginia plantations were too far apart for neighbors to make formal calls. When a planter wanted to see a friend he went to his home, often taking with him his entire family, and stayed a week if he liked. The many friends who came to Mount Vernon always received a cordial welcome.

Fishing in the summer months, card playing in the winter, and hunting all the year round were the favorite amusements for the gentlemen of the countryside. Deer stalking and duck shooting were good sport, but not to be compared with a ride to hounds.

The ladies of the party entertained themselves with drives, walks in the garden, and knitting.

Late on summer afternoons tea was served to all on the

broad veranda. At the usual early hour the party broke up for the night. Candles were lighted, and the guests went upstairs to stow themselves away in the great canopied four-post bedsteads. Some of these were so high that to get into them one had to climb the little carpeted steps kept for the purpose.

Such was the home life of George Washington during the years that saw the Stamp Act passed and repealed; the duties on glass, paper, and paints imposed and removed; and the trouble over the tea tax, which resulted in the Boston Tea Party.

When, in 1774, England planned to punish Boston by closing her port, it was the Virginia House of Burgesses which proposed that a congress of all the colonies be called to consider the plight of Massachusetts and the best course open to her sister colonies.

While serving as a member of the House of Burgesses, Washington was chosen one of Virginia's representatives to this congress, which was to be known as the First Continental Congress. It met at Philadelphia on the 5th of September, 1774.

Before the colonial delegates left Philadelphia, they agreed to meet again the following spring if their petition to the King and their declaration of rights were still unheeded. Both petition and declaration were ignored; so in May, 1775, the Second Continental Congress was held.

By the time the members reached Philadelphia, word of Lexington and Concord had thundered throughout the land. The effect was remarkable. Fighting with the mother country had actually begun. Was there then no other way for the colonies to maintain their rights than by taking up

READING NEWS OF THE BATTLE OF LEXINGTON.

arms in defense? It began to look so; and even while sending one last petition to their King, begging that their wrongs be righted, the Second Continental Congress was voting to raise an army.

Already thousands of colonial soldiers had gathered to the siege of Boston. They must be recognized as acting not only for New England, but for the whole thirteen colonies. They must be organized as the Continental Army. They must have a commander, and this at once. George Washington was unanimously chosen for the position. It was a great honor, but an even greater responsibility.

"I beg it may be remembered by every gentleman in this room, that I this day declare with the utmost sincerity I do not think myself equal to the command I am honored with," said Washington.

However, he accepted on condition that he should receive no salary, merely being repaid for his actual expense. His commission was signed on the 19th of June, and the 21st saw him already on the road to Boston.

THE CAMPAIGN BEFORE BOSTON AND AROUND NEW YORK

It was the 2nd day of July when Washington reached Cambridge, the headquarters of the colonial army. And, as he rode within the lines, the English shut up in Boston knew, by the soldiers' shouts of welcome that he had come.

Next day, while the colonial troops were drawn up on the Cambridge common, Washington rode out on horseback under the now famous elm and took command of the army.

There were fifteen or sixteen thousand soldiers, men who knew little about fighting and less about military discipline; and Washington had work ahead of him to get them into shape and enforce the necessary obedience. Moreover the

FORTIFYING DORCHESTER HEIGHTS.

supply of arms and powder was so small that an attack on the English was out of the question for months. Messengers were sent flying over the country to beg powder from every town and village, and fifty cannon were dragged all the way from Ticonderoga to Cambridge on ox sleds.

At last when March, 1776, came, Washington felt that all was ready to try what the colonial army could do. One evening he moved troops, artillery, and all that would be needed in building fortifications, to Dorchester Heights overlooking Boston.

It was like another Bunker Hill surprise. The next morning there were the Americans in a position to fire right into the British camp. It was apparent that the English General had his choice of leaving the town or of being destroyed with it. He chose to leave, and sailed away on March 17, 1776.

On the 18th, Washington marched into Boston in triumph, after his bloodless victory. In their retreat the English had been obliged to leave behind them two hundred cannon and more muskets, powder, and balls than Washington's army had ever owned before.

It seemed likely that New York would be the next place to be attacked by the English. Therefore Washington left part of his troops in Boston and with the rest hurried to New York. Here raw recruits joined his force until it numbered eighteen thousand.

Let us leave the army at work building defenses for New York and go back to the Continental Congress in Philadelphia. You will remember that last petition which the Continental Congress sent to England. As usual it was received with contempt. The King would do nothing for his disobedient colonists. And what was more, to end their rebellion, he had

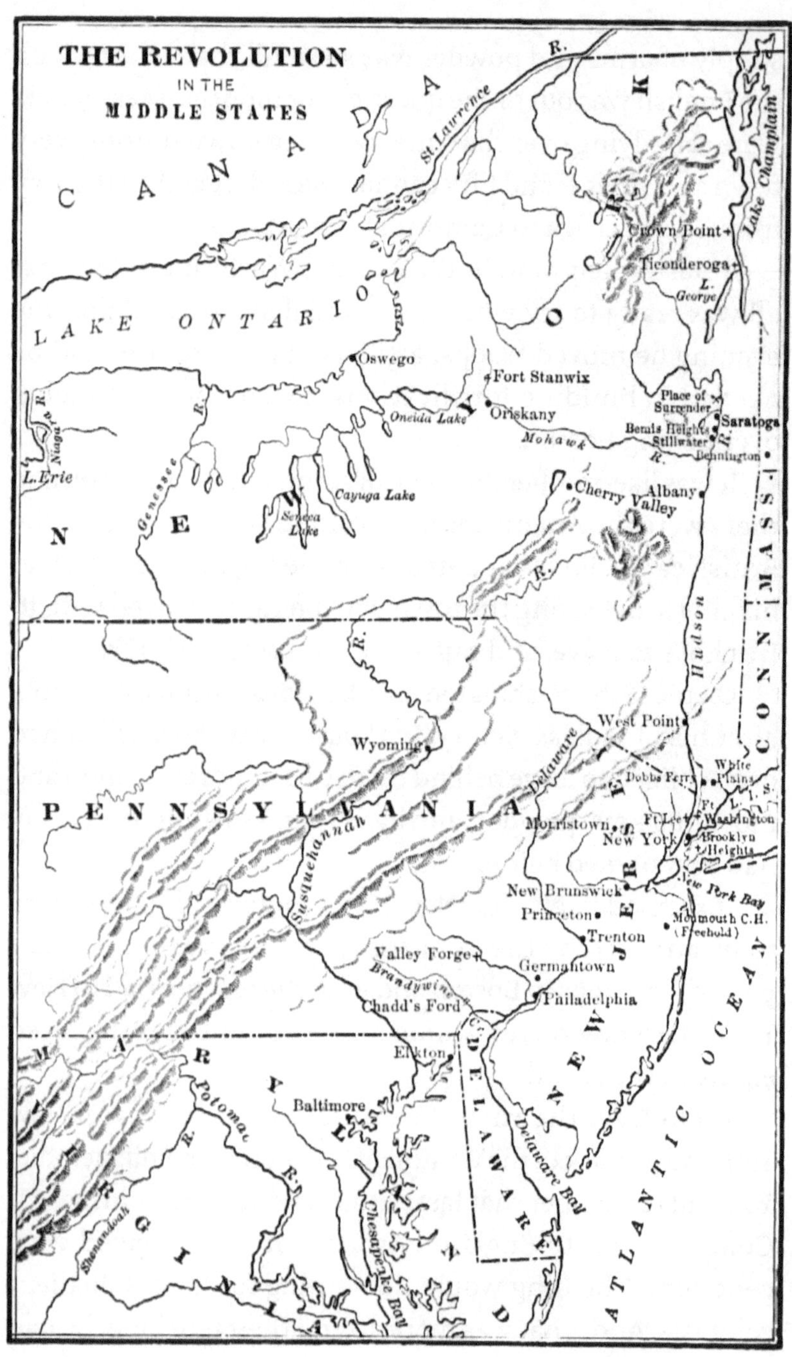

THE REVOLUTION
IN THE
MIDDLE STATES

CANADA
St. Lawrence R.
LAKE ONTARIO
L. Erie
Niagara R.
Genesee R.
NEW YORK
Oswego
Oneida Lake
Cayuga Lake
Seneca Lake
Fort Stanwix
Oriskany
Mohawk R.
Cherry Valley
Albany
Crown Point
Ticonderoga
L. George
Lake Champlain
Place of Surrender
Bemis Heights
Stillwater
Saratoga
Bennington
MASS.
CONN.
Hudson R.
West Point
Dobbs Ferry
White Plains
Ft. Lee
Ft. Washington
L. I. S.
Morristown
New York
Brooklyn Heights
New Jersey
New Brunswick
Princeton
Trenton
New York Bay
Monmouth C.H.
(Freehold)
Wyoming
PENNSYLVANIA
Susquehannah R.
Delaware R.
Valley Forge
Brandywine
Germantown
Chadd's Ford
Philadelphia
Elkton
Baltimore
MARYLAND
Potomac R.
Shenandoah R.
VIRGINIA
Chesapeake Bay
DELAWARE
Delaware Bay
ATLANTIC OCEAN

hired German troops to go to America and do this work for him in short order.

The colonists were outraged. All thoughts of peace were at an end. Daily the break between England and her American colonies grew wider, until finally, on the 4th of July, 1776, a Declaration of Independence was adopted by Congress, and the thirteen English colonies became the United States of America.

When this glorious news reached Washington and his men, they had barely time to celebrate before British ships entered New York Harbor, and a British army, far larger than Washington's, took possession of Staten Island.

One half of Washington's force was stationed on Long Island, on Brooklyn Heights just opposite New York. It seemed a simple thing to the English commander, General Howe, to defeat these nine thousand men. And with Brooklyn Heights once in his hands, he could take New York from Washington as surely and as easily as Washington had taken Boston from him.

However, it was late in August before he put his plan to the proof. Twenty thousand trained soldiers were landed on Long Island and began the advance on the Americans. On the 27th, they attacked and defeated the troops sent out from the Heights to meet them. This force was made up of half the soldiers sent by Washington to defend Brooklyn Heights.

If General Howe had persevered in his undertaking, the Heights would certainly have fallen into his possession. But after the battle his men were tired, night had come, and it seemed easier to wait for his final victory. His troops encamped at the foot of the Heights and took their needed rest.

While the British troops rested, Washington and more soldiers came by boat from New York, until ten thousand Americans were ready for the attack which they expected at any time.

But no attack came. Instead, General Howe had decided to lay siege to the Heights and starve out this handful of the enemy.

Before many hours Washington learned of this decision. Here indeed was danger. If once the British ships got between New York and the Heights, all hope of escape would be at an end. Soon trusted messengers were on their way to New York to collect all the boats, large or small, which were to be found.

The night of the 29th was foggy, and under cover of the darkness the boats were brought to the Brooklyn shore. There they were quickly and quietly filled with men, small arms, ammunition, supplies, and even cannon, all of which were safely landed in New York. Washington himself was the last to leave the now deserted fortifications.

Can you imagine General Howe's amazement the next morning? Washington was proving himself a veritable will-o'-the-wisp to the British. Where they least expected him, there he was; and when they counted him in their grasp, he faded away.

The Retreat Across New Jersey

With English troops on Brooklyn Heights and English vessels in New York Harbor, Washington felt that it would be asking the impossible to expect his small force to keep the English out of New York City. However, he did not mean to give up more ground than was absolutely necessary. Although

WASHINGTON CROSSING THE DELAWARE.

obliged to retreat, he yielded each step only when forced on by the British, who were constantly at his heels.

He crossed to the west bank of the Hudson, and was gradually crowded back into New Jersey. His men, disheartened, discouraged, poorly fed, and worn out, deserted by the score.

And all the while the English relentlessly kept up their hot pursuit. By breaking down bridges, when once his army had crossed them, Washington did what he could to delay his enemy. All to no avail. Before their superior numbers he had no choice but retreat. At last he reached the Delaware River.

Here he saw a chance of stopping the English for a while at least. Seizing every boat for miles up and down the river, the Americans crossed the Delaware to the Pennsylvania side. The English would have followed; but there was no means of doing so, and they were obliged to camp along the shore until the December weather should freeze the river hard and fast.

While they were waiting, Christmas day came and Christ-

mas night. And on Christmas night something happened of which the English had not dreamed.

During that December night of 1776, Washington, at great peril, recrossed the
Delaware. The next morning he
fell upon the British encampment at Trenton and captured
a thousand of the King's hired
soldiers.

Such was the battle of Trenton, and great was the rejoicing
it caused.

But though the discouraged
soldiers now took heart, Washington was sorely troubled. The
year was nearly over; and with
the first days of 1777, the term of
enlistment of many of his men
would end. They had suffered
much during their service, and
so had their wives and children
at home with no one to earn
their living. Money was necessary to buy what they needed,

A SOLDIER OF CONGRESS.

and money Washington must have if he hoped to induce
his soldiers to reenlist.

Where was he to get it? That he could not tell, unless his
friend Robert Morris would come to his aid.

This Robert Morris was a wealthy merchant and banker
in Philadelphia. In an imploring letter Washington begged

him to send $50,000 in cash as soon as possible, as cash was all that would now hold his army together.

Robert Morris had already given large sums to aid the Revolution, and it was out of the question for him to produce $50,000 more at a moment's notice. Still he could not fail Washington now; the sum must be raised. And it was raised. Going from house to house, Morris laid the case before man after man and got from each all that he could or would give. Nor did he stop until the entire amount was collected and ready to send to Washington.

Meanwhile in New York the English general, Cornwallis, was celebrating Christmas and preparing to sail back to England. In his opinion, the revolt was about over. With the British troops so closely pursuing, this upstart American commander must surely give up in a very short time.

Then came news of the battle of Trenton with its thousand prisoners taken. Cornwallis was amazed. Perhaps after all it did need a master hand to end this war once and for all. So, putting off his sailing, Cornwallis himself hurried to Trenton with eight thousand soldiers to conquer Washington.

It was late in the day when he reached Trenton. By that time, Washington had withdrawn his army across a small river, along whose banks he had placed his batteries.

Tired out from their day's march, the British put off their attack overnight. Cornwallis, sure of success, was in the best of spirits. "At last we have run down the old fox and will bag him in the morning," was his confident assertion.

But, foxlike, Washington was not to be run to earth quite so easily. All through the night the English sentries pacing back and forth watched the gleam of Washington's camp fires and listened to the thud, thud of falling earth as the

Americans worked on their intrenchments. Little did they suppose that only a few men were making all that noise and tending all those fires. Such was the case, nevertheless. While the camp fires blazed and the digging went on, Washington and his army were slipping away toward Princeton.

Washington had reasoned that in Princeton he would find so small an English force left to guard the stores that his army could defeat it and capture the supplies.

About sunrise Princeton was reached, and the battle was on. In less than half an hour it was over, and Washington had once more come off victorious. This was on January 3, 1777.

From Princeton, Washington took his soldiers to the Heights of Morristown, where the English dared not attack him. Here he spent the rest of the winter, raising new troops and doing what he could to strengthen his army. As for Cornwallis, he returned empty-handed to New York.

In Pennsylvania; Arnold's Treason

During the early summer of 1777, General Howe made an attempt to reach Philadelphia by an overland march from New York. Washington's force was still too small to risk meeting the English thousands in open battle. However, he so annoyed and worried their commander by keeping just out of reach and yet in the way, that General Howe gave up and went back.

Next, General Howe put his troops aboard ship, sailed them up Chesapeake Bay to its head, and set out for Philadelphia from that point. At Brandywine Creek there was Washington again. He had marched south in the hope of once more turning the English away from Philadelphia. On

WASHINGTON AND LAFAYETTE AT VALLEY FORGE.

September 11th, the armies met in battle, and Washington was defeated.

Soon after, the English entered Philadelphia and took possession of the capital of the United States. Nothing daunted, Washington decided to try another attack; and on the morning of October 4th he appeared at Germantown, where part of the English were encamped. At first, success seemed sure. But a heavy mist soon caused confusion and misunderstanding, and the Americans were once more repulsed.

Another winter was at hand. It was evident that General Howe meant to spend it in Philadelphia. Therefore Washington went into camp at Valley Forge, where he could keep an eye on his foe.

This winter at Valley Forge was terrible for both the American army and its General. The cold was intense and persistent. The men were poorly clothed and half starved.

Shoes were a luxury. The soldiers walking barefoot over the ice left bloody tracks behind. Money was scarce, and the army unpaid. All night men sat huddled around the camp fires. They had even no blankets in which to roll themselves.

Washington did all he could to provide for his troops and earned their loyal love and devotion by his constant sympathy and his willingness to share in their privations. His courage encouraged them.

In his turn Washington found help and comfort in the companionship of certain of his brave officers. His friend and right hand man, General Nathanael Greene, was with him through all this long, hard winter. And there were two other men at Valley Forge who earned not only Washington's thanks, but the thanks of all Americans. These were the Marquis de Lafayette and Baron von Steuben. Lafayette was a young Frenchman; Steuben, a Prussian. Lafayette not only gave his services to our country, but generously used his private fortune to supply with clothes and arms the soldiers under his command. Steuben, trained soldier that he was, drilled Washington's troops and taught even their commander the meaning of true military discipline.

At last the winter broke; and the spring of 1778 came, bringing good news to America. France had recognized the United States of America as a nation, and had agreed to send us aid in our fight against her old enemy.

The English general, Clinton, now succeeding General Howe, decided to abandon Philadelphia and unite his forces in New York.

Hardly had the British march begun when Washington, too, took to the road. He fully believed that if a battle were now to take place, his army could and would defeat Clinton's troops. Accordingly, he ordered a detachment to push on and attack the English, while he followed with reinforcements.

Now this detachment was under the command of General Charles Lee; and, but for him, Washington's plan would probably have succeeded. Already Lee had nearly brought ruin upon Washington's forces by direct disobedience; already he had played false to America by secretly giving information to her foe; and now, once more he was to show his treachery.

The American troops advanced on the English forces at Monmouth, and at first everything seemed in their favor. The battle was begun, and the patriots were fighting like tigers, when suddenly Lee ordered a retreat. Naturally his men obeyed. All would have been lost, had not Washington just then ridden up. Dashing straight to Lee, he fiercely demanded "What is the meaning of all this, sir?" Lee began some excuse. To Washington there was no excuse for such cowardly behavior. He ordered Lee to the rear while he himself rallied the soldiers, led them back, and saved the day. Lee was later dismissed from the service in disgrace.

One other of Washington's officers proved himself a traitor. This was Benedict Arnold. During the early part of the Revolution, Arnold gave America brave and valiant service. But later he was made bitter by lack of promotion; and when his conduct raised enemies for him, their attacks so stirred up his anger that he betrayed both his country and his honor, and offered his services to the English.

At the time General Clinton was in New York, he was very anxious to get possession of the Hudson River; but strong fortifications at West Point held him in check. Now, Arnold's offer opened up a possibility. The plan was for Arnold to ask

Washington for the command of West Point, and then allow the English to capture it.

Suspecting nothing, Washington gave Arnold the coveted command. The very next month Arnold and Andre, General Clinton's young adjutant general, met one dark night in a thicket on the river's eastern shore. Here Arnold gave Andre maps of the fort, and papers telling just what steps the English should take.

With these papers in his stockings, Andre started back to New York on horseback. But half-way back to the city he was captured, and finally he was hanged as a spy.

As soon as Arnold heard of Andre's capture, he fled down the river and joined the English army. This was in September, 1780. Years after, he died in England, praying God to forgive him for deserting his country. Nothing came of the plot but soreness of heart to Arnold's betrayed commander, and disgrace to the traitor himself.

Yorktown

During the two years following the battle of Monmouth, the war for the most part was carried on in the South, where such men as Daniel Morgan and Francis Marion, "the swamp fox," won lasting fame by their brave and daring deeds.

Although Washington himself stayed in the North, where he could have a watchful eye on the English in New York, he still kept in touch with conditions in the South.

Back and forth through the southern states went Cornwallis and the English troops, until, in the summer of 1781, he followed Lafayette up into Virginia. Then he betook himself and his troops to Yorktown, where he and Clinton could be in communication by sea.

Yorktown is on a cape, three sides of which are surrounded by Chesapeake Bay. At the first word of his enemy's move, Washington was on the alert. Carefully going over in his mind the position of his forces, he realized that the fleet sent us by France

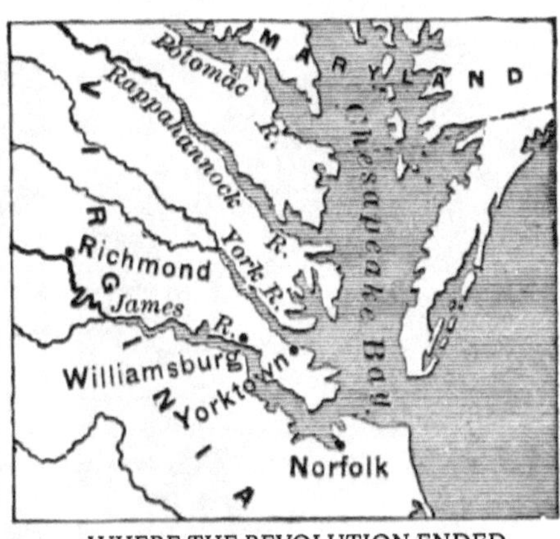

WHERE THE REVOLUTION ENDED.

could be placed so as to prevent Cornwallis from escaping by sea. And if his own New York troops could possibly be mustered with the French soldiers, and those under Lafayette, so as to shut Cornwallis into this land pocket, a deadly blow could be aimed at England's power.

It must be done and done at once. Misleading Clinton by seemingly preparing an attack on New York, Washington slipped away south.

After a long forced march the soldiers reached Chesapeake Bay and went by ship to Yorktown. There was the French fleet, and there was Cornwallis ready to be shut in exactly as Washington had foreseen. For days the English held out against Washington's attack. But no help came to them; and at last, on October 19, 1781, Cornwallis was obliged to surrender. To the tune of "The World Turned Upside Down" the British marched out of Yorktown between the two long lines of Washington's victorious army. And the American Revolution was practically at an end.

A few years later the United States adopted their Constitution and set up their government. Then through loving gratitude and just appreciation of his value, they chose as

PRESIDENT AND MRS. WASHINGTON.

their first President, the loyal commander of the army which had won their independence.

Washington was President of the United States for two terms. At the close of this service, he went back to Virginia to the happy home life awaiting him. For a little while he gathered up the reins of control on his plantations, but they soon slipped from his fingers forever.

December 14, 1799, was a day of grief for the entire country—grief which spread in every direction with the news that, at Mount Vernon, George Washington lay dead.

V

Philip Schuyler and Burgoyne's Campaign

THE ENGLISH PLAN AND BURGOYNE'S ADVANCE

While Washington and his army were encamped in the hills about Morristown, the English were laying plans which promised quick success.

Their scheme was to gain control of New York State, thus completely separating New England from the other colonies. As New England was Washington's chief source of men and supplies, such a step would be full of danger to him and would surely prove a tremendous stride toward final victory for old England.

The English had good reason to expect this plan to succeed. Not only was New York City already in their hands, but Canada was theirs as well. They were in a position to invade New York State from the north, south, or west; and they concluded to attack from all three directions.

One army under General Burgoyne was to enter New York State from Canada, by way of Lake Champlain. General Howe, with a second army, was to move up the Hudson from New York City. Colonel St. Leger, with still another army, was to land at

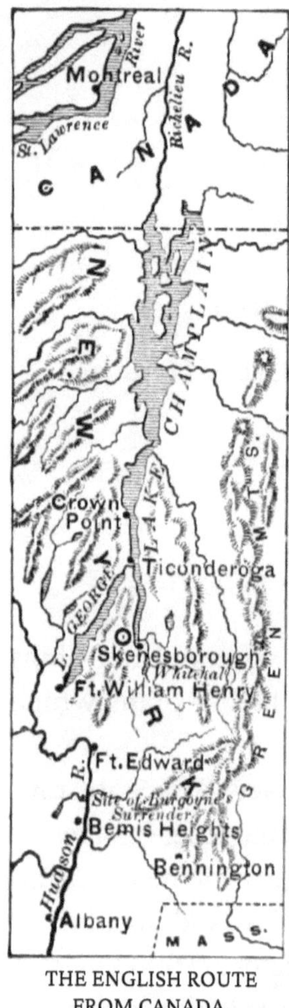

THE ENGLISH ROUTE FROM CANADA.

Oswego and, conquering as he came, march through the Mohawk Valley. With their work done, all three armies were to meet at Albany.

The summer of 1777 saw this plan set in motion, and down from the North came General Burgoyne with a force of nearly eight thousand soldiers and Indians.

The Americans had placed General Philip Schuyler in command of the Northern Department of the army, and so it fell to his lot to defend New York State against the three English armies.

Knowing that General Burgoyne would aim his first blow at Fort Ticonderoga, General Schuyler started for that place to reinforce its garrison. On the way he stopped at Fort Edward, where, to his great disappointment, he met the very troops that were supposed to be protecting Ticonderoga. An unexpected thing had happened, and Ticonderoga was lost.

It seems that to the south of Ticonderoga there towered a crag so steep that the Americans had not thought it possible to fortify it. But what the Americans had not thought possible to do, the English had done. "Where a goat can go, a man may go; and where a man can go, he can haul up a gun," one of Burgoyne's generals had said. And so it proved; for great cannon had been dragged up the side of the crag and placed so as to fire directly into the American fort.

It was the morning of July 5th when the Americans discovered this appalling fact. They waited only for the darkness to hide their movements, and then slipped away from Ticonderoga that same night, abandoning the fort to the English.

This was bad. General Schuyler saw that in some way time must be gained. If

Burgoyne were allowed to advance before more troops were recruited, the result would be disastrous. Something must be done to check him, and that at once.

Hurrying to the head of Lake Champlain, Schuyler's men fell to work with a will. Guns were laid aside, and axes took their place. Hundreds of trees were chopped down and left to block the roads. Bridge after bridge was burned; the streams themselves were choked until they overflowed, and all the country for twenty miles was laid waste.

Then, while General Schuyler retreated to Stillwater, the English tried to advance. But their path was so obstructed that a mile a day was the best they could do.

Meanwhile, men from all the country round were rushing to enlist in Schuyler's army. With each day's delay the American force was growing and threatening more and more to cut Burgoyne from his source of supplies.

At last the English neared the deserted post of Fort

Edward. While they were still a little way from the fort, Burgoyne's Indians indulged in a piece of cruelty which, though not unusual in itself, proved the cause of serious trouble to him. This was the murder of Jane McCrea.

The poor girl was visiting at the home of a Mrs. McNeil, probably in the hope of meeting her lover, who was an officer in Burgoyne's army. The story goes that this officer promised a party of Indians a barrel of rum if they would bring Aliss McCrea to him, so that they might be married in the English camp. Be that as it may, a band of savages seized both the girl and her hostess and carried them off into the woods. Mrs. McNeil managed to reach the British lines, but she came without her friend. The next day a gigantic Indian strode into the camp, bringing a scalp from which hung tresses over a yard long. It was the scalp of Jane McCrea, whose lifeless body was soon found pierced by three bullets.

Burgoyne was horrified. To put an end to such bloody acts, he ordered that no party of Indians be allowed to cross the British lines without an English officer. This was more than the Indians would endure. So, deserting the camp, they skulked off and left the English to fight alone. Nor was the loss of the Indians the only way in which Jane McCrea's murder hurt Burgoyne's cause. Her story was told far and near, and her fate roused many a man to join the American army and march against the invaders that had employed such cruel allies.

THE TABLES TURNED

Burgoyne's hard and tedious march from Lake Champlain had been severe on his horses and had nearly exhausted his provisions. By the time he had been a few days at Fort

GENERAL STARK AT THE BATTLE OF BENNINGTON.

Edward, he began to feel the want of fresh horses, and the need of new supplies. It was a long way to Canada. Therefore the General decided to get them from Bennington, Vermont, where the New England militia kept their stores.

In August Burgoyne sent out a detachment to capture the Bennington supplies. But he was doomed to disappointment. Before his men even reached Bennington, they were met by Colonel John Stark at the head of a force of trained militia.

As the Americans were about to attack the English, John Stark shouted to his men, "There they are, boys! We beat them to-day, or Mollie Stark's a widow!" Mollie Stark was not made a widow by the battle of Bennington. Neither did the English get the New England stores. When the battle was over the Americans had seven hundred prisoners, one thousand stand of small arms, and all the detachment's artillery to show for their pains.

Imagine General Schuyler's joy on hearing of this victory! These were anxious times with him. Not only was he trying to keep posted on Burgoyne's movements, but also he was trying to prevent Colonel St. Leger from carrying out his part of the English scheme.

St. Leger, according to the arrangement, had sailed up the Ft. Lawrence to Lake Ontario and had landed at Oswego. Here he had been joined by friendly Indian tribes and certain of the colonists who had remained loyal to their King.

Marching east from Oswego, this combined army had appeared before the American post of Fort Stanwix within a few days after Burgoyne had taken possession of Fort Edward. As St. Leger's army numbered more than twice the force that garrisoned the American fort, he confidently demanded that the Americans surrender. A prompt refusal was his answer. Very well, then, he would lay siege to the fort and force the soldiers to surrender.

And it is quite likely that the Colonel would have succeeded in starving out the plucky little garrison, had it not been for a stalwart German patriot named Nicholas Herkimer.

By dint of great perseverance, Nicholas Herkimer rallied eight hundred men to follow him to the relief of Fort Stanwix. On the morning of August 6, 1777, they left Oriskany to march to the fort, less than eight miles ahead. In their path lay a ravine. Suspecting nothing they pushed eagerly forward. But hardly had they entered the ravine when bang! bang! resounded from every side, and a deadly fire was poured from all around.

Colonel St. Leger had been warned of Herkimer's approach and had sent his Indian and loyalist allies to

THE WOUNDED HERKIMER.

entrap the patriots. Volley followed volley. Turning back to back, the Americans fought like mad. For five hours they battled hand to hand with their foe. It was a desperate fight. Early in the struggle Herkimer was shot through the leg. Still he was undaunted. Asking his men to place him at the foot of a beech tree, he lit his pipe and coolly went on directing the battle.

All at once the crack of muskets sounded in the distance.

THE FLAG OF THE UNITED COLONIES, 1775-1777.

THE FIRST FLAG OF THE UNITED STATES, ADOPTED JANUARY, 1777.

The Indians took to their heels in terror. And after them went the loyalists, leaving the ravine to Nicholas Herkimer and the remnant of his courageous followers.

Herkimer had not succeeded in reaching Fort Stanwix; but in spite of that fact, he had rendered its commander an immense service. By merely being in the neighborhood he had induced Colonel St. Leger to send a detachment to attack him, thus dividing the besieging army. And seizing the opportunity, the Americans had made a sortie; had driven away what was left of St. Leger's force, and held possession of the English camp until they had captured blankets, food, clothes, ammunition, and five British flags.

Then, with all these needed supplies and their trophies, the soldiers had retreated to their post. And the five British flags soon appeared floating from the fort, while over them waved the first American flag with stars and stripes. Made from an old blue coat, a white shirt, and a red flannel petticoat, it must have looked pretty rough compared with the beautiful English banners. But it unconsciously foretold how these thirteen states, newly joined together, were soon to triumph over proud old England.

St. Leger Routed and a Change of Command

When the Americans had withdrawn from the English camp, Colonel St. Leger returned to the siege of Fort Stanwix.

The gallant commander of the Fort needed help, and General Schuyler called a council of war to decide what was to be done. At this council General Schuyler stated that he thought it was of the utmost importance to destroy St. Leger's army, and that he favored the prompt sending of a strong detachment to Fort Stanwix. Several officers disagreed, some perhaps honestly, but others because they were opposed to whatever General Schuyler might desire.

Pacing anxiously up and down, Schuyler overheard one of these unfriendly officers say, "He only wants to weaken the army."

He turned like a flash, and said, "Enough! I assume the whole responsibility. Where's the brigadier who will take command of the relief?"

"Washington sent me here to make myself useful. I will go," spoke up Benedict Arnold. Yet this was the man who so soon proved himself a traitor to his country!

Twelve hundred men volunteered to follow Arnold to the relief of Fort Stanwix, and the next day saw the expedition on its way.

When they were still about twenty miles from the Fort, two captured boys were brought before Arnold. As they were known to belong to the Loyalist party, Arnold threatened to have them killed. Soon, however, he changed his mind and offered to spare the lives of both if the elder one would do as he was bid. The boy agreed. His coat was then shot full

WASHINGTON'S COAT OF ARMS
WHICH SUGGESTED THE DESIGN
FOR THE NATIONAL FLAG.

of bullet holes. And in this same coat, he was sent rushing into St. Leger's lines to tell of an approaching American army as numerous as the leaves on the trees.

The story was believed, and panic reigned in the English camp. St. Leger lost all control. The Indians fled; and by noon the next day even St. Leger himself had given up the siege, deserted his camp, and taken to the woods. With all haste he headed for Oswego, and from there embarked for Montreal.

Arnold's trick had saved not only Fort Stanwix, but the Mohawk Valley. His services were no longer needed in that section, so he went back to General Schuyler.

Let us see in what condition he found this noble hearted commander. You remember how Schuyler's officers behaved when he suggested sending aid to Fort Stanwix. That was only one of the many times when his motives and acts were misinterpreted. Again and again he had been unjustly accused of being in sympathy with the English, and unjustly blamed for losses which he had been powerless to prevent.

All this was due to the fact that he had a rival for the command he held. General Gates was an officer who desired much, while deserving little. And General Gates so strongly desired General Sclluyler's position that he was willing to go great lengths to get it. With the help of his friends he so misrepresented General Schuyler's every move, that finally Congress was deceived. General Schuyler was removed, and General Gates was appointed to succeed him.

On August 19, 1777, General Gates arrived and took command, just in time to claim the credit for the happy turn affairs were taking. It must have been a bitter thing for General Schuyler to be obliged to step aside thus for Gates. However, when Gates appeared, General Schuyler received him with great politeness, gave him all the information he could about the enemy, and offered to help him in every way possible.

BURGOYNE'S SURRENDER

What of General Burgoyne all this time? He had started out confident of success, but he now found himself in a grave predicament. Colonel St. Leger had been defeated and had fled. No help had come from General Howe, who had gone off south instead of ascending the Hudson, as Burgoyne had fully expected him to do. The Americans had sent a force to cut off his retreat, should he attempt to return to Canada. Moreover, his orders were positive and left him no choice. He was to march through to Albany, nothing more nor less.

Therefore, in the middle of September, Burgoyne left Fort Edward and once more began his advance. On the 19th, he reached Bemis Heights, where he found Gates and the American army encamped. During the morning Burgoyne attacked the Americans. All afternoon the battle waged with fury. Then darkness came to put an end to the fighting. Neither side had lost or won. The Americans fell back to their fortifications, and the English camped on the battlefield.

Here they stayed for over two weeks, watching each

other's every move. At last, on October 7th, Burgoyne determined to see what another attack would do toward opening the way to Albany.

The Americans came forward to meet their foe. This time there was no drawn battle. When night came on October 7th, the English had been utterly defeated.

Burgoyne now fell back to Saratoga. He no longer had any hope of reaching Albany. American troops surrounded him on every side. No supplies were to be had; starvation stared his army in the face.

He laid the case before his officers. Forced to it, they advised surrender. Hence a flag of truce was sent to General Gates. Details were arranged, and on October 17, 1777, General Burgoyne and his army surrendered to the Americans.

This surrender proved a turning point in the Revolution. In it, England saw the failure of her cherished plan to divide the colonies. By it, the Americans gained great stores of arms and ammunnition. And because of it,—so pleased was she to see her old enemy defeated,—France decided to give us the aid we sorely needed.

It was to General Gates that Burgoyne gave up his sword. But it was to General Schuyler that he and his friends owed their thanks for endless kindness in their misfortune.

The surrender complete, Burgoyne was at last to go to Albany. Schuyler sent his aid-de-camp to act as Burgoyne's guide in the strange city. And to Burgoyne's surprise the aid-de-camp led him direct to Schuyler's own home, where he and those with him were made cordially welcome and were shown every courtesy as long as they were in Albany.

You will be glad to know that even before the close of the

GENERAL SCHUYLER'S HOUSE AT ALBANY.

Revolution, General Philip Schuyler's disinterested services were recognized. His noble generosity to Gates was appreciated, and Congress acquitted him of all charges against his loyalty, "with the highest honor."

VI

Nathanael Greene

Early Life

Nathanael Greene had a busy happy boyhood. His home was in a little Rhode Island town. His Quaker father was a preacher and a miller, and an anchorsmith as well. He owned a gristmill, a flour mill, a sawmill, and a forge. And, better than all, he had eight sons.

In the elder Nathanael Greene's opinion, his mills, his fields and his forge furnished a good school for his boys. Of other learning they had little. They were taught to read that they might read the Bible, and taught to write and cipher as a help in business.

Theirs was a simple, healthy life with work and play all mixed together. Many a field was plowed in testing who could turn the deepest furrow. Many a harvest was gathered in proving who could cut the widest swath, or shape the best and firmest stack of new-mown hay. Then, too, there were jolly husking bees, for the love of which a boy would gladly tramp six good miles.

Well content with such a life, Nathanael Greene reached the age of fourteen. But now a chance acquaintance, talking of college life, showed him how meager his learning was;

and he began to think and wonder about things that he had never considered before.

At last his new thirst for knowledge led him to ask his father for more schooling, and a new master was arranged for. Under his guidance Nathanael studied Latin and geometry, and laid the foundation for the good general education which he finally acquired through his steady perseverance. Thus the boy came to early manhood, in the years when his country needed the help of every strong arm and active brain at her command.

At Covington, about ten miles from his home forge, the elder Nathanael Greene owned a second forge; and in 1770 he decided that one of the sons should leave the old home, move to Covington and take charge of the smithy there. Nathanael was chosen. It was a great event when his neat two-story house was finished, and he went to live in it. Hardly had he learned to feel at home in his new surroundings when he was chosen a member of the General Assembly of Rhode Island. This was the beginning of his public life.

Soon came the stirring times of the tea tax, the Boston Tea Party and the closing of Boston's port. All Covington was aroused; and in 1774 Nathanael Greene had a hand in organizing a military company, which was called the Kentish Guards. Greene joined the company as a private. But as he was a soldier without a gun, he resolved to go to Boston and get one.

Even for an enemy there was a certain fascination in the well-trained British redcoats. And while in Boston, Greene went both morning and evening to see the regulars drill. Strong, vigorous, broad-shouldered and full-chested was this Rhode Island recruit, whose keen eyes watched every move, from under his wide-brimmed Quaker hat.

What he saw must have pleased him well, for before he left Boston he had engaged a British deserter to go back with him to drill the Kentish Guards. Having bought his musket, he was in doubt as to how he could get his gun out of Boston. At last a farmer agreed to hide it under the straw in his wagon. And following the wagon at a safe distance, Greene set out for home.

In Washington's Army

In April, 1775, a messenger rushed into Providence with the news of Lexington and Concord. A few days later the Rhode Island Assembly voted to raise an army of fifteen hundred men, and Nathanael Greene was chosen brigadier general and placed in command of the fifteen hundred. In due time he led them to join the American forces; and so it was that Greene was already in the army that waited before Boston to welcome Washington, when he came to be its chief.

Washington was quick to see Greene's sterling qualities, and a close and lasting friendship grew up between the two. In the battles of Trenton, Princeton, Brandywine, and Germantown, Greene led a division of Washington's army. And while at Valley Forge, he accepted the position of quartermaster general, to please Washington. Thus the Commander-in-chief came to know his friend's value both in the camp and on the field of battle. Was it not natural, then, that, when the English turned their attention to the South, Washington's choice for commander of the Southern Department was Nathanael Greene? But Congress did not see with Washington's far-sighted eyes.

In carrying the war to the South, the English reasoned somewhat in the following way: We have not been very successful so far. These northern colonies are surely strong in their rebellion. However, the South does not seem equally determined. Would it not be our wisest plan, therefore, to subdue the southern colonies first? Then, if worst comes to worst, and we are obliged to make terms with the North, at least we shall still have a foothold in the colonies.

The conquering of the South was to begin with Georgia. In December, 1778, an expedition attacked Savannah; and with three men to our one the British found the city an easy prey. A few more minor victories followed, and the English soon claimed Georgia as their own.

Till the end of 1779 the conditions were practically unchanged. But early in 1780, the English reopened their southern campaign with vigor. This time South Carolina was attacked; and a mighty army advanced against Charleston, and completely surrounded it. It would have been a waste of life for the American force, gathered to protect the city, to have risked battle with such an army. Even the citizens of Charleston petitioned that terms be made with the British. They were accordingly made, and the city surrendered. The English at once sent detachments to take possession of Camden, and other points throughout the State.

At this time Congress put Gates in command of what

THE SIEGE OF CHARLESTON.

was left of the southern army, even though Washington had recommended Greene. Puffed with pride over his stolen victory at Saratoga, Gates had dreams of promptly defeating the English. He determined to surprise them at Camden before Lord Cornwallis could reach there. But Lord Cornwallis got to Camden first, prepared a warm welcome for Gates, and even advanced to meet him.

When the battle began, the English came on with such a rush that the Virginia troops threw down their loaded guns and took to their heels. Seeing them disappear, others did the same; and the troops that did stand their ground were soon routed. Nor was General Gates left behind in the headlong flight. Deserting his artillery, his baggage, and his few stanch followers, he covered sixty miles before night.

Although the Americans won a brilliant victory at King's Mountain in October, the disaster at Camden had convinced

Congress that, after all, General Gates was not much of a success as a commander.

Washington was now asked to suggest some one to take the place of Gates. Thoroughly convinced that Nathanael Greene was the man of all men, Washington again unhesitatingly recommended him.

IN THE SOUTH

In December, 1780, General Greene arrived in North Carolina and took command of the American forces. These forces were so small that Greene himself said they seemed but "the shadow of an army." And they were a disheartened, discouraged, unpaid, and poorly fed shadow at that. Still the man who had come to command them was the best general the Americans had, Washington alone excepted. His very presence soon inspired his forlorn troops, and they took heart once more.

MAP OF GENERAL GREENE'S CAMPAIGN IN THE SOUTH.

Before he had been long in the camp, General Greene sent part of his men, under Morgan, to threaten the English in the northern part of South Carolina. Then General Cornwallis, in his turn, sent out a detachment to drive Morgan back. Morgan heard that the English were coming, and he waited for them at Cowpens.

Here, on the 17th of January, 1781, he was attacked by the British. But so well had he planned his defense, and so bravely did his men do their part, that the English were terribly and utterly defeated.

Cornwallis was astonished. More determined than ever that Morgan should be crushed, he hurried against him before Greene could come to his aid. However, Morgan did not intend to be crushed, and started north before Cornwallis could get to him.

Here was General Greene's chance. His army was far too small to risk meeting the English in open battle. He must find some other way of getting the best of them. And what other way could be better than to tire them out by leading them a long, merry chase, all the time coaxing them farther and farther from their base of supplies?

With all speed, therefore, he hastened to join Morgan; and together they retreated, while Cornwallis followed in hot pursuit. Across the State of North Carolina went the Americans; and a few hours behind them came the British. Realizing that more than one river lay in his path, Greene had wisely ordered boats to be mounted on light wheels and taken along on the retreat. When a river was reached, it was an easy matter to put the wheels into the boats and carry the army safely to the opposite shore.

At last Greene and his men came to the Dan River, which was too deep for Cornwallis and his men to ford. Once in Virginia, General Greene received reinforcements until he felt his army could hold its own with the English. Then he went back into North Carolina once more, bent on battle with his enemy.

Cornwallis, too, was willing and anxious to meet the Americans. And on March 15th the two armies came together at Guilford Court House. It was a furious and

TOUCHING OFF THE FIRST GUN AT THE SIEGE OF YORKTOWN.

bloody battle. General Greene was defeated. But though the English loudly boasted of their victory, they had paid dearly for it. So heavy had been Cornwallis's losses that he dared not stay where he was. He retreated therefore nearly as fast as he had come, and made his way to Wilmington on the shore of North Carolina.

From Wilmington, Cornwallis marched into Virginia. Meanwhile, General Greene had begun his campaign to retake South Carolina and Georgia. It was no simple matter; but by patient, tireless effort, he at last won back the conquered southern states.

In marching into Virginia, Cornwallis was unconsciously marching toward his surrender. Finally he went to Yorktown. Washington came and shut him in, and the Revolution was over.

Soon after its close, the State of Georgia gave General Greene a plantation; and to this Georgia plantation he moved with his family. But his pleasure in his new home was to be short. In June, 1786, he died of sunstroke, at the age of forty-four.

His boyhood in the forge, the mill, and the field, had given him strength. His efforts to become a scholar had broadened his mind. Vast common sense and good tact were his by nature. A lasting patriotism came to him from seeing his country oppressed. These were what he had to give America, and he gave them with all his heart and all his energy. Great is the honor due Nathanael Greene.

VII

John Paul Jones

FROM SCOTLAND TO AMERICA

Far away from the American colonies, near the western shore of Scotland, lived a gardener, John Paul. His youngest son, John Paul, Jr., left his Scotland home, came to America, and later was the first man to raise an American flag over an American war ship. Let us see how it all came about.

John Paul's eldest son was called William. While William was still a mere boy, a wealthy Virginia planter, named William Jones, had come to Scotland to visit, and had taken a great fancy to young William Paul. Having no children of his own, Mr. Jones offered to adopt this boy and take him to Virginia to live. The offer was accepted; William Paul became William Paul Jones and left Scotland for America.

All this had happened before John Paul, Jr., was born. But though he had never seen this brother, the fact that he dwelt in America set the sturdy lad to dreaming of that distant land.

All his life, John Paul, Jr., had lived by the sea. He was naturally strong, daring, and plucky; and he quickly learned to handle a boat. Often, when the little fellow should have been in school, he was sent to sea in a fishing yawl to do his part toward providing for the family. His great ambition was to gain his father's permission to sail on some vessel bound for America. He was only twelve years old when good fortune and his own scorn of danger won for him his heart's desire.

One summer afternoon, in 1759, an ugly squall made sailing difficult. When the wind was at its worst, a small fishing boat was seen beating its way toward the harbor of John Paul's home village. The villagers watched anxiously. Among those gathered on the shore were the gardener, John Paul, and a merchant named Younger, who had come to the village to look for sailors.

FROM A PRINT MADE IN ENGLAND DURING THE LIFETIME OF PAUL JONES.

The little boat was having a rough time. Mr. Younger did not think it could reach the harbor. But, bit by bit, it made headway against the squall, until at last the watchers could see those on board. There were only a boy and a man. The boy was steering and handling the sails, while the man was merely trimming the boat according to the boy's directions. By this time, John

Paul had recognized the boat. He no longer seemed alarmed, but turning to Mr. Younger said, "That is my boy, John. He will fetch her in. This isn't much of a squall for him." And so it proved. The little boat came safely to shore, and her twelve-year-old commander was presented to Mr. Younger. The merchant congratulated the youthful seaman and offered him the position of master's apprentice on a fine new ship about to sail to Virginia and the West Indies.

In the face of such an opportunity the father could hardly refuse his consent. Arrangements were quicky made, and a few days later the young John Paul sailed from Whitehaven on the good brig *Friendship*.

It was nearly five weeks later when the *Friendship* came to anchor in the Rappahannock River, not far from the wharf of William Jones. While the ship lay in the river, John Paul paid his longed-for visit to his brother William and William's adopted father.

John, too, quickly found his way into the heart of William Jones, who wanted to adopt him also. However, the boy's love of the sea kept him from accepting; and when the *Friendship* headed for the West Indies, he was on board. The next spring the ship returned to Whitehaven, and John Paul's first voyage was at an end.

Other voyages followed. Time and again during the next twelve years he crossed the Atlantic; and gradually he rose from shipmaster's apprentice to captain, with an interest in the profits of the voyage.

In April, 1773, he once more went to see his brother. He found William at the very point of death, and this death made a great difference in Captain Paul's future.

Soon after John Paul's first visit to Virginia, William Jones had died. He had left his estates to his adopted son, William Paul Jones. But he had added that, if William were to die without an heir, the plantation was to go to John Paul on the one condition that he, too, should take the name of Jones.

In obedience to this condition, John Paul became John Paul Jones. As the Virginia plantation was now his own, he sent his ship to England in charge of the first mate and settled down to take his brother's place. And so it was that this Scotch laddie came to be an American citizen, fitted and ready to serve in America's first naval squadron.

IN AMERICA'S NAVY

During his first two years in Virginia, John Paul Jones led a care-free life, dividing his time between studying and dispensing the open-hearted hospitality of colonial days.

This brought him to the year 1775, and the beginning of the war between England and her American colonies. When fighting began, John Paul Jones offered his services to Congress, and later in the year he was appointed senior lieutenant on the *Alfred*. The *Alfred* was the flagship of the pioneer squadron of our American navy. And a weak little squadron it was, compared with the proud English ships which threatened our coast.

Early in 1776 the American fleet put to sea and headed for the Bahama Islands. After capturing two English vessels on the way, it reached Nassau, took the governor prisoner, and seized nearly a hundred cannon, besides large quantities of military supplies.

Later in this same year, John Paul Jones was appointed to the command of the *Providence*, with which he captured sixteen English ships, and had many narrow and daring escapes.

PAUL JONES WITH BENJAMIN FRANKLIN AT THE FRENCH COURT.

In 1777, Captain Jones concluded that America's best course was to send a ship, or a number of ships, to cruise along the British coast. So earnestly and persistently did he urge this plan that he convinced Congress of its wisdom. And as commander of the *Ranger*, a new sloop which had just been launched, he set out for foreign seas.

His first errand was to deliver to Benjamin Franklin in France certain despatches from Congress, telling the good tidings of Burgoyne's surrender. You remember that Franklin had gone to France to secure her sympathy and aid; and we have seen how these tidings stirred the French and led to the signing of their alliance with the young American nation.

When the spring of 1778 came, Jones left France and steered the Ranger to prowl about the coast of England. His audacity was past belief. Slipping into the harbor of Whitehaven, he surprised the forts, spiked the guns, and attempted to burn the shipping.

The English were alarmed, and sent out their sloop: of war, the Drake, to capture this intruder. The well armed Drake and the Ranger met in the Irish Sea.

"What ship is that?" queried the Drake.

"The American Continental ship Ranger. Come on, we are waiting for you," answered Jones.

At almost the same instant the two vessels opened fire. For an hour and four minutes broadside followed broadside. Then, the Drake, almost a wreck, struck her colors and followed her victor to France.

From France the Ranger was sent home to America, while Captain Jones remained to command a promised larger ship. For weeks and months he waited before this promise was fulfilled. In fact, it was the summer of 1779, when he at last sailed away from France with a squadron of four vessels besides his flagship, the Bon Homme Richard. This name, the French equivalent for "Poor Richard," John Paul Jones gave his ship in honor of Dr. Franklin.

The squadron spent a month or more capturing vessel after vessel and spreading consternation all along England's coast. By the latter part of September, Jones had sailed around the north of Scotland and was coming down the east of England. On the 23d, he spied a British fleet off Flamborough Head and immediately gave chase. It proved to be merchant vessels under the protection of two war ships, the *Serapis* and the *Countess of Scarborough*. Seeing that they were pursued, the merchant vessels spread full sail and escaped, leaving the field to the two English men-of-war, the *Bon Homme Richard*, and three of the American squadron. One of these three was soon busy forcing the *Countess of Scarborough* to surrender; another was too small to be of much account; while the captain of the third, by disobeying orders, did far more harm than good. Thus the *Serapis* was left for the *Bon Homme Richard*.

It was past seven o'clock when the two ships came within hailing distance. Both commanders knew that the encounter meant a battle to the finish. Little time was wasted in useless signals. The roar of cannon from each ship said all that was necessary.

With the first volley, two of the *Bon Homme Richard*'s guns burst, killing several men and damaging the ship. This lessened her power, but did not check the battle.

In the soft light of the rising moon, the two ships drifted nearer and nearer together. And all the while cannon answered cannon, and ball after ball tore through the rigging, or crashed its way through the decks. Once, for a moment, the British commander lost sight of the American flag.

"Have you struck your colors?" he shouted.

"I have not yet begun to fight," doggedly answered Jones.

But the *Bon Homme Richard* was old, and the battle was telling on her. She could not hold out indefinitely. At last the ships came close. Jones determined to keep them so, and seizing heavy ropes he lashed the two together.

Up into the rigging climbed the best shots in his crew and, firing down on the enemy's deck, quickly picked off every man who showed himself. Hand grenades were thrown into the portholes of the *Serapis*, and before long one was dropped through the hatchway. In an instant there was a terrific explosion. The hatch was blown open, and flame and smoke poured out. The grenade had struck in the midst of a line of cartridges and had fired them all. This was the beginning of the end. And when John Paul Jones ordered a party of his men to board the *Serapis*, the English commander, seeing them swarm forward unopposed, lowered his flag with his own hands.

It was now past ten o'clock. After the English commander had surrendered his sword to Jones, the ships were separated, and they drifted apart.

The condition of the *Bon Homme Richard* can hardly be imagined. Her dead and wounded lay stretched out on her decks. Water was pouring through many shot holes, and flames were threatening to destroy what little the battle had left. The vessel was a complete wreck.

Jones ordered all hands aboard the *Serapis* and left his ship to her fate. With her torn and tattered flag still flying, she slowly filled and sank from sight, while John Paul Jones sailed away in the conquered *Serapis*.

Great was the effect of his victory throughout all Europe. The King of France, the King of Denmark and the Empress of Russia each conferred honors upon him. Congress also gave him a vote of thanks, appointed him to the command of a new and splendid ship, and presented him with a gold medal in

recognition of his ines-
timable services to our
infant navy.

After the American
Revolution, John Paul
Jones entered the ser-
vice of Russia with the
rank of Rear Admiral.

Later he went to
Paris, and there he died
in 1792. His body was
carefully embalmed
and was put into a

THE MEDAL PRESENTED TO
PAUL JONES BY CONGRESS.

leaden coffin and quietly buried in a cemetery on the out
skirts of the city. As the city grew, the property was sold to a
building contractor; the cemetery was effaced; houses were
built over it; and the grave of America's first naval hero was
lost sight of.

His fame fared better. Although at the time of his death
the American people allowed the body of John Paul Jones to
be buried without pomp or honor, they have never forgotten
the immense debt they owe him. And at last, after more than
a hundred years, the nation he so loyally served has paid his
memory well-deserved tribute.

In 1899 General Horace Porter, our American Ambassador
to France, undertook to find the remains of John Paul Jones.
Through old letters and records he succeeded in locating the
discarded cemetery, and the city authorities gave him permission to search the ground. This work was begun in 1905;
and in a little under two months, the leaden coffin which
held the body of Paul Jones was dis covered. So perfectly

had the body been preserved that the features of the hero could be unmistakably identified with those of his portrait on the Congressional medal.

Then the United States sent a squadron to France to bring the body to Annapolis, the home of America's Naval Academy. And here the remains of John Paul Jones now lie in the crypt of a new chapel erected in his honor by the land of his adoption.

VIII

Lafayette

It is night in Philadelphia. In spite of their worries the members of Congress are in bed. Quiet is over all, and the only sound that breaks the stillness is the lagging footsteps of the drowsy watchman going his rounds. "One o'clock, and all is well!" he cries. "Two o'clock, and all is well!"

The minutes wear on. Then his ear catches a distant sound. He listens. Muffled at first, it grows nearer and nearer, louder and louder. It is the even hoof beats of a horse ridden at full speed. The rider comes in sight. "What news?" shouts the watchman. What news indeed!

His steps no longer lag. The tones of his voice are jubilant now, as he shouts from house to house, "Past three o'clock, and Cornwallis has surrendered! Past three o'clock, and Cornwallis has surrendered!"

Let bells peal! Let cannon boom! Speed the good tidings from man to man, from town to town, from colony to colony! Let all America know and rejoice that victory is ours!

Not many days behind the bearer of the glorious news, another man journeys from Yorktown to Philadelphia. He is young, tall, and slender. He is the French Marquis de Lafayette.

Four years before, at the very time when our future looked

THE MARQUIS DE LAFAYETTE
WHEN A YOUNG MAN.

the darkest, Lafayette came to America a boy of nineteen and offered Congress his services without pay. Loyally and well he has played his part in the Revolution. Now the hour of victory is come. America no longer needs his help, and his heart yearns for France. Congress gladly gives him leave to go. So journeying to Boston, he sails back to France; back to his young wife; back to all the luxury, position, and honor due his rank and wealth at home. All these lie left behind to take up arms in the cause of a stranger people's liberty; and to all these he returns, while that people exults in its triumph over oppression.

Years go by. The United States of America adopts a constitution, sets up a government, and takes her place among the nations of the earth. Meanwhile, the Marquis de Lafayette passes through fortune and misfortune at home. Often his thoughts turn back to America and the countless friends his ready sympathy and generous ways won for him there.

In 1824 a welcome invitation comes. The United States bids him once more to her shores, this time as the guest of the American nation.

In the man she greets again in this year of 1824, America

still sees the youth who paid from his own purse for that first ship that brought him to take up arms against her foe. She has not forgotten how he used his wealth in her behalf; how the starving, ragged troops of Washington's army were fed, warmed, and clothed at his expense. She has not forgotten the wounds he received while bravely fighting at Brandywine. She has not forgotten his gallant behavior at Monmouth.

It was at Monmouth that Lafay-

WASHINGTON'S EYE-GLASSES, TREASURED BY LAFAYETTE IN MEMORY OF HIS FRIEND.

ette was given a trusted command. Washington sent him ahead in charge of the detachment that was to attack the British. But no sooner was he well away than Lee claimed the right to lead the advance and, overtaking Lafayette, deprived him of the command. Though bitterly disappointed, Lafayette accepted the conditions without complaint and fought his best under Lee's ill-starred orders.

Then did he not also have a hand in the final victory? He led Cornwallis a chase through Virginia until, reinforced, he was able to turn the tables, follow the

LAFAYETTE AS HE APPEARED IN 1824.

HILT OF THE SWORD PRESENTED TO LAFAYETTE IN 1824 BY THE NINTH REGIMENT, NEW YORK STATE ARTILLERY.

enemy to Yorktown, and keep him there while Washington marched south.

The forty-odd years since the surrender of Cornwallis have in no way dimmed America's gratitude to the French Marquis, and she rejoices in his return. In August he reaches Staten Island and spends the night there. The next day, gayly decorated ships come to escort him to New York. There he is welcomed by booming cannon, and cheering thousands follow his four-horse carriage through the streets.

For over a year Lafayette stays in America. He travels through New England, through New York, to Philadelphia, to Washington, where the President welcomes him to the White House. He goes to Mount Vernon, although Washington, his revered friend, has long since died. He visits Yorktown and the South. He goes even to New Orleans and ascends the Mississippi River and the Ohio. What a difference between the thirteen struggling colonies and this fast growing nation! Can it be that one lifetime compasses it all?

Everywhere crowds line the roads to greet him. Everywhere he passes under arches raised in his honor, while each town and city vies in the length of its processions and the brilliancy of its balls and dinners. September, 1825, finds Lafayette in Washington, where he receives from Congress the gift of two hundred thousand dollars and two large tracts of land.

His visit is now near its end. The new ship *Brandywine* waits to carry him to France. And Lafayette sails down Chesapeake Bay while a grateful nation bids her guest God-speed.

IX

Alexander Hamilton

STEPS TO FAME

Alexander Hamilton was born in 1757 on the little island of Nevis in the West Indies, and there he spent his childhood. He was left motherless when he was very young, and was brought up by relatives. The future could not have seemed particularly bright for this lonely little boy. Yet he grew to be one of the greatest men of his time.

While still a lad, he was employed as clerk in a store; and he showed such ability and industry that soon he had almost complete charge of the business. But the life of a West Indian merchant was not to his taste, and his relatives were induced to send him to New York to continue his studies. He was now fifteen years old.

Hamilton wanted to enter Princeton and to get his college education as rapidly as possible, without regard to classes. However, the rules of Princeton did not permit of this; so Hamilton entered King's College, now Columbia University, instead.

At this time the colonies were on the eve of their struggle for liberty. Young as well as old were interested. Large numbers of the most able, upright, and conscien-

THE BATTLE OF GOLDEN HILL.

tious men were opposed to the idea of separation from the mother country. They argued that the wrongs complained of could and would be settled peaceably. These men came to be called Tories or Loyalists. On the other hand, many patriotic young men in the different colonies formed themselves into bands called "Sons of Liberty." They stood for the rights of the colonists; and in their enthusiasm they raised liberty poles, around which they held their meetings.

One of these liberty poles was put up in New York City. But in January, 1770, some of the English soldiers in New York took down the pole and cut it up. This caused great excitement among the patriots and led to a fight between the citizens and the soldiers. In this battle of Golden Hill, as it is called, the first blood of the Revolution was shed, five years before the battle of Lexington. However, it was little more than a street brawl, not an heroic fight, and no one was severely hurt.

The Sons of Liberty also took an active part in New York's "Tea Party" which, although not so celebrated as the one in Boston, seems to have been just as effective when the ship *Nancy* arrived with a cargo of tea, early in 1771, she was stopped at Sandy Hook. Her captain was brought to the city and told that he could not land his tea. He was then escorted by a large procession to the pilot boat, and carried out to his ship, which was compelled to turn back to England. About the same time the tea from another vessel was emptied into the harbor.

It was in the midst of such exciting scenes that Hamilton entered college. On July 6, 1774, he was present at a great meeting held by the patriots in New York to favor the First Continental Congress. Young, impulsive, thoroughly interested, he listened to the cautious luke-warm speeches. Finally he could stand it no longer and, stepping to the platform, began to address the meeting himself. The impression made by this boy orator of seventeen was great, and deep. His eloquence struck his hearers with surprise, and from that hour he was important to the cause of liberty.

In the fall of 1775 the patriots in New York removed some of the guns that were located on the Battery. They were discovered at work, and were fired upon by the English war ship *Asia*. The crowd grew excited, enraged, and sought to avenge themselves by injuring some of the Loyalists. They marched to King's College, whose president, Dr. Cooper, was unpopular because of his English sympathies. Hamilton, always ready to help the weak and unprotected, leaped to the steps of the building and began to harangue the mob,

thus giving the good doctor time to escape. As the story is told, at first the doctor did not understand what was going on. Looking out of his window and seeing, as he supposed, one of his students urging on the crowd, he called to them not to listen to the young rascal. Before many minutes, however, he was glad to get away under cover of the young man's oratory.

Once aroused, Hamilton's keen interest in the fight for liberty never lagged. During the campaign around New York he acted as captain of a company of artillery, which he had trained so well that it attracted general notice. He had a share in the victories of Trenton and Princeton, although by that time his company was reduced to a mere handful of men. And at Yorktown he headed the assault on one of the British outworks, which he gallantly captured.

Early in the war, Washington was attracted by the young soldier: and in March, 1777, he appointed Hamilton his aide, with the rank of lieutenant colonel. His duties as aide were to take charge of the correspondence of the Commander-in-chief, to prepare and draw up his orders, proclamations, and other important papers.

There can be no doubt that this discipline was of immense value to Hamilton. It developed him and gave him a grasp of national affairs. And best of all, for four years it kept him in intimate touch with Washington and cemented the friendship between them.

DEPRECIATION OF THE CURRENCY

The affairs of the Government, after the close of the war, were in a disheartening condition. The soldiers were unpaid. Congress had no power to raise money by taxation; had not even the power to protect the lives and property of the citizens. Commerce was at a low ebb. The states, jealous of each other, fell to quarreling and bickering.

New York and Virginia said that they owned most of the western land claimed by Massachusetts and Connecticut. Feeling ran high. Finally New York ceded all of her western claims to the Government. Connecticut, Massachusetts, and Virginia did the same. In this way a great national domain was created, and one of the interstate disputes was settled.

It was not so simple to solve the country's financial difficulties. The only way in which Congress was allowed to raise money for its many debts was by making requisitions on the states. These requisitions were paid grudgingly by some of the states; by others not at all. And Congress had no power to enforce payment.

The distress of the country was great. Almost everyone was in debt. Between 1775 and 1780 the Continental Congress had issued paper money to the amount of about $200,000,000. But it is not enough merely to print paper and call it money. People will not accept it as money at its face value, unless it represents gold or silver—something of value which can be had in exchange for this printed paper. Because there was no gold or silver behind the paper money

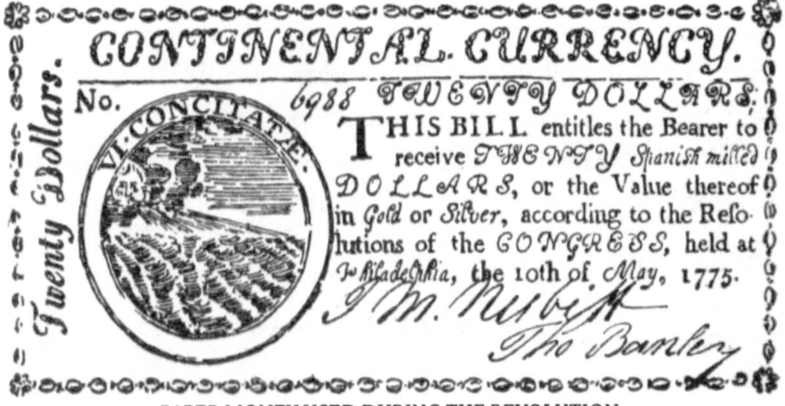

PAPER MONEY USED DURING THE REVOLUTION.

of Congress, it rapidly fell in value until, in 1780, a man had to pay forty dollars in paper money for what would cost one dollar in gold or silver. And later in the South it cost one thousand of Congress's paper dollars to buy one gold dollar's worth of goods. This depreciated paper money gave rise to the expression "not worth a continental."

Besides the worthless paper money issued by Congress, there was also the paper money issued by most of the states. This added to the confusion. As there was no Government mint, practically the only coins in use, besides a few pennies, were foreign coins. It was not always easy to be sure what these foreign coins were worth, and any moderately cautious man had to keep at hand a small pair of scales with which to weigh the gold or silver.

Therefore much of the trading was done by exchange. That is to say, if a farmer bought a suit of clothes, he would probably pay for it in flour or some other product of his farm. Thus we read of an editor of a paper offering to take subscriptions for his paper in salt pork.

With all these complications, the country was rapidly going from bad to worse. So a convention was called at

Annapolis, in 1786, to consider the question of setting up a uniform financial system. Alexander Hamilton was sent to represent New York. The convention did little. But from it originated the idea of calling all the states together in another convention to reorganize the government of the country.

The New Constitution and Financial Reform

New York appointed as her delegates to the proposed Federal Convention, John Lansing, Robert Yates, and Alexander Hamilton. The first two were bitterly opposed to the idea of giving great power to a National governing body. They feared that the importance of the State of New York might be lessened. Hamilton, with a broader view, was earnestly in favor of any movement to strengthen the Central Government.

The convention met at Philadelphia in May, 1787. Hamilton did his utmost to show up the dangers of the system of government under which they were living, and used his influence to have measures adopted that would remedy these evils. To his delight it was decided to draw up a new Constitution which would give greater power to Congress, would regulate the rights of the states, and would provide a president to see that the laws were carried out. The various articles of the Constitution were finally agreed upon and were signed by the majority of the delegates, ready for the states to ratify. During the fall of 1787 and the first months of 1788 the fight between the friends and enemies of the new Constitution waxed hot and furious.

Hamilton suggested the writing of a series of essays explaining the advantages of the Constitution, and the

WASHINGTON'S RECEPTION AT THE BATTERY, NEW YORK CITY.

reasons why it should be adopted. This suggestion was acted upon; and from time to time arguments appeared in the newspapers of New York, which did much to remove the prejudices and fears of those opposed to the Constitution. Later these essays were collected and published under the name of *The Federalist*. *The Federalist* is one of the most famous books ever published in America. Of its eighty-five essays, fifty-one were written by Hamilton.

When the New York convention met to decide whether that state should accept the Constitution, Hamilton was put to his wits' ends. Forty-six of the delegates out of sixty-five were bitterly opposed to the ratification. But by arguments so strong that they convinced enough of his opponents, he won a majority, and the ratification was approved. It was a great triumph for Hamilton. Eleven

THE PRESIDENTIAL COACH DRAWING UP IN FRONT
OF FEDERAL HALL IN WALL STREET.

states having accepted the Constitution, it went into effect in 1789.

Washington was unanimously elected to act as the first President under the new Constitution. His inauguration was to be held in New York, and great preparations for the event were made in that city. Washington reached New York from Mount Vernon on April 23rd. On his journey he received a constant ovation from a loyal and enthusiastic people. From New Jersey he was rowed to New York in a gorgeous barge, manned by thirteen masters of vessels, dressed in white uniforms. Every vessel in the harbor was gay in holiday attire. On April 30, 1789, at the old Federal Building in Wall Street, George Washington took the oath of office as the first President oft he United States.

When President Washington chose his cabinet he made Hamilton his Secretary of the Treasury. With the country deeply in debt, with no money in the treasury, and with the endless number of important questions that must be decided before the new government could be placed on a sound financial basis, Hamilton had a stupendous task before him. He bent all his great ability to the straightening out of America's tangled financial condition. Where others would have ended with dismal failure, Hamilton succeeded.

As the result of his work he brought out a series of financial pleasures which quickly and firmly established the credit of the country. He advocated the payment in full with interest of the enormous National debt and the debts of the states. He established methods of taxation by imposts and excises; he provided for the establishment of a National Bank and a Mint. All of these measures and many more besides, under his leadership, were adopted by Congress, though not without bitter controversies.

After Hamilton had rendered this valuable service to the country he retired from public office, and again took up the practice of law which he had begun years before. This was in 1795.

The Duel and Hamilton's Death

Hamilton was worshiped by his friends and hated by his enemies. He never ceased to take an active interest in the politics of the time; and it was largely through his efforts that Thomas Jefferson, and not Aaron Burr, was elected President in 1800. Then four years later, Hamilton prevented Burr from being elected governor of New York. Whereupon Burr became Hamilton's bitter enemy, and determined to kill him. So, claiming that Hamilton had defamed him, he picked a quarrel with the New York lawyer and challenged him to a duel.

According to the code of honor of those days, Hamilton could not well refuse to accept the challenge, although he did not believe in dueling. Weehawken, in New Jersey, was chosen as the place for the fight. Arrangements were made; and on the morning of July 11, 1804, the two statesmen and their seconds were rowed to the Jersey shore. Pistols were to be the weapons. The principals took their places. The signal to fire was given. Hamilton did not even attempt to shoot Burr. But, in his hatred, Burr took calm and deliberate aim. His bullet struck Hamilton in the body, and he fell. He had received a fatal wound; and although he lived to be taken home, before many hours he died. He had barely passed the prime of life, for he was but forty-seven years old.

The grief for his loss was deep. Burr was indicted for murder and was compelled to flee. The misfortunes that came to him in his after life must have seemed sufficient penalty for his revenge. Disliked, suspected, with the stain of Hamilton's death on his reputation, this brilliant man died in misery and poverty thirty-two years later.

Hamilton was buried in New York in Trinity churchyard, at the head of Wall Street. His tomb of white marble, now yellow with age, is surrounded by stately buildings. He lies near one of the great financial centers of the world—a center which his genius did much to create.

Perhaps the love and admiration of his countrymen is best told in the epitaph on his tomb. It reads in part:

The PATRIOT of incorruptible INTEGRITY
The SOLDIER of approved VALOUR
The STATESMAN of consummate WISDOM
Whose TALENTS and VIRTUES will be admired
By
Grateful Posterity
Long after this MARBLE shall have mouldered into
DUST.

X

Thomas Jefferson

STUDENT AND LAWYER

The treaty that closed the American Revolution was signed at Paris, in 1783. Before the new year the British soldiers

had gone home; the Continental troops had disbanded; and the American people had begun to test their ability to use in peace the freedom that they had declared to be theirs by right.

On that day, long before, when Patrick Henry offered his resolutions against the Stamp Act, he had other hearers besides the members of the Virginia House of Burgesses. Near the door stood a tall, gawky young

114

man with sandy hair, freckled face, and large hands and feet. He was Thomas Jefferson, who was later to write America's Declaration of Independence.

Jefferson was the son of a well-to-do Virginia planter. In 1760, when seventeen years old, he came to Williamsburg and entered William and Mary College. After two years he left the college and took up the study of law.

These were happy years which Jefferson passed in Williamsburg. Cheery, genial, and fond of fun, he made many friends. But especially did he enjoy the evenings of violin playing, story-telling, and laughter spent with Patrick Henry, the rising young lawyer.

Fortunately for Jefferson, his legal instructor as well as certain of his college professors were among the ablest men of the time. He attracted their attention and won their friendship because he was interested in his work and wide awake to everything around him. And under their influence he learned to think clearly and to express his views simply, but with force.

In 1767, Jefferson's student life came to an end, and he began the practice of law, at which he proved himself a great success.

Two years later, he was chosen a member of the House of Burgesses. He was still a member when, early in 1775, the Burgesses met at Richmond. Here he heard Patrick Henry's second stirring speech—the speech in which he denounced all efforts at peace and for himself chose liberty or death. Jefferson was thrilled by his eloquence and heartily approved Henry's motion that Virginia "be immediately put into a state of defense."

Later in the same year Jefferson was sent to represent Virginia at the Continental Congress, which met in Philadelphia.

AUTHOR OF THE DECLARATION OF INDEPENDENCE

The crisis had come. England had thoroughly roused the blood of her American colonists. Fighting had begun, and dependence on England was no longer to be endured. It was time for America to declare her rights and claim her freedom. So in June, 1776, John Adams, Benjamin Franklin, Roger Sherman, Robert R. Livingston, and Thomas Jefferson were appointed to draw up a declaration of the colonies' independence.

Thanks to Jefferson's early training, he had developed into a powerful writer; and it now fell to his lot to draft this all-important paper. He worked on it for three weeks. By the end of June it was ready, and Jefferson submitted it to the Continental Congress.

Congress spent a few days in going over it, making changes here and there. As a whole, they were well pleased with Thomas Jefferson's work; and on July 4, 1776, the Declaration of Independence was formally adopted. The first to sign it was John Hancock, the President of Congress. He wrote his name in a clear, bold hand and, as he put down the pen, exclaimed, "There, John Bull can read that without spectacles!"

Meanwhile, about the State House throngs packed the streets. Would Congress adopt the Declaration? If so, the old State House bell was to announce the fact. While the anxious crowd watched and listened, up in the building a small boy waited for a signal from the doorkeeper. At last it came. Away to the old bell ringer rushed the boy shouting, "Ring!

ring! ring!" And in an instant the great bell pealed out the joyous news.

The excitement was intense. Cheer rose after cheer; and there were hand-shakings and shout-ing, and even tears of joy. Then a copy of the Declaration was sent to each colony. And everywhere by, fireworks, cannon firing, and flag flying the American people proclaimed their new-born freedom.

It was the 4th of July, 1776, when this greatest, this most prized blessing—independence—became the possession of America. That day marked the founding of the American nation. And on each 4th of July, we, the American people, still proclaim our undying love of independence by patriotic speeches, cannon firing, and flag flying.

"Sage of Monticello" and President

But to return to Thomas Jefferson. Two months after the adoption of his Declaration of Independence, he resigned from Congress and went home to Virginia. Some say that he did this because his wife was ill and needed him; others hold that he left Congress because he was anxious to bring about certain reforms in the laws of Virginia.

CROWDS IN BOSTON LISTENING TO THE DECLARATION OF INDEPENDENCE.

His first attack on the laws was on those of inheritance. At this time a Virginia landowner was obliged to leave his property to his eldest son. He could not divide it among all his children, nor could he will it away from his family without a special act of legislature. This seemed all wrong and unfair to Thomas Jefferson, and he succeeded in having these laws annulled.

Another law that he attacked was that which required the people of Virginia to pay taxes for the support of the Estab-

MAP SHOWING THE TERRITORY OF THE UNITED STATES BEFORE THE LOUISIANA PURCHASE.

lished Church. Jefferson felt that no one should be compelled to attend or support a church against his will; and this law, too, was abolished through his efforts.

For two years he was Governor of Virginia. For five years he was abroad as envoy to France. On his return to America he was appointed Secretary of State under President Washington. And later, so well had the American people come to know his value, he was elected the third President of the United States.

Jefferson was the first President to take the oath of office in the city of Washington, the new capital of the country, named for George Washington and founded on a site of his choice. At the time, Washington was a city of but a few thousands, and the Capitol was an unpretentious building.

This fact must have well suited Thomas Jefferson. Both Washington and John Adams, Washington's successor, had felt that the President of the United States should stand a little apart from the people. They had kept up a dignity and formality befitting their idea. All this was very unlike Jefferson. He believed in "Republican simplicity"; believed that all men are equal, and that the President should be always

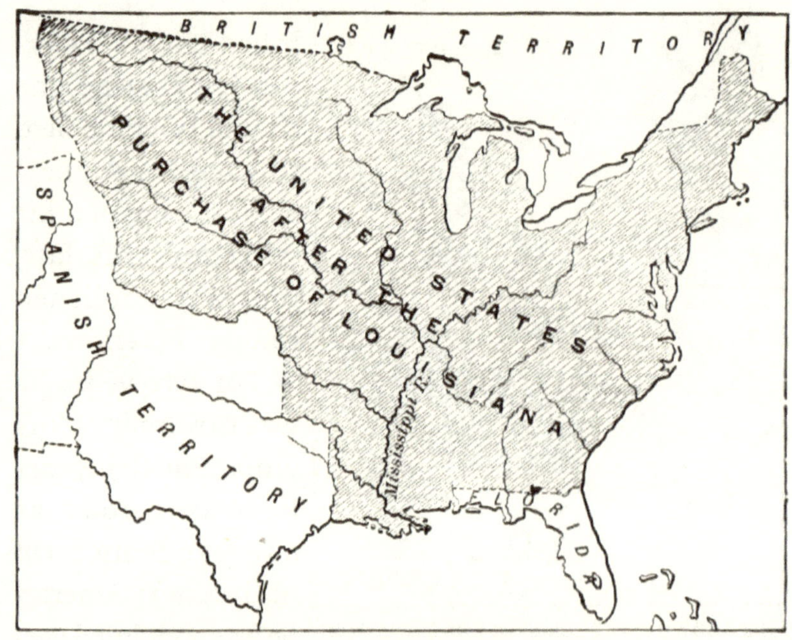

MAP SHOWING THE TERRITORY OF THE UNITED STATES AFTER
THE LOUSIANA PURCHASE.

ready to exchange a friendly handshake with anyone. On the day of his inauguration, dressed in his everyday clothes, he went on foot to the Capitol.

Thomas Jefferson was President for eight years. One of the wisest things he did while in office was to buy from France the land known as Louisiana. This was not merely the present state of Louisiana; it was a great stretch of land containing nearly nine hundred thousand square miles, lying between the Mississippi River and the Rocky Mountains, and between Canada and the Gulf of Mexico.

All this Jefferson got from Napoleon Bonaparte, at a veritable bargain. At the time, Napoleon was in sore need of money; so he was glad to sell Louisiana to America for fifteen millions of dollars—less than three cents an acre. Now that Louisiana was the property of the United States, Jefferson wanted to know what it was like. Few, if any, Americans had ever crossed that part of the country; so no one could tell him. Accordingly he sent out an expedition under two young men named Lewis and Clark. They started from the log cabin village of St. Louis and went by boat up the Missouri River to the Rocky Mountains.

They were away nearly two years and a half, and when they came back they brought with them tales of adventure and descriptions of the natural wealth and beauty of Louisiana, and a carefully made map of their trail.

In 1809 President Jefferson's term ended, and he went back to Monticello—his beautiful home near Charlotteville—to live with his daughter in a house full of rollicking grandchildren. His wife had died many years before; but Jefferson still kept up the hospitality of their home, receiving and entertaining the many who came, drawn either by friendship or to ask advice of the "Sage of Monticello." Nor did he lose his keen interest in the welfare of Virginia. He had long wanted to see a new university in his State, and during these peaceful years at home he himself founded the University of Virginia.

Jefferson lived until 1826. It is a strange coincidence that his death should have occurred on the 4th of July, the fiftieth anniversary of the adoption of the Declaration of Independence. His body was laid in the family cemetery at Monticello, and on the stone which marked his grave were written the words, "Here was buried Thomas Jefferson, author of the Declaration of Independence."

XI

Daniel Boone

THE YOUNG HUNTER

When white men first came to America they planted their settlements here and there along the Atlantic coast. For many years the great unbroken forest, extending westward from these settlements, deterred the early colonists from pushing their way into the wilderness. However, a few, bolder than the rest, and with a stronger love for adventure, did penetrate some little way into the unexplored country. And then there came a pioneer whose energy and fortitude helped to set the pace for the great migrations west. This was Daniel Boone. Boone was born in Bucks County, Pennsylvania, in 1735, and when still a boy went with the rest of the family to build a new home on the banks of the Yadkin River in North Carolina. Here he went to school for a short time and studied the "three R's." His spelling was original—what one might expect of a boy who spent nearly all his time in the fields and the woods.

Boone was a hunter born, and passionately loved the forest. In its depths he learned to track the deer and the elk; to imitate the calls of the birds; and to seek out the hiding

PIONEER SETTLEMENTS ON THE WESTERN FRONTIER.

places of the panther, bear, and wolf. He grew up to be a strong, lithe, sinewy man with muscles of iron.

At twenty-five Boone started out to explore. He pushed his way as far west as Boone's Creek, a branch of the Watauga River in eastern Tennessee. Here still stands a birch tree on which can be seen the words he carved: "D Boon cilled A BAR on this tree year 1760."

These early explorations only made Boone long for more. He wanted to find the great hunting grounds of the far interior, the land we now know as Kentucky. To the Indians this meant "The Dark and Bloody Ground." Although the region was fair to look upon, the savages were not far wrong when they gave it such a name. This blue-grass country lay midway between the northern and southern Indians. No one tribe owned it, but all used it as their hunting grounds and were jealous of anyone else who came there.

At last Boone decided to visit the "Bloody Ground", and

on May 1, 1769, set out accompanied by five other men. After a long and tedious journey of five weeks, the explorers saw before them a beautiful level region which they knew to be the land they were seeking.

Boone and his companions built a rude shelter of logs, open on one side. Here they lived, and in the country around they hunted until December without being molested by Indians. Then one day they were attacked, and Boone was captured. For days there was no chance of escape. But, at last, he succeeded in creeping stealthily away by night. A year from the next spring Boone returned to North Carolina.

The Wilderness Road and Boonesborough

Some time after, a certain Richard Henderson concluded a treaty with the Cherokees by which they agreed to allow white men to settle on the Bloody Ground. When the treaty was concluded, Henderson sent Boone with a company of thirty men to open a pathway from the Holston River, over the Cumberland Gap, to the Kentucky River. This was the first regular path into the wilderness, and it is still called, "The Wilderness Road."

When Boone's party reached the Kentucky they built a fort which they called Boonesborough. The fort was oblong in shape. There was a loopholed blockhouse at each corner. The log cabins were so arranged that their outer sides formed part of the wall, with a stockade twelve feet high filling the spaces between. This stockade was made by driving into the ground heavy timbers, pointed at the top.

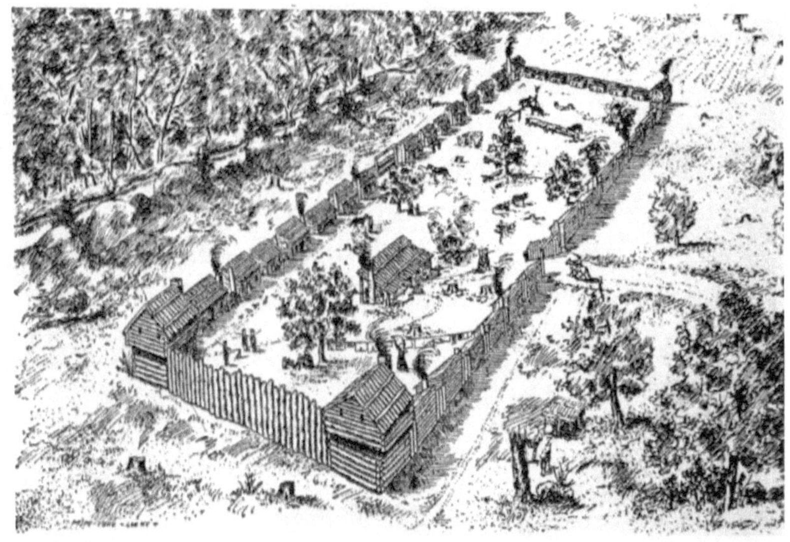

THE FORT AT BOONESBOROUGH.

The building of Boonesborough at this time was most important, as it offered protection for the settling of Kentucky.

After building the fort, Boone went back to North Carolina. When he returned to Boonesborough a little later, he brought with him his family and a band of settlers.

Not long after this, Boone's daughter and two girl companions were surprised by Indians and taken captive. As they went along, the eldest girl broke off twigs and dropped them in the path. Seeing her, one of the Indians threatened her with his tomahawk. However, she managed to tear off bits of her dress instead and, unnoticed, scatter them along the trail.

When the girls did not return to their home, Boone knew at once what had happened. With some neighbors he started in pursuit. Guided by the twigs and bits of cloth they overtook the savages just as they were cooking supper. Firing into the camp, they killed two of the Indians and frightened the rest away. The girls were unharmed, although badly scared.

At another time the Indians captured Boone himself and carried him off. But because they so admired his courage and skill, they decided to adopt him into their tribe in place of killing him. Accordingly he was made to go through some curious ceremonies. First, all his hair was taken off, with the exception of a tuft on the top of his head. Next, he was ducked in the river and scrubbed well in order to wash out his white blood. With a coat of paint on his face, with feathers in his scalp lock, and dressed in Indian costume, Boone certainly resembled his adopted brothers.

Although they treated him as one of themselves and seemingly gave him the utmost freedom, the Indians were ever watchful lest he should get away. Cunning and sagacious as the Indians were, Boone was a match for them. Apparently he was quite contented. One day he learned that his savage friends were planning an attack on Boonesborough. Then by great good luck he managed to escape. He had a hundred and sixty miles to cover and food enough for but one meal. He did not dare shoot game for fear the savages would hear him. Four days he traveled, almost without stopping. On the fifth day he arrived in safety at the fort.

The settlers immediately prepared the defences; and when the Indians came to make their attack, they were repulsed and Boonesborough was saved.

For many years Boone continued to be a useful citizen of Kentucky. But in due time, Kentucky became too crowded to suit him. He needed more elbow room. So, toward the close of the eighteenth century he went farther west and finally reached Missouri. This state was then the outpost of civilization. Here he lived until his death.

Boone's passion for hunting and solitude was a part of

A TYPICAL PIONEER WOODSMAN.

him until the end. Even in his eighty-second year he went on a long trapping expedition into the wilderness. He lived to see younger men pushing still farther west, and it saddened him that he could no longer equal them in endurance.

Daniel Boone was a typical backwoodsman. In his life and character we have a good picture of the western frontiersmen of the eighteenth century, men whose courage and perseverance opened the way to civilization.

XII

Whitney and Howe

Eli Whitney

Few men have done more for the welfare of mankind than did Eli Whitney. He did not discover a new land, nor did he explore the untrodden wilderness or win a great battle. He invented a machine which revolutionized the cotton industry.

Eli Whitney was a native of Massachusetts. At nineteen he made up his mind to go to college. As his father did not see fit to send him, he earned the necessary money himself. Partly by teaching and partly by odd jobs at carpentry, he gathered enough to pay his way through Yale University. In 1792 he was graduated. Soon after, Whitney secured a position as tutor in a Georgia family. But when he reached the South, he found the place filled. So he decided to study law. On the trip south he had become acquainted with Mrs. Greene, the widow of General Nathanael Greene, of Revolutionary fame. Hearing of his disappointment, Mrs. Greene now cordially invited him to make her plantation his home while he was studying law.

Whitney did many little things for his hostess to show that he appreciated her kindness. He made toys for the children and an embroidery frame for Mrs. Greene, which was an immense improvement over the awkward old-fashioned one she had been using. In fact, he had what has long been known as "Yankee ingenuity."

One day Mrs. Greene had as guests a number of plantation owners. They were speaking about the raising of cotton, and of how the value of the crop would be vastly increased if only some one could invent a machine that would strip the seeds from the cotton fiber. Mrs. Greene advised the men to lay the problem before her young friend, Eli Whitney. They explained the matter to him; but as he had not even seen the cotton fiber and its seeds, he was afraid he could do nothing. However, he said he would try.

At the time Whitney went to Georgia, cotton seeds were picked from the fiber by hand. It used to take a negro a whole day to clean a single pound of cotton, and it took many slaves several months to clean an entire crop. Because of this vast amount of labor, the planters could not raise cotton at a profit. But if only some one could invent a cotton cleaner, the profits on cotton would be immense. This then was Whitney's problem.

All winter long he tinkered. By the spring of 1793 he had

A SECTION OF THE COTTON GIN, SHOWING THE COTTON PASSING FROM THE FEEDER OVER THE CYLINDERS.

succeeded in contriving a machine with which one man could clean one thousand pounds of cotton in one day.

The machine consisted of two cylinders. On one were rows of teeth, which pulled the cotton through a grating too fine for the seeds to pass through. The other cylinder was covered with little brushes, which, as they met the teeth, brushed the cotton from them into a place prepared to catch it. And all this was done without in any way harming the seeds for the many uses they could be put to.

Whitney called the machine a cotton gin, "gin" being a contraction of the word "engine." He let only Mrs. Greene and a few others see his model. Yet, before long, nearly everyone in the South was talking about his wonderful invention; and, careful as he was, his shop was broken into, and his model was stolen. Before he could make another and get it patented there were several cotton gins in operation. All were copied from his stolen model, and it was years before Whitney recived justice in connection with his great invention.

Immediately after the invention of the cotton gin the planters began to increase the size of their cotton fields, and every year more and more cotton was raised. In 1784 America exported three thousand pounds. In 1803, ten years after the cotton gin came into use, forty million pounds were exported.

Since Whitney's time, the increase in production has lowered the price of cotton goods from a dollar and fifty cents a yard to as low as five cents a yard, thus enabling the very poorest to buy cotton cloth.

And all this is due to Eli Whitney's cotton gin, and has been brought about in a little over a century. The cotton gin has helped not only the Southern cotton growers, but also the manufacturers of both North and South. It has done much to improve our foreign trade, and so has helped the commerce of the country at large. Improvements have been made upon the original cotton gin, but the Americans of the twentieth century owe as much to Eli Whitney's invention as did those of a hundred years ago.

ELIAS HOWE

In colonial days making clothes was no easy matter. There are many, many stitches in even one simple garment. And when you think how many garments are necessary for one child, you can imagine how busy the mother of a large family must have been, when each stitch had to be done by hand.

There were traveling tailors, it is true, who would come and stay with a family and make the coats and trousers, and there were traveling cobblers, who made the shoes. But every family could not afford to pay these helpers, and even those who could, had to make many other things besides coats and trousers and shoes. So, day after day and evening after evening saw the women of the family busily sewing, sewing, sewing, one stitch at a time, and all done by hand.

One mother whose evenings were spent in this way was Mrs. Elias Howe. Her husband was a poor young man. They lived in Boston and Mr. Howe worked in a Boston shop where machines were made for spinning and weaving. The old way of spinning and weaving was very slow, but by the use of these machines much time and labor were saved.

Mr. Howe was not very strong and his day's work tired him out. At night, fairly exhausted, he would lie down and rest. And as he rested, his eyes watched his wife's patient fingers sending her needle in and out, in and out. He knew she was tired, too, for she had three little children to care for all day as well as her house work to do. Still, she could not rest in the evening. She must sew every night to keep the children in clothes and add to her husband's small earnings. It seemed a pity. Wasn't there some easier way to do the same thing?

Several men had tried to make a sewing machine but none had succeeded. Surely, it was possible to make such a machine and Elias Howe decided to try. At the shop he gave every spare minute to his plans. His first machine had a needle pointed at both ends with an eye in the middle. For more than a year he tried to make this succeed. Next, he used two threads, making the stitch by means of a shuttle. This time he used a curved needle. And, this time, he had a machine which would actually sew.

By now Howe had given up his place in the shop and

was poorer than ever. Fortunately, he was able to interest a Mr. Fisher in his machine, and Mr. Fisher took Howe and his family to board and furnished him the money to make a better machine than his rough model. In return for all this Mr. Fisher was to be half owner of the patent when it was secured.

By the spring of 1845, the new machine was made and, in 1846, was patented. Can you believe that such an invention was feared rather than received with joy? Tailors admitted that it might be useful, but they would have nothing to do with it. They and others who made their living by sewing thought it would ruin their trade. They talked against it and said it would throw many people out of work.

Mr. Fisher grew discouraged and withdrew from his agreement. Howe took his family to his father's home. And, now, came harder times than ever for the inventor and those dependent on him. He even went to England and tried to make something out of his invention over there. But, when he reached New York again, months later, he had less than a dollar in his pockets.

What was worse, while he was away, others had made copies of his machine and sold them. Sure of his patent, however, Howe began suits against these people and finally, after years of poverty and struggle, his rights were fully established and all manufacturers of the machine were forced to pay him a royalty.

Gradually, the usefulness of the sewing machine over-came the opposition to it, and it became a necessity. In 1863 Elias Howe's royalties were said to be $4,000 a day.

Of course, many improvements on Howe's machine were later made by others. In these he was much interested, and doubtless remembering his own hard times, he gladly helped their makers with advice, or money, or both. In his triumph, he was the soul of generosity to those working to follow where he had led.

XIII

Robert Fulton

Travel by Water in Colonial Days

There was a time long, long ago when America was like the land of fairy tales "where no one lived but a strange people and many animals." The people who lived in America were the red-skinned Indians. And it was to their land of forest wastes that the early colonists came. These colonists must have been lonely indeed as they stood on the shore and watched the ship that had brought them fade away in the distance, bound for home. There must have been a great longing in their hearts for the time when the ship would come again, bringing other colonists and news of far-away friends. And perhaps there was fear, too, of days when they might watch anxiously for a ship bearing fresh supplies. What more natural than that they should build their homes near the coast or on some navigable river, where ships from home could easily come to them?

As other colonists came, they, too, for the same reasons, settled near the shore. Moreover, if a man from one settlement wished to visit another, clearly he must go by land or water. If he went by land, there was greater danger from Indians, and he must travel through the rough forest, guided only by the blazed trees that marked the way. To go by water was a far simpler matter.

So it was that colonial towns grew up along the Atlantic coast, or on the shores of some stream that ran into the sea.

The small boats of these pioneer settlers were for the most part canoes copied after those of the Indians. There were two ways in which the Indians made canoes. One was by hollowing out a great pine or cedar log. This was done either by burning the wood, or by chipping away piece after piece with some sharp tool. The other form of Indian canoe was a light framework covered with birch bark.

As time went on the settlers built small boats of other kinds, and vessels large enough for ocean use. These last were all sailing vessels, and the best of them took weeks and sometimes months to cross the sea. Slow as they were, the sailing vessels were the only means of ocean travel for many years after the founding of the American colonies.

The world of long ago wasted time and strength in slow, tedious travel. So, too, its people were handicapped in endless directions by their lack of knowledge of steam and electricity and the uses to which they could be put.

It is the proud boast of America that to her citizens are due many of the inventions and discoveries that have changed

POLING A FLAT-BOTTOMED BOAT.

the clumsy methods of long ago into the effective ways of to-day. Among this number stands Robert Fulton.

The Boy Fulton

Robert Fulton was born in a Pennsylvania village, in 1765. When he went to school his schoolmaster found it hard work to keep the boy's attention. He did not appear interested in the lessons set before him, but liked much better to spend his time drawing pictures with pencils that he had hammered out of pieces of lead.

However, Fulton was far from being stupid. He had ideas of his own, and good ones.

Shortly before the 4th of July, 1778, the people of Fulton's town stopped as they went along the street to read a public notice. The notice said that inasmuch as candles were at present very scarce, the citizens were requested not to illuminate their houses that year in celebration of Independence Day. This was a bitter disappointment to Robert, who was full of patriotism and eager to express it. He simply could not have the streets dark on the Fourth of July. So he bought some gunpowder and pasteboard, and went to work.

Fourth of July came, and he was ready for it. He had made some sky rockets, which not only

ROBERT FULTON.

illuminated the town but surprised and astonished all the people.

When young Fulton and his friends went fishing, they went in a heavy, flat-bottomed boat, which had to be poled along from place to place. As this was slow and rather hard work, Robert made a pair of paddle wheels, one of which was fastened to each side of the boat. They were turned by a crank and were far easier to manage than the long poles whose place they took.

But while Fulton enjoyed making all sorts of things, he still took chief pleasure in drawing and painting. And when he was seventeen years old he went to Philadelphia to take up the life of an artist.

The "clermont"

Soon after Fulton became of age his friends began to urge him to go abroad, as in Europe he could learn to do better work and could win a wider reputation as an artist than in America.

The voyage was made in a sailing vessel. Now and again a fair wind filled the sails, and the ship made good headway. Then came days of calm when the vessel rocked to and fro on the waves and drifted idly. It seemed a long journey. At last England was reached, and Robert Fulton went to London.

For a while he devoted his time to art, but gradually his love for invention grew upon him and enticed him more and more away from his painting. During his stay in England he invented several useful machines. Idea followed idea.

At length he went to France and, while in that country, made a diving boat that would move about under the water. This diving boat was to carry torpedoes, one of which could be fastened to the bottom of a ship so that, when it exploded, it would blow the ship to pieces.

Fulton thought that such a boat would be a mighty protection to a country with a weak navy. Should an enemy's warship on mischief bent enter a harbor, down could go the diving boat with its torpedo; and in no time the dangerous visitor would be a hopeless wreck. But in spite of the inventor's belief in his boat, he could induce neither England nor France to adopt it for her navy.

Another thing that Robert Fulton tried to do while in France was to make a boat that would run by steam. Others had already attempted to do this, but with very indifferent success. Fulton remembered that old flat-boat to which he had fastened the paddle wheels. Why not try the same plan on a large boat and make a steam engine turn the crank?

At that time Robert R. Livingston was America's minister to France. He grew so interested in Fulton's scheme that he offered to furnish the money necessary to carry it out.

When the boat was finished it was launched on the river Seine. Fulton was well pleased; but just as the day of its trial trip was at hand, the boat broke in two and sank. The machinery had proved too heavy for so light a framework. A stronger one was made; but now the engine was not powerful enough to move the boat with any speed.

Still Fulton was not discouraged. In 1806 he and Mr. Livingston went to New York, determined to try their luck once more.

The building of their boat was soon under way, and almost every day saw Fulton down at the shipyards directing just how it should be done. He named the boat the *Clermont,* which was the name of Mr. Livingston's home on the Hud-

THE "CLERMONT".

son. Others called it "Fulton's Folly," so absurd did it seem even to try to make steam run a boat. Out of sheer curiosity, men visited the shipyards to look at "Fulton's Folly"; and they spoke of it with scorn and ridicule.

It was August, 1807, when the *Clermont* was done, and her owners invited their friends to join them on a trip up the Hudson.

So Fulton really thought that boat would go! It was too ridiculous. Great crowds gathered to see the fun of the start, which they felt would be no start at all. Even the invited guests stepped to the *Clermont*'s deck with grave misgivings. No one enjoys being in an absurd position, and this certainly looked like one.

The signal was given. The side wheels began to churn the water, and—wonder of wonders!—the *Clermont* moved steadily away from the dock.

A great cheer rose from the amazed crowd on the shore. But it died again as quickly as it rose. The boat had stopped.

Now indeed the guests on board wished themselves out of their predicament. Why had they come? They knew all the time just how it would be.

Fulton frankly admitted that he did not know what was wrong. But he asked his passengers to give him half an hour in which to set things right. He promised that, if he could not start the boat in thirty minutes, he would give up the trip and put his guests ashore. Then, hurrying to his engine, he looked it over anxiously. The trouble was only a small matter, and in a few moments Fulton's skilled fingers had made the needed readjustment. Again the *Clermont* started, and this time she steamed straight up the Hudson. All the rest of that day and all that night she went on and on toward Albany. Fishermen in their boats, sailors on sailing vessels, watchers on the shore heard the strange sound of the *Clermont's* engine, and saw the smoke pouring from her stack. All were filled with wonder, and many were overcome with terror.

To Albany and back the *Clermont* went, covering the distance of one hundred and fifty miles between Albany and New York in thirty-two hours. This was only the first of many trips she made up and down the Hudson, carrying passengers.

Robert Fulton was now a great man. He had succeeded where all had expected failure; he had made a boat that would go in spite of wind or tide. And more than that. He had found the means for the better, quicker water travel which our country needed. Before many years steamboats were running on the Mississippi and the Missouri rivers and on the Great Lakes. The great west lay open to emigrants, and Robert Fulton had furnished a way for them to go there.

The first steamboat to cross the Atlantic sailed from an

American port in 1819. This was the *Savannah* and it took her twenty-six days to go from Georgia to Liverpool, England.

The record for Atlantic travel between Queenstown and New York to-day is five days and a few hours. Seven hundred and ninety feet long by eighty-eight feet wide are the dimensions of the two largest ocean steamers now afloat. Each is built to carry two thousand two hundred passengers, besides its crew.

Do the passengers, living for a few days in all the luxury and comfort of a modern ocean palace, realize that only a century lies between Fulton's ungainly little *Clermont* and the stately steamships that sail the seas to-day?

XIV

George Stephenson

Land Travel Before 1830

As late as the end of the first quarter of the nineteenth century a land journey of any length was a matter not lightly to be undertaken. One had to go either on foot, or by horse. In the modes of travel the people of that time were no better off than the Romans under Caesar, more than eighteen hundred years before.

In early colonial times two or more persons traveling in the same direction often used the "ride and tie system," as it was called. That is to say, one would start on horseback, the other following on foot. The one on horseback, after riding about a mile would dismount, tie the horse, and walk on.

TRAVELING BY STAGE COACH.

The one on foot, coming to the horse, would mount, ride past the one ahead for a distance, tie the horse, and walk on in his turn, leaving the horse once more for the first rider.

In 1776 a coach took thirteen days to journey from London to Edinburgh; and in this country in the same year a coach between New York and Philadelphia, the weather favorable, took two days for the trip.

Now we travel at the rate of over fifty miles an hour and think nothing of it. This great change in the method of transportation is due, in large measure, to the genius and ability of George Stephenson.

THE MINE ENGINE AND THE COAL ROADS

George Stephenson was an Englishman. His father was a poor worker in the coal mines, and as a boy, he too worked in the mines. He did not know how to read or write till he was past seventeen, yet he became one of the most prominent men of his country.

England has always been celebrated for its coal mines; and in the years of Stephenson's childhood, the need of a quicker and a cheaper method of transporting the coal had long been felt. In some of the mines rough rails had been used, the loads being pulled by horses.

Stephenson was put to work as engine boy for the stationary engines used in lifting the coal. He had a mechanical mind and was fond of machinery. So he soon became familiar with the construction of machines, and at an early age was an expert engineer.

By studying after his working hours he learned to read and write. He was so poor that in order to increase his earnings, he made and repaired shoes in the evening. Later he gained

GEORGE STEPHENSON

quite a local reputation from the skill with which he cleaned and repaired clocks.

As he matured and his knowledge of mechanics increased, he became more and more interested in solving the question of transporting coal more cheaply. As early as 1815 he had built an engine which was used in drawing coal from a mine to the place of shipment several miles away.

A few years later he constructed another road, the Stockton and Darlington Railroad. At that time no one supposed that travelers would care to be carried in this way; for, as an English newspaper of those days said, "What person would ever think to pay anything to be conveyed...in something like a coal wagon...and to be dragged...by a roaring steam engine?" At the celebration of the opening of this road a rider on horseback with a flag led the procession in front of the engine. You see that the train was not expected to go very fast.

Passenger Railroads

But the Stockton and Darlington Railroad proved successful and led to the construction of the Liverpool and Manchester Road. In order to decide the best engine to be adopted on this new road, a contest was held in which four engines

THE "ROCKET".

took part, and the prize of five hundred pounds was won by Stephenson's engine, the *Rocket*.

The Liverpool and Manchester Railroad was opened in the summer of 1830; and the occasion was honored by the presence of the Duke of Wellington, many members of Parliament, and other prominent men. At this opening the first railroad accident is recorded, Mr. Huskisson, a distinguished member of Parliament, being killed.

The famous little *Rocket* is still preserved in London in the Kensington Museum. It weighs only four and a quarter tons and is a great contrast to the monsters of to-day, some of which weigh one hundred and twenty tons. But small though it be, it is, so to speak, the grandfather of the present locomotive.

RAILROAD TRAVEL IN NEW YORK STATE IN 1831.

In the United States, railways were quickly introduced. The first one was only about thirteen miles long and ran from Baltimore, Maryland, to Ellicott's Mills. Over its rails in 1830 went the first American locomotive. Ten years later there were nearly three thousand miles of railroad in the different states. On May 10, 1869, the last spike was driven in a railroad that ran clear across our country from the Atlantic to the Pacific. And to-day one can travel the 3,322 miles between New York and San Francisco in about five days, the same length of time it took the early colonists to journey from New York to Boston.

XV

Oliver Hazard Perry

BEFORE THE WAR OF 1812

A sailor himself, Christopher Perry destined his son, Oliver, for the sea. The boy was born in South Kingston, Rhode Island, was sent to school in Newport, and lived the life of all boys until he was nearly fourteen.

At this time his father was given command of the United States ship *General Greene*, bound for Cuba. What better chance for Oliver to become a sailor? The *General Greene* put out to sea in the spring of 1799, with Oliver Hazard Perry acting as her midshipman.

It was on this West Indian cruise that the lad first learned practical seamanship, satisfying even his father by his readiness. Thanks to Christopher Perry's training and his own aptness, Oliver, when he left his father's service, was fitted for the seaman's life that lay before him.

Now came years when England and France were at war with each other. England needed all the sailors she could get. She even went so far as to stop American ships on the high seas to search them for Englishmen sailing under the American flag. "Once an Englishman, always an Englishman," she said. "If we find native born Englishmen on your vessels, we shall treat them as deserters to be returned to the English navy."

Once aboard an American vessel, the British officers commanded the crew to be drawn up for inspection. Then began the selecting of sailors, who, the intruders insisted, should be serving England's king. It mattered little that many of these sailors said they were American born. They were able-bodied men; England wanted them, and they were

made to board the English ships and were carried off.

Not only did British men-of-war stop our vessels on the open sea. They were so bold as to lie in wait near the entrance of our harbors. When over six thousand sailors had been seized, and hundreds of vessels had been overhauled, the end of American endurance was reached. And in 1812 war was declared on England.

The Victory on Lake Erie

At the beginning of the War of 1812, Perry was stationed at Newport. Since the days of his first cruise on the *General Greene*, he had had a hand in putting down the pirates of the Mediterranean. He was no longer a midshipman, but was in command of a flotilla of American gunboats. Seeing little prospect of actual fighting if he stayed at Newport, Perry asked to be transferred. And, according to his wish, he was sent to the Great Lakes, where Commodore Chauncey put him in command of the forces on Lake Erie.

By the capture of Detroit the English had gained control of Lake Erie, where they had a fleet which was a serious menace to the Americans. It was Perry's task to rid the country of this danger.

Perry was a man who believed in doing things; and from the time of his arrival on the lakes, things began to happen. When he reached Erie in March, 1813, he found two brigs, two gunboats, and a small schooner being built from the green timber of the forest trees. Leaving the shipbuilders to complete their work, Perry rushed to Pittsburg to hurry up the equipment for his little fleet. He hastened to get additional boats. He hurried them to Erie before the English could intercept them. And such was his alacrity that, by the end of July, his fleet was ready, except for the crews. These arrived slowly. Perry named his flagship the *Lawrence* in honor of a gallant American captain who had recently died in battle, calling to his men, "Don't give up the ship!"

August went by, and the first days of September. Then on the 10th of September, 1813, Perry met the English fleet near Put-In Bay. In the American fleet were nine boats, large

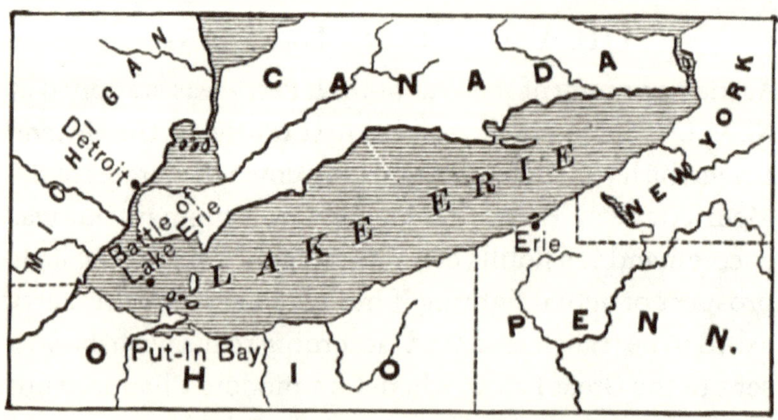

WHERE THE BATTLE OF LAKE ERIE WAS FOUGHT.

and small. In the English there were six. But the English six carried more guns than the American nine.

Running up a blue flag bearing the brave words of Captain Lawrence, "Don't give up the ship," Perry ordered his fleet to advance toward the approaching English. The *Lawrence* with two little schooners forged ahead. The rest of the fleet was delayed in starting, so the first of the English attack fell upon the flagship. Her masts were shot away, her guns were disabled, and she was completely crippled. The English had wrecked Perry's ship. Had they conquered the commander? No! Flag in hand, he slipped over the Lawrence's side, dropped into a small boat, and amidst the whizzing balls of the enemy was rowed to the *Niagara*.

Taking command at once on this second ship, Perry sailed straight into the enemy's line and raked the vessels with a

PERRY LEAVING THE "LAWRENCE".

deadly fire. The English could not endure long under such conditions, and one by one they struck their flags.

With his victory won, Perry went back to the deck of the *Lawrence* and there received the English surrender. His message to General Harrison was written on the back of an old letter. It read in part, "We have met the enemy, and they are ours."

This victory gave the United States the control of Lake Erie, and the English abandoned Detroit. Commodore Perry lived only six years to enjoy the fame earned through his triumph. In 1819 he was sent to protect American commerce from attack by the privateers of Venezuela. He sailed up the Orinoco River and settled with Venezuela the disputes that had arisen. But on his return voyage, the brave young seaman was stricken with yellow fever; and as his ship was entering the harbor of Port-of-Spain, Trinidad, he died.

XVI

Thomas Macdonough

THE BATTLE ON LAKE CHAMPLAIN

A year and a day after the battle of Lake Erie, the battle of Lake Champlain was fought. This was on September 11, 1814. The hero of the encounter was Thomas Macdonough.

In 1814, the English planned to attack 'New Fork by way of Lake Champlain, as General Burgoyne had done more than thirty-five years before. While a British fleet entered the lake, a British army advanced on Plattsburg. The army and the fleet were to make a joint attack.

To oppose this, the Americans had a small force at Plattsburg and a few war vessels on the lake under the command of Thomas Macdonough. Reaching Plattsburg, the English troops waited for their fleet to begin the battle. The first broadside had just flashed forth when, on the American flagship, a pet game cock flew upon one of the guns and gave a defiant crow. Macdonough's men raised cheer after cheer and, encouraged by the happy omen, plunged into the fight.

THOMAS MACDONOUGH.

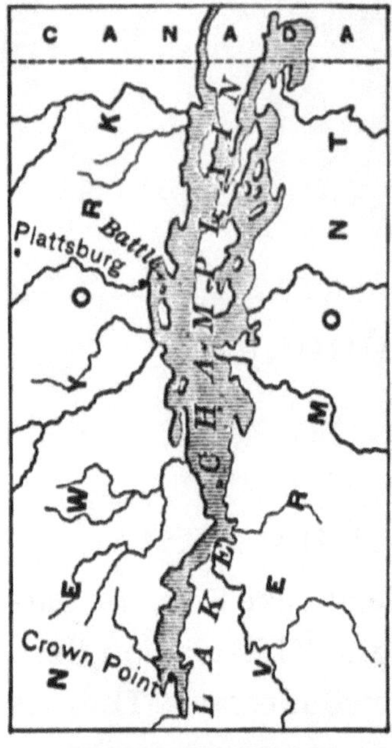

WHERE THE BATTLE OF PLATTSBURG WAS FOUGHT.

At length not one of the flag-ship's starboard guns was fit to use. Then Macdonough, with the utmost coolness and bravery, turned his boat around so that the guns on the other side could be brought to bear. The fresh attack was too much for the English. Soon their flagship surrendered, and the other vessels were overcome.

On the defeat of his fleet the British General and his army retreated to Canada. Macdonough by his victory had put an end to the invasions of New York.

THE BARBARY PIRATES

Although Thomas Macdonough's fame as a warrior rests on the battle of Plattsburg, that was not the only service he rendered our country. Eleven years before he had distinguished himself against the Barbary pirates. Along the north of Africa lie Algiers, Tunis, and Tripoli. From their ports for years the Barbary pirates had sallied forth on the Mediterranean, capturing merchant men, confiscating their cargoes, and holding their crews for ransom, or selling them as slaves. England and the countries of Europe had long paid an annual tribute to free their shipping from these piratical pests.

When American ships began to frequent the Mediterranean, the Barbary pirates welcomed them as a new source of profit. And our ships too were plundered, and our crews

DECATUR'S MEN FIGHTING PIRATES IN THE MEDITERRANEAN.

held for ransom. So for a time the United States likewise paid an annual tribute to Algiers.

This roused the envy of Tunis and Tripoli, and they began to make demands on our Government. It seems now almost amusing to read how the ruler of Tunis ordered the American Consul to furnish him ten thousand stand of arms, as peace depended on compliance. Tripoli went even further and, in 1801, actually declared war on the United States.

In the course of this war, the American frigate, *Philadelphia*, wrecked near Tripoli, was captured, towed into the harbor, and anchored under the guns of the port. Here she was repaired and fitted up to fight against us. This was adding insult to injury. But how to prevent it?

Stephen Decatur, a gallant officer, asked permission to try, and called for volunteers to go with him. There was a hearty response. And one night Decatur with a few men stole into the harbor of Tripoli, boarded the *Philadelphia*, and burned her to the water's edge, under the very guns of the enemy. It was a valiant deed, and one of Decatur's little band was Thomas Macdonough.

XVII

Andrew Jackson

THE EMIGRANT'S BOY

About the time the injustice of the Stamp Act was common talk in the thirteen colonies, a poor Irish emigrant and his family set sail for America.

The father was Andrew Jackson. He and his wife and two sons, Hugh and Robert, landed in America and made a clearing on Twelve Mile Creek, a branch of the Catawba River.

THE BIRTHPLACE OF ANDREW JACKSON.

After two short years of struggle to gain a living for his family, Andrew Jackson died. The wife was left to care for Hugh and Robert, and a baby boy, who was born on March 15, 1767, a few days after the father's death. The mother named her little boy after his father. And now we have come to the hero of our story, Andrew Jackson.

On the death of her husband, Mrs. Jackson moved from the clearing and, with two of her boys, went to the home of an invalid sister. Here she did what she could to support her children.

When the boys were old enough, Mrs. Jackson sent them to school, where they learned reading, writing, and arithmetic. As Andrew's mother wished him to become a minister, he was later sent to another and better school. But school was a sort of bugbear to Andrew. He was not much of a student.

He was a thin, barefooted, freckle-faced lad, with reddish hair and eyes of a beautiful clear blue. He loved all out-of-door sports—hunting, running, jumping, and wrestling. He was so full of tricks and fun that he was called "mischievous Andy."

He was very wiry and active; and, although the stronger boys could throw him three times out of four, he was so quick in getting to his feet that they couldn't keep him down. He was never afraid of the older lads, and always took the part of the smaller and weaker boys. But Andy had his faults as well as his virtues. One of these was his quick temper, which was always ready to blaze forth. As he grew older he learned to control it; but even then it sometimes ran away with him, and he did things for which he was very sorry afterwards.

Although still a little fellow when the Revolution began, Andrew took the liveliest interest in it; and when the campaign in the South brought the fighting near his home, he learned a lesson in British cruelty, which he never forgot.

In the summer of 1780 he and Robert attached themselves to a band of dragoons. It is hard to tell just what work was assigned to such young boys, but they saw at least one battle during that summer. This must have been an anxious time for the mother, especially as her son Hugh, who had enlisted in the American army, had already died.

The next year Robert and Andrew Jackson were captured by the British. One day, while they were prisoners, an officer ordered Andrew to clean his muddy boots. The boy's temper was up in an instant and he flashed out, "Sir, I'm not your slave. I am your prisoner; and, as such, I refuse to do the work of a slave."

Angered at the lad's boldness, the officer raised his sword to strike. Andrew parried the blow, but received two severe wounds, the scars of which he carried to the grave.

He and Robert were soon sent to the prison pen at Camden. This was a large yard around the jail. The poor soldiers had no shelter and hardly any food. Some of them had smallpox, and everything was as wretched as could be. Day by day the men waited for the help that did not come. Andrew's mother had been pleading for her sons' release and finally succeeded in getting them exchanged for British prisoners. When they left the prison, both boys had smallpox. Robert died, and Andrew recovered only after a long illness.

As soon as his mother could leave him, the patriotic woman went to care for the soldiers on the prison ships is Charleston Harbor. There she took a fever; and she, too, died. Poor Andrew was now left to face the world alone.

Lawyer and Fighter

For a while after his mother's death Andrew Jackson tried his hand as saddler and school-teacher. Then he decided to study law; and for this he went to Salisbury, North Carolina.

At the age of twenty-one, after he had been admitted to the bar, young Jackson joined a party that crossed the Blue Ridge Mountains into Tennessee and settled in Nashville. The freckle-faced schoolboy had grown into a man, six feet and one inch tall, with the same thick reddish hair and sharp blue eyes.

When he had been in Nashville a while, he was appointed by President Washington to the office of United States Attorney. This was an honor attended with much danger. In Jackson's new position it was his duty to punish horse stealing, land stealing, and to settle all kinds of quarrels. He had to go from one place to another to hold court, and on his journeys through the forests the danger from the Indians and his enemies was great.

Tennessee was the far West of that day, and many rough adventurers flocked there. These men had no respect for law, nor did they care what they did to avenge supposed wrongs. It was among such people that Jackson had to preserve order. But in spite of difliculties, he did his utmost to fulfill the duties of his office. Once he even drew out two large pistols and laid them on his table by way of subduing a bully who had vowed he would not be tried. A fight followed, then and there. But in the end, Jackson restored order and tried the man. This is merely one incident out of many such, in his life as United States Attorney.

In 1791 Jackson married. His home during his married life

"THE HERMITAGE".

was on a large plantation not far from Nashville. Here he built a house, which he called "The Hermitage." Rich and poor alike were welcome here, and "The Hermitage" was always famous for its hospitality.

On his plantation Jackson devoted much time to his horses, of which he had a goodly number. He was passionately fond of them, and none knew better than he how to raise and train thoroughbreds.

Once he had a quarrel about a horse race, with a man named Dickinson. In consequence the two fought a duel, as was the customary way of settling quarrels in those days. Dickinson was a "dead shot" and boasted that he would surely kill Jackson. They met at the appointed time. Dickinson fired. Then Jackson fired, and the boaster fell to the ground, dying soon after. Jackson, with his surgeon and a friend, had left the scene of the duel and gone some distance when his companions saw blood oozing from Jackson's clothes. He had had two ribs shattered, but had told no one that he was wounded. Such was his fearless courage and his great endurance of pain.

This same ability to endure won for him in his military life of later years the loving title of "Old Hickory." "He is as tough as hickory," his soldiers were wont to say.

A few years rolled by; and then one summer the Creek

Indians attacked Fort Mimms in Alabama and massacred about five hundred men, women, and children who had taken refuge there. Jackson, who had long before been elected Major General of the Tennessee militia, took command of a detachment and marched against the Indians.

Before he had succeeded in routing them, Jackson found himself out of provisions. For days the men had but small rations. Then, because of their sufferings, and because their short terms of enlistment had come to an end, they said they were going home. It took all the patience and tact that Jackson had to keep his men together, and three different times he had to use one part of his army to keep the rest from marching away.

After this campaign, in which the power of the Creeks was broken, Jackson received the title of Major General in the United States army. His greatest triumphs were yet to come.

The War of 1812 was now in progress; and a few months after subduing the Creeks, General Jackson and his troops were ordered south to keep the British out of the Mississippi valley.

In Florida, which still belonged to Spain, the British had been allowed to land at the town of Pensacola. When Jackson heard of this he marched against the sleepy little Spanish town and drove the British back to their ships. Then he went to the defense of New Orleans, as that city was the key to the Mississippi.

The English soldiers sent to take New Orleans were veterans just from the wars with Napoleon. Their foreign victories were still fresh in their minds, and they thought what short work they would make of the backwoodsmen of America.

On the 8th of January, 1815, the British made their last

GENERAL JACKSON KEEPING WATCH OF THE ENEMY FROM THE ROOF OF
HIS HEADQUARTERS IN NEW ORLEANS.

advance against the city. All their previous attacks had been
repelled by the vigilance and activity of General Jackson. Nor

did he mean to be beaten now. "Old Hickory" was everywhere on that memorable day. "Stand to your guns!" "See that every shot tells!" were his commands. And so well did the soldiers obey, that when the battle was over they could claim an overwhelming victory. The British had lost more than twenty-five hundred men.

The saddest thing about the whole war was that the battle of New Orleans was fought after peace had been declared. The agreement was made in Europe; and just because there were no cables or fast ocean steamers in those days, the news of peace did not reach this country until after these many lives had been sacrificed.

The victory of New Orleans made Jackson very popular throughout the country. On his return home he was welcomed with great joy by the people of Tennessee.

Famous visitors now came to "The Hermitage." Among them was General Lafayette on his last visit to America. Lafayette said of Jackson, "That is a great man. He has much before him yet."

It was not long before this prophecy came true; for in 1828 Andrew Jackson was elected President of the United States. Mrs. Jackson died a short time after the election, and Jackson was heartbroken. He had now no desire to go to Washington and be President, but he faced the duty bravely.

PRESIDENT

As President, Andrew Jackson showed the same fearlessness that he had displayed in battle.

The South at this time was opposed to the law which put a high tariff, or tax, on imported goods. The northern states wanted this tariff because they were manufacturing states. They said that Americans ought to buy goods

made in America, and that the way to make them support the home industries was to force a high price on foreign manufactures. The southern states were not manufacturing states, and so had to buy their finished woolen and cotton cloth from either the North or Europe. Before the tariff, they had been able to get it from Europe for less than they could buy it in the North.

Now all this was changed. With the duty that must now be paid, foreign cloth was even higher in price than cloth made in the North; so the South was practically forced to buy from the North at her price. The South claimed that this was an effort to enrich the North at the expense of the South. South Carolina, especially, resented such a step and said that she would disobey the law.

Senator Hayne from South Carolina made a powerful speech in Congress, in which he set forth the right of any State to disobey the laws of the nation.

Daniel Webster answered him. Webster stated that, according to the Constitution, every state must obey the laws of Congress and no state had the right to withdraw from the Union as South Carolina had threatened to do. He ended with these memorable words: "Liberty and union, now and forever, one and inseparable."

President Jackson was a southern man, so the South thought that he would not oppose them. Imagine their surprise then, when, at a banquet of Southern sympathizers, he offered the toast, "The Federal Union. It must and shall be preserved." Jackson agreed with Webster that the Union should stand ahead of the states, and that no state had the right to withdraw from it. When he found that South Carolina was firm in her refusal to pay the tariff, he said, "Send for General Scott." Troops were immediately ordered south, and South Carolina withdrew her opposition. Jackson's firmness of decision had put off the day of secession.

At the end of his second term of office, Andrew Jackson retired to his plantation home, where he spent the few remaining years of his life in peace and quiet. He will always be remembered for his fearless devotion to what he believed to be right, and will live in the hearts of all loyal Americans as one who helped to preserve the union of our country.

XVIII

Henry Clay

Early Training

Have you ever heard of the "Mill Boy of the Slashes"? He was born in Virginia in 1777, in a part of the country that had many low, swampy lands, called "The Slashes." This "Mill Boy" was Henry Clay.

Henry Clay's father died when this boy of his was four years old, and the care of the large family of children fell to the mother. As soon as Henry was old enough, he did his share of work. The neighbors often saw him walking bare-

THE BIRTHPLACE OF HENRY CLAY.

foot behind a plow, or riding to the mill seated on a bag of corn thrown across his horse's back. The people all along the way called him "The Mill Boy of the Slashes."

Although the Clays were poor, Henry was sent to school. Then, when he was fourteen, he went to Richmond where he found employment as clerk in a small store. Here he did the odd jobs which fell to him to do.

By this time Mrs. Clay had married again, and the step-father was not satisfied to have Henry where he was. So he secured for the boy a clerkship in the office of the High Court of Chancery. The clerks in the office smiled when they saw the awkward country lad, and imagined they were going to have some fun with him. But he was ready with a telling answer to all their jokes, and soon they learned to respect him for his faithfulness in the office and for his habits outside. He was forever reading, when not at work. Much of his future character and success was due to the fact that by so much reading he made up for his lack of education.

Soon young Clay attracted the attention of Chancellor Wythe, who asked him to be his private secretary. For four years Clay worked for the Chancellor, and it was during these years that he was inspired with the desire to become a lawyer—a desire which he fulfilled when he was twenty. Not alone by being associated with Chancellor Wythe, had he had advantages. He had belonged to a debating club, many of whose members became famous lawyers in after days. Henry Clay himself was a chief spirit in the club, and the practice he had in speaking before its members told in his years of public life.

As there was little chance in Richmond, Clay, like Jackson, concluded to go west when he had become a full-fledged lawyer. So, when he was not quite twenty-one, he set out for the land of Daniel Boone.

He settled down in Lexington, Kentucky, where he hoped his profession as a lawyer would bring him fair returns. And he was not mistaken. Before long he had his hands full. He was unusually successful, whether his case was defending a criminal or settling some dispute in regard to land or money. Many a time did he give his services free of charge to some poor widow or orphan, to slaves struggling for their freedom, to free negroes, and to the poor and oppressed who came to him for help.

His success as a lawyer grew so fast that he soon had money enough to enable him to marry; and in a few years he bought an estate, which he called "Ashland."

Meanwhile, he was gaining popularity. The people of Lexington and of the whole state loved and admired him. He was not yet thirty years old when they sent him to fill a vacancy in the United States Senate.

In Congress

In the Senate, Clay began at once to take part like an old hand at the business. He was all attention and ready to act whenever anyone made a resolution which had to do with "internal improvements."

At this time America was at peace with foreign nations, and the country was thriving. Thousands of people were pouring over the mountains into the fertile regions beyond.

But the roads were poor; there were snags, sand bars, and rapids in the rivers, and the hardships of a journey were great.

EMIGRANT AND FREIGHT WAGON OF PIONEER DAYS.

So, as the West grew, there was constant cry for better roads and for canals and bridges between the East and the West.

Henry Clay knew how hard the journey was, because he, too, had been an emigrant. And from the days of his first term in the Senate he became a veritable champion of the cause of internal improvements. One of the most useful of these improvements was the famous Cumberland Road, which in due time was opened from the banks of the Potomac at Cumberland, Maryland, over the mountains and across the country, until it almost reached the Mississippi.

Clay's first term in the Sen-ate was soon over. But in 1809 he was sent again to fill the unexpired term of another senator. He served for two years, and when the two years were up he was elected a member of the House of Representatives.

Late in 1811 Henry Clay arrived in Washington to take his place in the House. On his very first day of service he was chosen Speaker.

In this position Clay had great influence, and it was largely due to his leadership that the War of 1812 was brought on as soon as it was. He said that America must stand up for the rights of her sailors, and not allow England to seize them. He felt and preached that war must come, and war came. New England was against the war. But Clay insisted that a sailor who works or fights for his country has a right to be protected by that country. The flag under which he sails should be his protection. If a country cannot protect its sailors by peaceable means, then it ought to do so by force.

The War of 1812 was not much of a success from a military point of view. It was our plucky little navy which taught England that she must keep her hands off American sailors.

In 1814 Henry Clay was one of the men who went to Europe to arrange the treaty of peace that put an end to the war.

The Great Pacificator

In the early days black slaves were brought by shiploads from Africa and were sold to the colonists. No matter how long or how hard the slave worked, he could never earn his freedom; and he might, at any time, be sold away from his family. Occasionally a master gave a slave his freedom, but this happened rarely. Many of the slaves were kindly treated and had comfortable homes; but others had little to eat and wear, and many hardships to endure.

Before the Revolution all the states had slaves. But in the years that followed the war, the North gradually gave up slavery. The northern states were turning their attention to manufacturing; for their swift flowing streams gave excellent water power for mills and factories. The negroes of those days were not educated enough to work in the factories, so slave labor was no longer practicable in the North. This fact doubtless made it easier for the North to recognize the evils of slave-holding, and one by one the northern states declared themselves free states—that is, states opposed to slavery.

The South still held firmly to its slave system and intended to do so. With their warm climate and broad stretches of fertile land, the southern states went on raising cotton, rice, and tobacco. And it is in no way surprising that they saw much good and little evil in the slave labor which was so cheap and which served their purposes so well.

Thus, little by little, the difference in business interests between the North and the South led to an ever-growing difference of opinion in regard to slavery.

The laws that governed the interests of the North and the South were made in Congress by the representatives of the different states. So it was only natural that North and South should each want on its side as many states as possible, in order to increase the number of its votes in Congress.

When Missouri asked to be taken into the Union as a slave state, there were eleven free states and eleven slave states—an arrangement of which neither side could complain. Now, if Missouri came in as a slave state, it would give the controlling votes in Congress to the South. Of course the South was in favor of admitting Missouri. And of course the North was set against such a step. For nearly two years the matter was debated. Neither side would give in to the other.

Then Henry Clay persuaded Congress to make a compromise which promised satisfaction to both North and South. By this compromise, Missouri was to be taken into the Union as a slave state, on the express understanding that any other

states that might be formed from the Louisiana Purchase land north of Missouri's southern boundary should be free forever.

The Missouri compromise was adopted in 1820. But even before Missouri succeeded in becoming the twelfth slave state, Maine had been admitted as the twelfth free state. And so neither North nor South could yet claim the balance of power in Congress.

In 1848 a short war between the United States and

Mexico came to an end. And at its close Mexico ceded California and New Mexico to the United States. Here was the old struggle back again. Should slavery be allowed in this new land or not?

California wanted to enter the Union as a free state. Again there was the same number of free and slave states, and again the state asking to come in would give one side the advantage over the other. So again there were hot disputes. These grew so bitter that the Union was in danger of being broken up. Once more, as in the case of Missouri, Henry Clay urged a compromise. This compromise contained so many points that it was called the "Omnibus Bill."

According to Clay's plan, California was to be admitted as a free state; the people in the rest of the new land were to suit themselves as to how their territory should come into the Union; and the North was to arrest, and send back to their owners, all runaway slaves found in the free states. For two days Clay spoke in the Senate. People had come from far and near to hear him, and all his old charm of voice and manner were used to convince his audience of the advantages of the compromise. He asked the North to yield, and appealed to the South for peace. Then followed a debate which lasted for months, but finally Clay's compromise was adopted. This was in 1850.

A fellow Kentuckian told Mr. Clay that this compromise would injure his chances of ever becoming president. "Sir, I would rather be right than be president," answered Mr. Clay.

In two short years after his struggle to keep the states together by his compromise of 1850, Henry Clay died. He has been called the great Pacificator. Though his compromises failed to secure to the country the lasting good he hoped for, they attest his patriotism—his pure love for his country, and his desire to see the Union great and glorious. The name of Henry Clay will always fill a place in the list of America's honored statesmen.

XIX

Daniel Webster

At School and College

One day, many many years ago, an eight-year-old boy hurried into a New Hampshire village store. His black eyes were bright, and he was eager, for he had come to buy a coveted treasure.

On a past visit to the store the lad had seen a cotton handkerchief on which was printed the new Constitution of the United States. How he had wanted this wonderful handkerchief! But it takes money to buy things; and for lack of the price the treasure had been left behind, while the boy went home to save up the needed twenty-five cents.

At last he had succeeded and, money in hand, had come to buy the longed-for copy of the Constitution. It was from his printed cotton handkerchief that Daniel Webster learned the

Constitution from end to end. Little did he think then that he would ever be called the defender of that same Constitution.

Daniel Webster was born in Salisbury,—now Franklin, —New Hampshire, in 1782. He was the ninth of ten children. From the very first he was a frail, sickly child, for whom the neighbors foretold a short life.

Because of his ill health little was expected of him on the farm, and he was allowed to roam at will over the hills and through the meadows. His companion on these rambles was an old soldier-sailor, who had deserted from the British ranks to help the Americans fight for freedom. And many thrilling tales did he pour into the willing ears of his little listener.

Ebenezer Webster, Daniel's father, had fought in the French and Indian and Revolutionary wars; and he, too, often told Daniel about his adventures. The boy liked to hear especially how his father had been on guard in front of Washington's tent just after Arnold's treason, and how the great general himself had come to Ebenezer and said, "Captain Webster, I believe I can trust you." Such stories filled Daniel with love for his country.

Reading was another pleasure of Daniel Webster's boy-hood. He read all the books he could get hold of, time and again. As he had great power of expression, people loved to hear him read; and teamsters, while they rested their horses near his home, often called Webster's boy to come out into the shade of the trees and read to them.

Whenever he could, Daniel went to school. As he learned easily and remembered well, he soon came to be considered the brightest boy in his class. Once his teacher promised a jackknife to the pupil who could recite the greatest number of verses from the Bible. When Daniel's turn came, he reeled off so many verses that the master had to stop him. There was no question as to who had won the knife.

His talents were a delight to his father, who had had little chance himself for study and appreciated what he had missed. Knowing that Daniel's poor health would prevent him from ever doing hard physical labor, Mr. Webster determined to give the boy an education. Ezekiel, who was two years older than Daniel, and strong and robust, was to stay at home and help his father on the farm. But Daniel was to be sent to school and, if possible, to college.

This was a great undertaking in those days, especially to people of small means. For the Websters it meant much sacrifice on the part of the whole family. Not only would the farm have to be mortgaged, but they would be obliged to pinch and save in order to live. Still Ebenezer Webster and his wife were willing to do without comforts, that their boy might be educated.

Mr. Webster told Daniel about the plan and spoke sadly of his own lack of schooling. Daniel was much moved and never forgot his father's words. The next spring Mr. Webster took the boy to Exeter Academy.

This was Daniel's first step in the outside world, and it proved a bitter experience for him. The boys at Exeter were mostly sons of wealthy parents. They were well dressed and came from cultured homes, and they laughed at Daniel's country clothes and manners. Such treatment hurt the sensitive boy, but he had the good sense not to resent it.

Although he rose rapidly in his classes, one thing he could not do. He could not face these schoolboys and declaim. Much as he had read and recited to teamsters, relatives, and friends, he invariably failed completely whenever he was called upon to speak before his schoolmates. Alone in his room, he would go over and over what he wanted to say; but as soon as he faced the boys, not a word could he utter. And yet in years to come, this lad was to be one of the greatest orators of modern times.

When Daniel Webster had been nine months at Exeter, his father took him to a Dr. Wood to be tutored. On the way there, Mr. Webster told his son that a college course was in store for him. Under Dr. Wood's tutorship, he was ready to enter Dartmouth College before he was sixteen.

During the first two years of life at college, Webster was not the best student in his class. He was never a scholar, in the true sense of the word; but he had the reputation of being one. Webster himself said that it was because he read so much and remembered so well what he read, that he could talk with ease; and that when he came to the end of his knowledge he was careful to stop and let other people do the talking.

Everyone wondered at his eloquence. He had overcome the bashfulness which made his life wretched at Exeter, and now he delighted in nothing so much as holding an audience spellbound by the music of his marvelous voice.

During his first two years in Dartmouth, Daniel Webster often thought of his brother Ezekiel. He saw the wide gulf that was beginning to yawn between him and his stay-at-home brother; and his heart felt a great pity. He knew his brother's talents to be equal to his own, and he wanted Ezekiel, too, to have a college education.

But how was it to be done? The farm had already been mortgaged, and how could he ask his father to sacrifice himself still more? It seemed too much. However, when Daniel went home on his vacation, he did ask his father if in some way Ezekiel could not be sent to college.

As all his other sons had now left home, Mr. Webster realized that, in Ezekiel, he was sending away the prop and stay of his last years. He gave his consent on condition that the mother and daughters also were willing, as they were the ones who would suffer most. They proved as self-sacrificing as Mr. Webster. "I will trust my boys," was all the mother had to say. And so it was settled that Ezekiel should go to college.

Daniel was graduated from Dartmouth in 1801. That summer he studied in a law office. But as he had offered to do his share toward earning the money for Ezekiel's education, he accepted a position to teach during the winter.

At the close of the school year Daniel returned home and again took up the study of law. He longed to go to Boston to finish his law studies, but saw no way to do it. Finally Ezekiel found a way, and they both went to Boston.

Daniel was fortunate enough to get into the office of a famous lawyer who taught him many things besides law. After being admitted to the bar in 1807, he went to Boscawen, six miles from home, and opened a law office. Here, before long, he had a fairly good practice.

When Ezekiel, too, was admitted to the bar, Daniel turned his business over to his brother and moved to Portsmouth.

In Congress

In Portsmouth, Webster practiced law and took an active part in politics. Soon he was elected to Congress, and took his seat there in May, 1813.

There were many noted men in the House at this time. Among them were Henry Clay and John C. Calhoun. Both

A SESSION OF THE HOUSE OF REPRESENTATIVES
IN THE DAYS OF WEBSTER AND CLAY.

were statesmen and born debaters and orators. They were leaders of the southern states; and, as Webster became a northern leader, he was often opposed to them on the great questions of the day.

One of these questions had to do with the tariff, or duty, on certain imported goods. Mr. Clay, and at that time the South, thought that there ought to be a tariff on these articles to protect the growing American industries. Webster did not agree with him and made several speeches against the different tariff laws as they came up from time to time.

But when the tariff bill of 1828 was before the House, to the general surprise Webster changed about, and spoke in favor of it and voted for it. The reason for his change was that New England had, by this time, increased her manufacturing and was now in a position to profit by a tariff that placed a tax on competing goods imported from other countries. With New England it was simply a matter of dollars and cents, not one of right and wrong. And being a New England man, Webster changed his views to accord with those of his home section.

By this time the South, too, had changed about, and was bitterly opposed to the tariff bill of 1828; for she had found that foreign goods were, on the whole, cheaper than goods made in the North. However, the bill was passed and became a law. As a result the enraged southern people held mass meetings and declared the new tariff a violation of the Constitution, claiming that Congress had no power to impose duties except those necessary for the expenses of the Government. South Carolina even went so far as to say that the law would not be obeyed and that, if force was used, she would withdraw from the Union.

It was in January, 1830, that Senator Hayne of South Carolina made his bitter attack on Massachusetts and on Webster, and in the Senate of the United States declared this southern doctrine—that any state has the right to disobey the nation's laws.

Webster, now Massachusetts Senator, agreed to reply to Hayne on the next day. He had only one night in which to prepare what he had to say. But none knew the Constitution better than he, for had he not been a close student of it ever since his childhood days?

By the opening hour of the following day the great crowd that had come to hear him packed the Senate Chamber.

"It is a critical moment," said a friend; "and it is time, it is high time that the people of this country should know what this Constitution is."

"Then," answered Webster, "by the blessing of Heaven, they shall learn this day before the sun goes down what I understand it to be."

His theme was "Nationality." His sole purpose was to strengthen the claims of the Union; to put the Union first and the State second. For four hours he held that vast throng spellbound, while he set forth the meaning of the Constitution. His whole life had been a preparation for this moment. And his closing words, "Liberty and union, now and forever, one and inseparable," inspired all loyal Americans with deeper devotion to the Union. These words were put into text-books; schoolboys used them in declamations, feeling their pride in the Union increase as they made Webster's words their own. Finally the time came when men were needed to preserve the Union. Then it was that these boys, whose love for their country had been fostered and kept alive by the undying words of Webster, became the "Boys in Blue" and fought to save the land they loved so well.

In his "Reply to Hayne" Daniel Webster reached his highest point as a public speaker. More than his eloquence was the influence of the man himself. Nature had been most lavish with her gifts to him. His voice, face, and form were perfectly suited to an orator. He lacked but little of six feet. He had a swarthy complexion and straight black hair. His head was large and well shaped. His brow was high and broad. His wonderful eyes were deep set, black and glowing. But perhaps his voice was the most remarkable of all. In conversation, it was low and musical. In debate, it was high and full, sometimes ringing out like a clarion and then sinking to deep notes like the tones of an organ.

By his splendid defense of the Constitution, Daniel Webster won a national fame which brought with it talk of the Presidency. This high honor dangled before his eyes all the rest of his public life—a dream never to be realized.

One reason why Webster failed to arouse general enthusiasm as a Presidential candidate in 1852 was the stand he had taken in regard to Clay's compromise two years before.

This period in our history was a most critical one. On the one side was the South anxious to extend slavery into the new territory acquired through the Mexican War; on the other side was the North with the feeling against slaveholding constantly growing stronger. Between these two came Henry Clay in 1850 with his great compromise, which he thought would settle all the problems. One term of his compromise was the enforcing of the fugitive slave law, which ordered that all escaped slaves found in the North must be returned to their masters.

Up to this time Webster had always been a foe to compromise and to the extension of slavery, and he had always spoken eloquently in behalf of the poor down trodden slave. Now he rose in the Senate and declared in favor of Clay's compromise, saving nothing at all about the horrors of slavery and, worst of all, urging the carrying out of the fugitive slave law.

It was a shock and disappointment to his friends in the North that Daniel Webster should speak coldly and calmly of sending the runaway slaves back to their owners. This was hard to believe. Why did he do it?

Many said that his purpose was to preserve the Union and that he had decided that this was the only way to do it. Whatever his motive, many of his friends deserted him.

WEBSTER'S HOUSE AT MARSHFIELD.

Through years of his long public career, Daniel Webster had taken much pleasure in his country home at Marshfield near the Massachusetts coast. It was to Marshfield that he came in disappointment over his failure to gain the Presidency in 1852. And it was here that he died in October of that same Year. From his boyhood he had loved the flag with an intensity which increased with his years. And now, when he lay dying, his eyes constantly looked through the window in the dark hours of the night to a small boat anchored at the shore, for over this boat were flying the stars and stripes, lighted by a ship lantern on the mast.

Daniel Webster was a true American citizen. His chief desire was to see the nation great and glorious. He wished only to procure the good of the whole country and always strove with all the ardor and force of his great soul to preserve the Union. For years he poured the message of nationality into the ears of the people. He it was who fostered and strengthened this spirit so that, when the South seceded, the North had the courage to perform her mighty task. This is the debt the American people owe to Daniel Webster, and in this lies his importance in the history of our country.

XX

De Witt Clinton and the Erie Canal

Though United States Senator, Mayor of the City of New York, three times Governor of the State of New York, De Witt Clinton is remembered to-day principally from his connection with the Erie Canal.

In the first years of the nineteenth century those who dwelt in the western part of New York State were shut away from Albany by days or even weeks of travel. A water route, it is true, connected Cayuga and Seneca lakes with Schenectady; and rough roads ran across the state. It took fully three weeks and cost fully ten dollars to haul a barrel of flour over them from Albany to Buffalo.

Seeing what a gain it would be to the state if the rich farming country to the west could be put

DE WITT CLINTON.

in touch with the markets of Albany and New York, one and another had schemes to suggest. But it was left for De Witt Clinton to champion the building of a canal from Lake Erie to the Hudson River at Albany. Every possible objection was raised to his plan; and the more he tried to convince people of the advantages a canal would bring, the more they scoffed. "Clinton's ditch," it was called in ridicule.

Because such a canal connecting the Great Lakes with the Atlantic would benefit many states besides New York, the United States Government was asked to pay the cost of building. Congress would have nothing to do with the project.

In spite of all opposition, Clinton held fast to his faith in the canal, and year after year worked away to persuade the New York legislators and the farmers to favor it. At last his efforts were rewarded, and the Legislature voted in favor of the Erie Canal.

The digging was begun at Rome, on July 4, 1817. It seems curious that the first part of the canal to be built was the middle section. One of the reasons for this, it is said, was because the friends of the canal thought that, with the middle section built, the people at either end would insist that their section be finished. And this would make it harder for the enemies of the canal to block the work.

These old-time diggers must have known how to make the dirt fly. In a little over eight years they had dug a canal forty feet wide and four feet deep, the whole length of the three hundred and sixty-three miles between Lake Erie and the Hudson.

By the end of October, 1825, the last rock had been blasted from the canal bed; the last lock had been finished to lift the boats up and down the grades, and the canal was ready for use.

A great celebration was planned for October 26th, and on that day the waters of Lake Erie were let into "Clinton's ditch." With their first rush into the canal, a cannon's boom started the news across the state. Five miles off the firers of another cannon heard the sound. The second cannon boomed the tidings to a third, the third repeated them to a fourth, and so cannon telegraphed to cannon till New York City heard the sound and knew that the canal was open.

At ten o'clock in the morning a gay procession of boats left Buffalo. In the lead came the *Seneca Chief* towed by four gray horses, and carrying the exultant Governor Clinton and other noted men.

After the *Seneca Chief* followed a brightly decorated flotilla of canal boats. Two eagles, two fawns, some fish, a bear, and two Indians rode in *Noah's Ark*. All were headed for New York.

Everywhere along the route cheering crowds welcomed the procession. On the 2nd of November, Albany, the eastern end of the canal, was reached. From Albany steamboats towed the fleet down the Hudson to New York, where a splendid reception was awaiting.

Aecompanied by boats large and small, Governor Clinton was taken out to sea that he might empty into the Atlantic a keg of Lake Erie water. This signified the uniting of the Great Lakes and the Atlantic Ocean, and the completion of De Witt Clinton's great undertaking. The Erie Canal has proved an astonishing success. Great as was the cost of building it, more than the amount was realized in tolls within its first ten years.

The charge of ten dollars for carrying a barrel of flour

A QUIET SPOT ON THE ERIE CANAL.

across the state was reduced to thirty cents after the canal was opened. And in 1906 a bushel of wheat could be sent all the way from Buffalo to New York by water for from four to five cents.

The canal also aided the growth of towns along its course. Of the seven cities through which the canal runs, only Albany and Schenectady boasted that title in 1825. Mica, Rome, Syracuse, Rochester, and Buffalo were mere villages, or settlements.

The Erie Canal is a worthy memorial of De Witt Clinton. It is a good lesson of what patience, ability, and energy can accomplish in the face of almost unsurmountable difficulties. It is a striking example of a gigantic undertaking, bravely and boldly begun and successfully accomplished.

XXI

Samuel F. B. Morse and his Successors

METHODS OF SIGNALING

"If danger threatens you from our direction, we will warn you by a beacon fire," agreed the early inhabitants of neighboring settlements. This way of sending a message from hilltop to hilltop by signal fires was a custom our ancestors brought with them from across the sea. At best it was uncertain, and the message to be sent had to be agreed upon beforehand.

Later another signaling device, the semaphore, came into use to some extent. The semaphore was made by fastening a movable arm to an upright post, the different angles at which the arm was placed indicating the different words of the message.

Then during the Civil War, flags and rockets were used in signaling on the battlefield, and to notify troops of the approach of the enemy.

The heliographic system was still another form of signaling, and was carried out by reflecting the sun's light from one station to another by means of mirrors. Heliograph signals have been sent more than one hundred and fifty miles. But even this system had its drawbacks. It was only a daylight and pleasant weather system, darkness or cloudy weather, putting an end to communication between the stations.

So you see that the invention of the telegraph supplied a great and pressing need. Here was a means of rapid communication, one that could be used by night as well as by day, and could carry a message long or short. Samuel F. B. Morse was the inventor of the telegraph.

Samuel Morse and the Telegraph

Morse was a Massachusetts boy born there in 1791. While in college at Yale, Morse had for professors two of the most noted scientists of the day in this country, and through them he first became interested in electricity. However, at the time of graduation his ambition was to become an artist, not a scientist. Accordingly he went to London where he worked for four years with splendid results and where, through his father's influence, he came to know many prominent Englishmen.

In 1815 he came back to America and set about earning his living through his art. He seems to have been a true Yankee with an active, inventive mind, quick to grasp the possibilities of a suggestion that to many would have meant nothing. At dinner one night, in 1832, when he was returning from another visit abroad, the conversation turned on electricity. Then and there the thought flashed through his mind that this mysterious force might be employed in sending messages.

For the next eleven years Morse's principal interest in life was pushing and perfecting the idea of an electric telegraph. He was so poor that it was with great difficulty that he managed to carry on his investigations at all. He was even compelled to build his own models and machines. Discouragement followed discouragement; but still he plodded on, always confident of final success.

In 1835 he was appointed professor in the University of the City of New York. Luckily for him one of his pupils became interested in the experiments and induced his father, the owner of brass and iron works, to furnish the necessary materials.

Then came the struggle to raise the money needed to put up a telegraph line. Morse exhibited his apparatus in Philadelphia. He exhibited it in Washington to the President and his Cabinet, and for several years sought an appropriation from Congress with which to build an experimental telegraph line. Finally, in 1843, an appropriation of $30,000 was granted by Congress. The Senate approved the bill late at night on the last day of the session, after Morse had given up all hope of its being reached and had gone home to bed. As he was coming down to breakfast in the morning, a young lady congratulated him on his success. Had the Senate passed his bill? He could hardly believe the news.

A year later the bearer of the good tidings was asked to send the first telegraph message in this country. "What hath

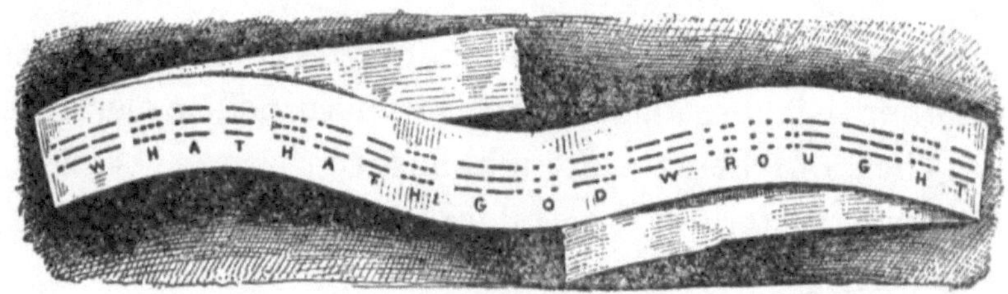

THE FIRST TELEGRAPHIC MESSAGE SENT BY THE MORSE
SYSTEM, NOW PRESERVED AT HARVARD COLLEGE.

God wrought!" were the words she chose. And on May 24, 1844, this message was flashed from Washington to Baltimore over Morse's new telegraph line. Of course the opening of the line created intense interest; and the Chamber of the Supreme Court, the Washington end of the line, was filled with excited people.

The practical use of the telegraph was shown in a rather dramatic way a few days later. The Democratic National Convention was being held in Baltimore, and Silas Wright was unexpectedly nominated for Vice President. The news was telegraphed to Morse at Washington, and Wright's refusal of the nomination was quickly sent back to Baltimore, and the convention was told of it.

This was beyond belief. It was not possible that a message had really been sent, received, and answered in so short a time. Surely it was some trick of Wright's enemies, nothing more nor less. So the convention adjourned, while a committee went to Washington to see Wright in person, only to learn that the message was correct and that he had refused the nomination.

Soon after the opening of the telegraph line a young lady came to Morse with a sealed letter and asked him to send it by telegraph to Baltimore. When he said that he could not do that, she asked if he would not send her. These and other queer notions about Morse's invention were held by many when it was first put into operation.

The influence of the telegraph was soon widely recognized, and Morse richly deserved the many rewards he received. By his genius and ability he had contrived a means of overcoming distance, enabling those separated by many miles to communicate with the swiftness of lightning.

CYRUS W. FIELD AND MARCONI

After becoming accustomed to the rapidity of communication by telegraph, ten days or more seemed a long time to wait for European news. So Cyrus W. Field interested himself in plans for the laying of an ocean cable.

Early in 1854 the New York, Newfoundland, and London Telegraph Company was chartered, and the preliminary work was begun. By August of 1857 all the arrangements were made; and on the 7th a steamer started from Ireland for Newfoundland, unrolling the cable as it went. But after a few hundred miles had been laid, the cable broke; and the attempt was put off for a year.

In 1858 another effort at cable-laying proved successful, and for eighteen days England and America were connected. Messages of congratulation were sent by the Queen and the President, and everyone concerned with the undertaking was happy. Then suddenly the cable ceased to work; a break had occurred somewhere.

No further attempt was made to carry out Field's plan until 1865, when the Great Eastern, the largest ship of that time, succeeded in laying more than a thousand miles of cable. At that point came another discouraging break.

Mr. Field still persisted, however; and finally in 1866 a cable was successfully stretched across the Atlantic Ocean. Ever since that time there has been cable communication between this country and Europe. There are to-day more than half a dozen cables across the Atlantic and Pacific; and, as far as news is concerned, New York is as near to the capitals of Europe as it is to Washington.

It is indeed wonderful to be able to send messages over a wire across land and sea. But a still more marvelous invention is now coming into use. This is wireless telegraphy. The inventor is an Italian, Guglielmo Marconi. By Marconi's system messages can be sent, miles through the air from station to station without a wire to carry them. And for the first time ships crossing the ocean can keep in constant communication with land.

ALEXANDER GRAHAM BELL
AND THE TELEPHONE

Eighteen hundred and seventy-six was the year of the Centennial Exhibition at Philadelphia, and at that time and place another great electrical invention was exhibited. But in spite of the fact that the telegraph by land and sea had already illustrated the marvelous uses of electricity, the telephone of Alexander Graham Bell was regarded by people generally as a toy.

Few, if any, credited that it could ever be of practical service. And yet there is hardly any modern invention that has done as much to add to the convenience of living as has the telephone. We use it to order our meals, to chat with our friends, or to transact business, near at hand or miles away. Most of us use it a hundred times where we use the telegraph once.

Mr. Bell, its inventor, was born and educated in Scotland, but has lived in this country for many years. His father, too, was a noted man. He it was who evolved the system of "visible speech," as it is called, by which the deaf are taught to speak by imitating the motions of another person's lips.

XXII

Abraham Lincoln Before 1861

Lincoln's Birthplace

On the roughly built bed over in the corner two little children lie asleep. Before the open fireplace the mother and father talk together in low tones.

It is winter, and outside a storm is raging. From time to time the wind beats with added fury against the lonely Kentucky log cabin. As its icy breath comes through the cracks between the logs, the mother shivers; and crossing to the bed she tucks the patchwork quilt closer about her children and spreads an extra deerskin over them.

A smaller skin, which is the only cover for the window, is flapping, letting in the cold. This then must be fastened better; and while she is about it, the

WHERE ABRAHAM LINCOLN WAS BORN.

mother looks to see if the doorway is covered as tightly as it can be. Sure that all is now secure she comes back to the fire and sits down on one of the wooden blocks that serve as chairs.

To a stranger this might seem a poor little place, with only the hard earth for a floor and only one room to hold the bed, the board table, the wooden bench, the shelf for dishes, and even the old Dutch oven. But to Thomas and Nancy Lincoln it is a house and they are happy in it. Suppose it is cold on a winter's night—summer will soon come again, bringing warmth, sunshine, and a free out-of-door life. Suppose their bread is made from corn meal, and potatoes are about the only vegetable they have—there is always plenty of venison and other game, or fish, to be boiled in the great iron pot, or broiled over the hot ashes.

Things might be much worse. The Lincolns' life is the life of those about them, and they are content in their little log cabin, the birthplace of their boy Abraham.

Lincoln the Boy

Abraham was four years old on the 12th of February, 1813. Within a few months after that date, his father sold the farm where the boy was born and moved to another about fifteen miles away. This second home was a log cabin much like the old one.

Naturally the neighbors were interested to learn something about the new family. They found Thomas Lincoln a cheerful, happy-go-lucky man. He was a carpenter by trade, a farmer by circumstance, and a do-nothing by choice.

Nancy Lincoln was a handsome young woman with far more energy than her husband. She was considered very well educated because she could read and write, things which few of her neighbors could do. She was a good housekeeper. She could spin and weave, could use a hoe or an ax as well as Thomas, and was as good a shot. Best of all she was a devoted wife and mother.

Then there was their daughter Sarah and the boy Abraham. Abraham was an awkward, homely child. He wore a rough homespun shirt, deerskin trousers and leggings, homemade shoes, and a coonskin cap.

There were no regular schools or churches near the Lincolns' new home. All the schooling these out-of-the-way settlers had was the few weeks' instruction they bargained for when a wandering teacher came along.

Soon after the Lincolns moved to their second farm such a teacher came to their neighborhood. One settler offered to give him board, another to lodge him, a third to mend and wash his clothes, while a fourth gave the use of an old log cabin in which to hold his school.

His scholars included, besides the two little Lincolns, some boys

A TRAVELING SCHOOLMASTER
TEACHING "MANNERS".

and girls almost grown up, many of whom did not even know their letters.

As it was with schooling, so it was with preaching. Except for the occasional visits of traveling preachers, the settlers heard no sermons. One of the traveling preachers was David Elkin. He was a good friend to the Lincolns, and Abraham liked nothing better than to hear him speak to the people. How much the child understood it is hard to say.

The Lincolns lived on their second Kentucky farm until the fall of 1516. Then the spirit of unrest tempted Thomas Lincoln to move again. This time he took his family to the timber lands of Indiana. The journey ended in a piece of lonely forest.

At once the father and son fell to with their axes, chopping trees, cutting poles and boughs. With these they built a "half-face" camp fourteen feet square. A "half-face" camp is practically a shed with three walls, the fourth side being open and entirely unprotected. In front of this open side the Lincolns kept a fire burning to shut out the cold. Here they spent their first winter—in fact, their first year in Indiana.

By another fall they had cleared a patch of ground, had planted it with corn, and had built a new log cabin. A happy year in the new home went quickly by, and then a great sorrow came. A sickness had broken out in the neighborhood, and Nancy Lincoln took it and died. When her husband had built her a board coffin, her family and neighbors carried her a little distance from her home and buried her. All was silence and grief. No minister was there to read a service over the grave.

The two children followed their father back to the desolate house, where the little girl made shift to do her mother's work.

Mrs. Lincoln had taught her boy to read the Bible and to believe in God. He knew what all this had meant to his mother, and it was a dreadful thing to him that she had been buried without prayer or service. If only some preacher had been there! If only some preacher would come even now!

There was his mother's old friend, David Elkin. Would he come if he knew about it all? It was worth trying. So Abraham wrote a letter to David Elkin in far-away Kentucky and begged him to visit Indiana and hold a service for Nancy Lincoln.

A long hard journey lay between David Elkin's home and the Lincoln farm. But the good preacher made it, and one spring day several months after Mrs. Lincoln's death he rode up to the cabin door. The funeral service at last was held over his mother's grave, and Abraham Lincoln was content.

SARAH BUSH LINCOLN,
LINCOLN'S STEP-MOTHER.

His mother's influence lasted all his life. And when he had come to be a man he still said, "all that I am or hope to be I owe to my angel mother."

Before long the influence of another good woman came into Abraham's life. Late in 1819 Thomas Lincoln married a Kentucky widow and brought her to Indiana. With her very arrival the dreariness of the last lonely months disappeared, and at once Abraham and his stepmother were good friends. She was a sensible, happy, thrifty woman; and the boy loved and respected her.

Years later she said of him. "Abe never gave me a cross word or look and never refused in fact or appearance to do anything I requested of him. Abe was the best boy I ever saw."

Had it not been for her, Abraham would have been far less happy. He loved to study and read and went to school whenever a teacher came along to make this possible. His father, uneducated himself, did not approve of the boy's reading so much, or going to school when he might be working. But the stepmother insisted on letting Abraham have his way, and even encouraged him in his study.

Most of his reading was done at night when the day's work was finished. Then the boy would curl up near the fireplace and read by the light of the flames. "Robinson Crusoe," "Pilgrim's Progress," "Aesop's Fables," a history of the United States, and the Bible, he read over and over. These were his favorites.

Once he borrowed Weems's "Life of Washington" and began to read it on his way home. It fascinated him, and all that evening and far into the night he read. When finally he closed the book, he tucked it into a crevice between the logs where he could reach it and read again as soon as daylight came.

During the night there was a heavy storm; and when Abraham reached for his treasure in the morning, his hand found a very wet and badly soaked book. With a heavy heart he carried it back to its owner. "If you work three days for me, you will pay me for the book, and you may keep it," the man declared. So for three days Abraham worked, and then went off with his book a proud and happy boy. He had paid for it with his labor, and it was his own—the first that he had bought.

From the time Abraham was ten years old he was kept busy. When not needed at home, he was hired out to the neighbors at twenty-five cents a day, which was paid to his father. Young Lincoln was very obliging, very capable, and, as he grew older, very powerful. He could and would do any sort of work there was to be done. It was not that he really liked to work. He didn't. But he accepted it as part of life and did his duty the best he knew how.

And so with plenty of hard work, many jolly times with his comrades, a little schooling, and all the reading and studying he could find time for, the years passed by, and the boy grew up and became a man.

Lincoln Starts Out for Himself

One summer Thomas Lincoln hired his son out as ferryman to take passengers across the Ohio. It was before the days of railroads, when the farmers of the new western states shipped all their saleable goods by water to New Orleans, the great business city of the West. The Ohio and Mississippi rivers were the highways to this market and were filled with craft of every sort.

Abraham saw the busy river life and wanted to try a hand at it himself, and before long his wish was gratified. A Mr. Gentry sent his son and the nineteen-year-old Abraham down the river on a flatboat to New Orleans with a load of provisions. Abraham's pay was eight dollars a month and his passage home on a steamer. What a trip it must have been

TRAVELING BY FLATBOAT DOWN THE MISSISSIPPI.

for a forest-bred boy! It was his first glimpse of the outside world, and the wonders he saw he never forgot.

In February, 1830, Abraham Lincoln became of age. Now he was free to use his time as he liked and to keep the money he earned. But that very month saw a great stir in the Lincoln household. Once more the family were packing up, saying good-by to friends and neighbors, and making ready for another move farther west. They had resolved to leave Indiana, through fear of the dread disease that had killed Nancy Lincoln. And because of the glowing reports sent from Illinois, they had chosen that state for their future home.

By the beginning of March the start was made. All their possessions were piled into large wagons, which were drawn by oxen. Two weeks they traveled before they reached the place where they were to build their new cabin. In a short time the cabin was done. And then such a chopping as went on before the men had made rails enough to fence in ten acres of ground! They must have worked fast indeed, because they not only split the rails but put up the fence, broke the ground, and raised a crop of corn on it that same year.

At this time Lincoln had no respectable clothes. But within a few miles of his father's cabin there lived a woman who could weave a material called jeans. Lincoln went to her and made a bargain to split four hundred rails for each yard of brown jeans necessary to make him a pair of trousers.

Now that he had helped his father move and settle, Lincoln decided to start out for himself. When he left home, he left empty-handed. He had nothing at all to take with him. Even his looks were not prepossessing. He was six feet four inches tall, his hands and feet were large, his legs and arms long and loose-jointed. But his muscles were like iron, his endurance remarkable, and his courage beyond question.

In the spring of 1831 Lincoln made a second trip to New Orleans. This time he went on a flatboat belonging to a Mr. Offutt. For a month he stayed in New Orleans seeing life as he had never seen it before.

One phase of life in the great city sickened Lincoln. This was the horrors of slave trade. For the first time he now saw men and women sold like animals in a public market. He saw them in chains, saw them whipped; and the cruelty of it all raised in him a hatred of slavery, which lasted all his life.

When the New Orleans trip was over, Lincoln went to New Salem, Illinois, to be a cleric in Mr. Offutt's store. New Salem was a little town of about fifteen houses and a hundred people. Its women came to the store for supplies; its men came to lounge, tell stories, and talk politics. With all of them Lincoln was soon in favor; for was he not the kindest, the most amusing, the most honest man that had ever come to New Salem?

He walked several miles one evening after the store was closed to return six cents to a woman who had over-paid him. Once a customer came in for half a pound of tea just at closing time. In the dim light Lincoln weighed out the tea. Next morning he found that he had taken a wrong weight and so had given this customer too little by half. So shutting up shop he carried another quarter of a pound to the belated buyer. For such things New Salem named him "Honest Abe."

Although New Salem was a promising town, keeping store there could hardly take all one's time. Lincoln could now begin to study again. He was becoming interested in politics and resolved to study grammar so that the speeches he meant to make might be correct.

But where could he get a text-book? The village school-master knew of one which belonged to a man living six miles away. Before night Lincoln had found time to walk the twelve miles to bring back the book. For weeks he studied it, learning the rules, reciting them to his fellow-clerk, and practicing them in his talk.

In the spring of 1832 there was an Indian uprising, known as the Black Hawk War. The frontier settlers were in terror, and the Governor called for volunteers to repel the savages. Lincoln was chosen captain of the company from his neighborhood, and marched off to war. In about three months the war was over, and Lincoln was back in New Salem without having fought in a single battle.

By this time Mr. Offutt's store had proved a failure and was closed. Lincoln now used his time for political work; for before he went away he had become a candidate for the General Assembly of Illinois.

The election was at hand. All the country round was

Democratic, while Lincoln was a stanch Henry Clay man. But just because it was Lincoln, the Democrats of New Salem worked for him as hard as if he had belonged to their own party. However, when the ballots from Springfield and other towns of the district were counted, it was found that he had been defeated.

The election over, Lincoln looked about for work. Everything considered, keeping store suited him best. As none of the three grocers of New Salem needed a clerk, he and a young man named Berry decided to buy one of the stores. Before they got through with it, they had bought all three—or at least they had taken the stock of all three and had promised to pay for it when they could.

The partnership was not a fortunate one. Lincoln wanted so to read and study that he left the management of the store largely to Berry and Berry was unreliable and worthless. Business was slack, and Lincoln gladly accepted the position of postmaster when it was offered him the next spring.

The duties of postmaster at New Salem were not very heavy. The mail usually consisted of a dozen or fifteen letters and a few newspapers. The letters Lincoln carried about in his hat until he saw the people to whom they were addressed. The newspapers he opened and read through before he handed them over.

One day soon after Lincoln and Berry opened their store a man drove up. He had in his wagon a barrel, which he asked Lincoln to buy. On dumping it to see what it held, Lincoln discovered a book which proved to be a standard authority on law. He had often wished that he could study law; so he wasted no time in getting to work on this book, which good fortune had tossed in his way.

People were now beginning to flock into Illinois. This meant that much land must be surveyed. The county surveyor needed all the help he could get; and he offered to make Lincoln a deputy surveyor if he would learn to do the necessary work. In six weeks Lincoln reported that he was ready to begin.

Although his surveying brought him in more money than any other work he had tried, he did not get ahead very fast. His father was still poor, and his family needed help. Then there was the store with its heavy debt. Under Berry's management, conditions here grew worse and worse, until the partners were so discouraged that it was given up. A few months later Berry died, leaving on Lincoln's shoulders the responsibility of paying off their debt of eleven hundred dollars. "That debt," said Lincoln, "was the greatest obstacle I ever met in my life. There was however but one way. I went to the creditors and told them that if they would let me alone, I would give them all I could earn over my living as fast as I could earn it." Fifteen years later he was still sending money to Illinois to apply on this debt. But "Honest Abe" at last paid every cent.

Lincoln the Lawyer

The summer of 1834 was a busy one for Lincoln. His surveying took him much about the country. Everywhere he met new acquaintances and won many friends. And the kindness shown him encouraged him to try once more for a place in the Legislature. This time he won. Hardly was the campaign over when he began to study law again. He was urged to do this by John T. Stuart, and many a trip did Lincoln make over the twenty miles between New Salem and Springfield to

BUILDING IN SPRINGFIELD, ILLINOIS, USED BY THE UNITED STATES COURT, 1850-1860: LINCOLN'S LAW OFFICE ON THE THIRD FLOOR.

borrow law books from his friend. He threw himself into the work heart and soul. Before long he was able to write deeds and other legal papers for his neighbors.

That winter and the next he spent in the Legislature, coming back to New Salem for the summer between—the summer of 1835—to go on with his law study and surveying.

In September, 1836, he was admitted to the bar. Another winter was given to the Legislature. And then in the spring of 1837 Lincoln moved to Springfield to accept a partnership with John T. Stuart.

He rode into town "on a borrowed horse, with no earthly property save a pair of saddlebags containing a few clothes." Being asked to room with a friend, he climbed the stairs, put his saddlebags on the floor, and announced, "Well, I'm moved."

Now came the years of building up a practice, riding the circuit and making a legal reputation.

What does riding the circuit mean? In Lincoln's time it was the custom to divide the counties into groups, assigning a judge to each group. Twice a year this judge visited the county seat of each county, to hear whatever cases people cared to bring before him. There were no railroads, so the judge and the lawyers who followed him rode on horseback from place to place. This was called "riding the circuit." Although Lincoln worked hard and had many clients during his first years in Springfield, he was not destined to become rich through the law. This was probably because he was too kind-hearted when it came to charging for his work. If his client was rather poor, he charged very little; if the client was very poor, he charged nothing. And all the while he was sending money home and slowly paying off his big debt.

In a social way Lincoln went about among the best people of Springfield. When he had been a while in the town a certain Miss Mary Todd came there to live with her married sister. She and Lincoln met, fell in love, and in 1842 were married.

For a while they lived at the Globe Tavern, paying four dollars a week for both. Then Lincoln bought a modest frame house, and he and his wife set up housekeeping.

LINCOLN THE POLITICIAN

For four terms Abraham Lincoln served in the Illinois Legislature. For one term he was a member of the National Congress. The term ended in the spring of 1849. He came home with the intention of dropping out of politics, and devoting his time to his law practice and his children. But these were the days of the great disputes over the spread of slavery. And how could a man be indifferent who had seen only the awful side of slavery, first in the New Orleans slave market and then in the slave market at Washington?

For a time it seemed that Henry Clay's compromises had settled the question of slavery in America's western lands.

LINCOLN'S HOUSE AT SPRINGFIELD.

According to the Missouri compromise, Missouri had come into the Union as a slave state on the condition that all the states which should be formed from the land north and west of Missouri's southern boundary should be free forever.

Clay's second compromise admitted California as a free state, leaving the people on the rest of the land obtained from Mexico to decide for themselves whether their states should be free or slave.

This was all well and good and apparently gratified North and South alike. However, four short years after Clay's second compromise was adopted, both sides were all excitement again.

In 1854 Stephen A. Douglas of Illinois brought up in Congress

a bill to make two territories of the lands beyond Missouri and the Missouri River. The northern of these territories was to be called Nebraska; the southern one, Kansas. And Mr. Douglas wanted the people of Kansas and Nebraska to be allowed to choose for themselves whether or not they should have slaves.

The North protested loudly against Douglas's bill. But in spite of the protest, Congress passed it, thus repealing the Missouri compromise.

And now would the new territories be for or against slavery? The South was anxious that they should adapt. The slave system. The North was determined that they should be free.

"So the matter is to be decided by the settlers. Then the

settlers shall be from our side," said both North and South. And a wild race for possession began. Slave holders from Missouri rushed over into Kansas, staked out farms, and commenced to build a town. About forty miles to the southwest of this town a band of settlers from the North built another town, which they called Lawrence. All were well armed, and both sides made use of their weapons. They burned each other's houses, shot each other without warning, and fought each other so furiously that the new territory was soon called "Bleeding Kansas." In the end the antislavery party won the victory; and when Kansas finally came into the Union, she came in as a free state.

One of the northern men who moved to Kansas was John Brown. When a boy John Brown had seen a young slave cruelly beaten, and from that time he had vowed to fight slavery. In Kansas he certainly had a good chance to fulfill his vow. At least he found ample opportunity to fight the upholders of slavery, and several of them were killed in attacks which he led.

Not content with fighting slavery in Kansas, John Brown attempted to carry his raids into Virginia. At the head of a band of not more than twenty men he went to Harper's Ferry, seized the Government arsenal, and made an effort to free the slaves of the neighborhood.

An alarm was given, soldiers turned out, several of Brown's men were killed. And after a hard fight, John Brown himself and six of his men were captured, and put into prison. He was tried, found guilty of treason, and finally hanged. He had paid the price of being unwisely zealous in a great cause.

While the fighting was going on in Kansas, another matter came up which increased the bad feeling between North and

South. Some years before, a certain slave holder of Missouri had gone to the free state of Illinois and had taken with him one of his slaves, named Dred Scott. After several years he took Dred Scott back to Missouri and there sold him. Scott said that his master had no right to do this, and claimed that since he had lived for a period of years on free soil he was now a free man and no longer a slave.

His case was carried to the United States Supreme Court; and in 1857 that Court decided that a negro who was descended from slaves was not an American citizen, and therefore could not sue for justice in the United States courts. And the court declared, moreover, that a slave-holder could lawfully take his slaves wherever he wished, just as he could take his horses and his cattle.

The North was dismayed. If a slaveholder could take his slaves where he liked, what was to prevent a Southerner from moving with his negroes to Massachusetts or New York? What was to prevent slavery from being carried into any or all of the free states? Resentment in the North ran high.

But to return to Abraham Lincoln. With the repeal of the Missouri compromise in 1854 his interest in the slave

ABRAHAM LINCOLN IN 1858.

question became so intense that he once more entered politics. And when in the fall of that year Stephen A. Douglas spoke in Springfield, justifying the repeal, it was Lincoln who was called upon to answer his arguments. This was only the first of many public debates on slavery between Lincoln and the "Little Giant," as Douglas was called.

In his speeches Lincoln voiced his honest opinion of the great question that was uppermost in all men's minds. He held that in the words "all men are created equal," the Declaration of Independence meant to say that black as well as white men were entitled to "life, liberty, and the pursuit of happiness." He said that he firmly believed that slavery should not be allowed in new states; and he stoutly asserted that the Government could not go on half slave and half free; that the future would see the whole country united on one policy in regard to the holding of negro slaves.

Most of the debates between Lincoln and Douglas were during the campaign of 1858, when the two men were rival candidates for the office of United States Senator. When the campaign was over, Lincoln was recognized as the abler talker, but Douglas had been elected to the Senate.

Lincoln was disappointed. "I suppose that I feel very

much like the overgrown boy who stubbed his toe....He was hurt too bad to laugh, and was too big to cry.”

But could Lincoln have looked even a little way into the future, he would have understood that he had no occasion to be disheartened over this defeat.

“Who is this man that is replying to Douglas in your state? Do you realize that no greater speeches have been made on public questions in the history of our country?” wrote a prominent Eastern statesman. And this statesman’s letter voiced the reputation which Lincoln’s sound logic, his insight into the subject, and his simple direct style were making for him all over the country.

The year 1860 was the time for the election of a new National President. Though this office is the highest honor the country can give, Lincoln’s enthusiastic friends felt that he was fitted to receive it. But when the idea was talked over with Lincoln himself, and he was urged to write out a sketch of his life, he replied with characteristic modesty: “I admit that I am ambitious and would like to be President. I am not insensible to the compliment you pay me and the interest you manifest in the matter; but there is no such good luck in store for me as the Presidency of these United States. Besides, there is nothing in my early history that would interest you or anybody else; and, as Judge Davis says, ‘It won’t pay.’ Good night.” And he hurried away.

However, in spite of his demur, Lincoln was nominated the Republican candidate for the Presidency in the spring of 1860.

Election day that year came on the 6th of November. By daylight Springfield was astir. About eight o’clock Mr. Lincoln went as usual to his room in the State House and calmly began to look over his mail. But if Mr. Lincoln was calm, his friends were not. They rushed in and out of his room until some one suggested that it might be well for him to shut them out and rest. No, indeed. Never in his life had he closed his door on his friends, and he did not intend to begin it now. So all day they came and went, until it was time for Lincoln to go home to supper.

A little after seven he was back, and now came the excitement of waiting for news from the different parts of the country. It was nearly morning before the reports were all received, and Lincoln announced that he "Guessed he'd go home now." He had been elected President of the United States.

XXIII

President Lincoln and The Civil War

THE DIVISION OF THE UNION

Although Lincoln was elected President in November, 1860, he was not inaugurated until March, 1861. In those four months great changes took place in the South.

When the thirteen American colonies joined together to form the United States, slavery was general. One by one, however, the Northern States became convinced that slavery was doing them more harm than good. So slavery was abolished in the North. The South still held to it.

Then having recognized the evils of the slave system, the North naturally wanted to keep it out of any new states which might come into the Union. The South, on the other hand, saw no harm in holding slaves and wanted slavery spread into America's western lands. At last, through this struggle for the control of the new states, the South came to believe that the North meant to crush slavery even in those of the original thirteen states which still favored it.

This was not true. And time and again Mr. Lincoln and

CHARLESTON

MERCURY

EXTRA:

Passed unanimously at 1.15 o'clock, P. M., December 20th, 1860.

AN ORDINANCE

"To dissolve the Union between the State of South Carolina and other States united with her under the compact entitled "The Constitution of the United States of America."

We, the People of the State of South Carolina, in Convention assembled, do declare and ordain, and it is hereby declared and ordained,

That the Ordinance adopted by us in Convention, on the twenty-third day of May, in the year of our Lord one thousand seven hundred and eighty-eight, whereby the Constitution of the United States of America was ratified, and also, all Acts and parts of Acts of the General Assembly of this State, ratifying amendments of the said Constitution, are hereby repealed; and that the union now subsisting between South Carolina and other States, under the name of "The United States of America," is hereby dissolved.

THE

UNION

IS

DISSOLVED!

FACSIMILE OF AN EXTRA ANNOUNCING THE SECESSION.

the Republican party which elected him stated that their great desire and firm purpose was to shut slavery from the new states, not to interfere with it in the South.

Still the South persisted in believing that their theory was right. And the very month after Lincoln's election, South Carolina withdrew from the Union. By the 1st of February six other slave states had followed South Carolina's example, and before many days these seven had formed a government of their own and named themselves The Confederate States of America.

The six states to follow South Carolina from the Union were Georgia, Alabama, Florida, Mississippi, Louisiana, and Texas. A few months later Arkansas, North Carolina, Virginia, and Tennessee joined the Confederate State and raised their new flag in place of the stars and stripes.

No sooner had the seven Southern States declared themselves out of the Union than they began to seize upon the United States forts and arsenals within their limits. This was the state of affairs when Abraham Lincoln left Springfield and journeyed to Washington, where he was inaugurated on the 4th of March, 1861.

The new President fully realized the gravity of the responsibility which had fallen upon him. In his inaugural address he went over the situation. But while he denied the right of the Southern States to secede from the Union and vowed to do all in his power to "preserve, protect, and defend it," he assured the Southern sympathizers that if civil war came it would be the South that would start it.

One month went by, and then the South put a final end to all hope of peace between herself and the North. A Southern general demanded the surrender of Fort Sumter, in

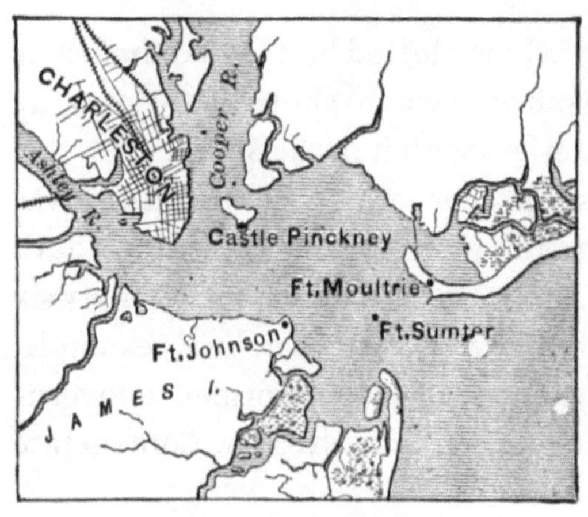

CHARLESTON HARBOR.

Charleston Harbor. The officer in charge refused. Whereupon, on April 12th, Southern batteries opened fire on Fort Sumter and kept on firing until the fort was surrendered.

This was too much. The North was ablaze with resentment. So when Lincoln called for seventy-five thousand men to defend the Union, more than ninety thousand enlisted. The first call for troops was quickly followed by another, and from the Northern States men came marching to the tunes of "Rally round the flag, boys" and "We are coming, Father Abraham, five hundred thousand strong." Washington was turned into a veritable camp and put into a state of defense.

So, too, the men of the South were hurrying to join the Confederate army and rushing to the protection of Richmond, the capital of the Confederate States.

"On to Washington!" was the cry of the South. "On to Richmond!" rang throughout the North.

July, 1861—September, 1862

In July, 1861, the two armies met on the banks of the little Virginia stream, Bull Run. In the beginning the Confederates fell back before the onslaught of the Union troops. Then the Southern general, Jackson, came to their rescue. And so like a stone wall did he and his men stand their ground that he was ever after called "Stonewall Jackson." First the Union advance was checked, and then the Union troops were driven from the field.

Now came a time of comparative quiet, while each side laid its plans and drilled its forces. Part of the North's plan was to close the ports of the Southern States and so keep them from getting supplies from abroad. Well-armed ships were stationed near the mouth of each harbor and did valiant work, capturing hundreds of vessels which tried to run the blockade.

Eight days after the firing on Fort Sumter, the Confederates had seized the United States navy yard at Norfolk, Virginia. But before they succeeded in getting possession, its Union commander had destroyed the shops and ships. One ship, the *Merrimac*, had burned to the water's edge and then had sunk.

Soon discovering that her engines were not damaged, the Confederates raised the *Merrimac* and rebuilt her. This time she was covered with plates of iron, was mounted with large cannon, and was made into an ironclad war vessel.

When the ironclad *Merrimac* was ready, she put to sea and set out to attack the three wooden vessels from the North, which were riding at anchor in Hampton Roads. Two of the three Union ships opened fire on the strange-looking sea monster. Their shots could not pierce her iron plates, and the *Merrimac* came on unharmed.

Steadily, steadily she drew near the *Cumberland*, until, with a mighty crash, she tore a gaping hole in the wooden ship. In rushed the water, and the *Cumberland* filled and sank.

Then turning to the *Congress*, the *Merrimac* forced this second ship to surrender, set it on fire, and left it to its fate.

THE BATTLE BETWEEN THE "MONITOR" AND THE "MERRIMAC".

The nest morning the *Merrimac* came sailing out to destroy the *Minnesota*, the last of the three Northern ships. But there beside the *Minnesota* lay another vessel—a queer-looking affair "like a cheese box mounted on a raft." It was the new Union war ship, the *Monitor*; and it, too, was ironclad.

Never before had two ironclad vessels engaged in battle. For hours they fought without being able to do each other serious damage. The little *Monitor* had saved the *Minnesota* and had held in check the dreaded *Merrimac*. A new era for naval warfare had begun.

The *Merrimac* had done all the damage she was ever to do. Some weeks later the Confederates were forced to give up Norfolk, and before they went they destroyed their ironclad vessel.

The news that the *Monitor* had repulsed the *Merrimac* must have been to Lincoln a ray of encouragement in a storm of troubles. When the war began, everyone felt that a few, short weeks would bring its close. But nearly a year had gone by, and still there were no signs of peace. And everywhere were people willing to blame the country's President because things had not turned out as they had expected.

Officers placed in high command proved unfitted for their work. Soldiers deserted, and still others turned cowards in the hour of battle.

As Commander-in-chief, Lincoln looked into these cases; and while he was severe on wilful insubordination, he was always ready to give a man the benefit of the least doubt. "Leg cases" was the name he gave for cowardice in the face of the enemy. And he was inclined to show pity to such offenders "because," he said, "if Almighty God has given a man a cowardly pair of legs, how can he help running away with them?"

The doorkeepers at the White House had standing orders to admit every person who came seeking a pardon for some one condemned to death. In every way Lincoln did all in his power to lessen the burden of those made to suffer through the war.

Early in 1862 New Orleans fell before Captain Farragut. This was a great victory and a great step gained toward conquering the rebellion in the West.

But in the East the army was still trying to take Richmond, and the Confederates were still successfully fighting them off. Late in the summer of 1862 the Southern general, Lee, crossed the Potomac and attempted to march on Philadelphia.

The Union troops hurried to stop him. The two forces met at Antietam, where, on September 17th, they fought one of the bloodiest battles of the war. The "Boys in Blue" defeated the "Boys in Gray" and drove them back across the river. But even with so signal a success to encourage them, the North could not see that the South was any nearer giving up than in the beginning.

JANUARY, 1863—APRIL, 1865

Lincoln constantly turned the situation over in his mind. For weeks he thought about it, until certain facts came to stand out from the rest clear and unquestioned. He was convinced that slavery was not only the cause of the war, but that it was also the means by which the South was keeping up her strength. Did not the slaves raise crops with which to supply the Southern army and carry those supplies to the camps? And were they not of the greatest help to the troops in the digging of trenches, the building of fortifications, and the daily work of camp life? To take away the slaves would be to strike a hard blow at the Confederate strength.

When elected President, Lincoln truthfully said that he had no intention of interfering with slavery in the South. However, at that time he had taken an oath to preserve, protect, and defend the Union. There now seemed but one way to keep that oath. This was to free the slaves. So on New Year's day, 1863, Abraham Lincoln issued his Emancipation Proclamation, which gave freedom to more than three million slaves living in the Confederate States.

Month after month the war went on. In June, 1863, General Lee made another effort to invade Pennsylvania, and for the second time crossed the Potomac. There were seventy thousand men in his army when it reached Gettysburg, and there he entered into a three-day battle with the Northern troops. But when, on the third day, utterly defeated, he fell back into Virginia, he had lost more than twenty thousand. This was the last attempt to enter Pennsylvania. The Northern army, too, had lost heavily. This battle of Gettysburg is the greatest and the saddest in our history.

ON THE BATTLEFIELD OF GETTYSBURG.

While the eastern armies were fighting at Gettysburg, another battle was taking place in the West. The Union General had been trying for weeks to capture the Confederate city of Vicksburg. Day and night he had kept up his attack. Night and day his big guns went on shelling the city. At last, on July 4th, the very day after the Union success at Gettysburg, Vicksburg surrendered.

The persistent general who had won this victory was Ulysses S. Grant. Lincoln soon saw in him the one man who could put an end to the war; and in March, 1864, Grant was given command of all the Union armies.

At once he made his plans and began to carry them out. Battle followed battle all through that year. In April, 1865, Grant finally raised the stars and stripes over the city of Richmond and a few days later received the surrender of General Lee and his army.

That very month the four years struggle came to an end. The Civil War was closed and the Union was saved.

LINCOLN'S DEATH

In the White House the President's family are at breakfast. All are happy, for Robert, the eldest son, has just come home from serving as General Grant's aide-de-camp.

There is much for Lincoln and his boy to talk over. But some of it must be kept for another time, as this is a morning on which the President meets his cabinet.

By afternoon he is free. The carriage is called, and Mr. and Mrs. Lincoln drive out together. The long years of the war have saddened Lincoln's face and cut deep lines in it. But to-day the lines are softened, and the face is bright. With a smile he turns to Mrs. Lincoln. "Mary," he says, "we have had a hard time of it since we came to Washington; but the war is over, and, with God's blessing, we may hope for four years of peace and happiness; and then we will go back to Illinois, and pass the rest of our lives in quiet."

Many a friend receives a hearty greeting, many an acquaintance a cordial bow. And late in the afternoon the drive is over.

Then comes dinner. And all too soon it is eight

PRESIDENT LINCOLN AND HIS SON "TAD" (THADDEUS).

o'clock, and Mr. Lincoln is due at the theater. This is the 14th of April, 1865—the night of a benefit performance; and guests have been invited to share a box with Mr. and Mrs. Lincoln.

When they reach the theater the play has already begun. But the people in the crowded house are watching the President's box; and, catching sight of his tall figure, they rise from their seats and welcome him with cheers, while the orchestra strikes up "Hail to the Chief!"

The play goes on. It is good, and Lincoln listens and laughs and enjoys it all.

The players are going through the third act. The people are pleased and do not notice a pale, handsome man who is making his way toward the President's box. Quietly he slips in, stands one instant behind Lincoln, and then deliberately aims a pistol at him and fires.

The shot rings out. A woman screams. The murderer leaps to the stage and escapes. All is now confusion. Some try to follow the murderer; some try to reach the Lincoln box. But in the midst of all the uproar, the President sits quiet. His head has fallen forward on his breast.

Strong arms lift him and carry him from the theater to a modest brick

HOUSE WHERE LINCOLN DIED.

house across the way. He is put to bed. His son and friends are summoned, and all watch beside him through the night. They have no hope. The assassin has done his work. Slowly the hours drag by. The dawn comes. It is a little after seven, and Abraham Lincoln has ceased to breathe.

The watchers bow their heads. A prayer is said; and in the stillness a solemn voice proclaims, "Now he belongs to the ages."

XXIV

Ulysses S. Grant

YOUNGER DAYS

If you had been in Georgetown, Ohio, any school day about 1835, and had stepped into the little frame schoolhouse there, you would have seen thirty boys and girls bending busily over their slates, and at the desk the teacher standing, probably with a long beech switch in his hand. Little did he dream that behind one of those slates sat a boy who in coming years was to lead the armies of the Union to victory, and was to sit for eight years in the Presidential chair. That boy was Ulysses S. Grant.

Ulysses Grant's father was a tanner in Georgetown and owned considerable land outside of the city. Ulysses disliked the tanning business, but loved the farm, especially when he could use the horses. When only eight years old

he hauled all the wood used in the house and in the shops. And from the time he was eleven until he was seventeen, he did all the plowing and hauling, besides taking care of the cows and horses, sawing the firewood, and going to school. For play he used to go fishing, swimming, and skating; and sometimes he rode on horseback to visit his grandparents fifteen miles away.

Just before Ulysses was seventeen, he received an appointment as a cadet to the United States Military Academy and, in May, 1839, went to West Point.

The four years at West Point passed rather slowly but pleasantly enough for Grant. He never stood very high in his classes. In French his work was such that he himself said, "If the class had been turned the other end foremost, I should have been near the head." On being graduated from West Point, he was commissioned an officer in the United States Infantry.

In 1844 the regiment to which Grant belonged was ordered to Louisiana. The young soldier was soon to have his first taste of real war.

Some years before, the great state of Texas had made herself independent of Mexico, to which she had formerly belonged. She now asked to become a part of the United States and, in 1845, was taken into the Union. But the Mexicans were not willing to grant her as much land as she claimed. Texas said that her territory extended to the Rio Grande River. Mexico denied this, and said that it extended only to the Nueces River, about one hundred miles north of the Rio Grande. An American army then seized the disputed land—a step which the Mexicans naturally resented. Blood was shed, and the result was war declared between the

United States and Mexico in 1846. This war General Grant said in later years, was "one of the most unjust ever waged by a stronger against a weaker nation."

However, whether Grant thought the war was just or unjust made no difference. It was his duty as a soldier to fight at his country's call. Late in the summer of 1846, the army under General Taylor was headed for Monterey, one of the important places on the road to the City of Mexico.

Monterey was built on a high plane, at the entrance to a pass in the Sierra Madre Mountains. The town was well defended. Upon the low flat-roofed houses were soldiers, protected by rows of sand bags. Over the tops of these sand bags the Mexicans could shoot with but little danger of being struck themselves. And it was only after a four day battle that the American troops succeeded in taking the town.

During this battle Lieutenant Grant performed a most daring feat. Ammunition was getting low, and some one had to go for more. It was a dangerous ride; and as the General in command did not like to ask anyone to take the risk, he called for a volunteer. Grant promptly responded. Hanging over the farther side of his horse he galloped through the streets so fast that the enemy's shots were always too late to strike him.

At another time, when near the City of Mexico, he caught sight of a church with a high steeple. With a few men he took a cannon up into the belfry and showered shots upon the enemy.

The city was finally taken, and a treaty was arranged between the United States and Mexico. By the terms of this treaty Texas extended her territory to the Rio Grande, as she had claimed, and New Mexico and California were secured to the United States. In return, the United States paid Mexico $15,000,000.

FARMER, BUSINESS MAN, AND GENERAL

For the next few years Grant remained in the army. In the meantime he married. Finding that he could not support a family on the pay of an army officer, he resigned his position and became a farmer near St. Louis, Missouri. Here he lived for four years, working hard in good weather and bad, until fever and age forced him to give up farm life.

In 1860 he went to Galena, Illinois, where his father had a store; and in this store he clerked until President Lincoln's first call for volunteers.

The night that the call reached Galena, Grant presided over a great meeting of the citizens, at the Court House. He never wrapped another package after that meeting. He was selected to take charge of the volunteers of the town, drill them, and take them to Springfield, where they would be assigned to a regiment.

One thing that made Grant a great commander was his power to drill and manage men. He could take men who knew nothing about handling guns or about military discipline and could make fine soldiers of them in a few weeks. He said very little, but thought a great deal, and did his thinking at the right time. When he did speak, he always said something worth hearing.

Grant was soon made Colonel of a regiment in General Pope's division of the Union army, and in August was promoted to the rank of Brigadier General.

At this time the Confederates held forts along the Mississippi River from its mouth to Columbus, Kentucky. They

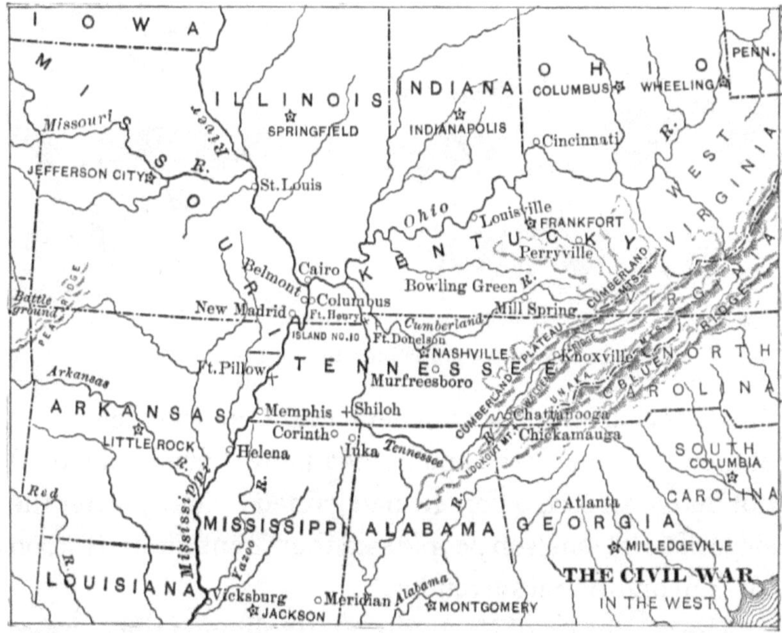

had also Fort Donelson on the Cumberland, and Fort Henry on the Tennessee. General Grant saw the importance of taking these two forts and gaining control of this section of the enemy's country. He talked over his plans with Commodore Foote, who had charge of the gunboats near Cairo. Both telegraphed to headquarters for leave to attack the forts and received permission in February, 1862.

Fort Henry was the first point of attack. Here the gunboats had the advantage. While Grant with his land forces was wading through the flooded creeks and the deep mud of the roads, Commodore Foote sailed up and took the fort.

At Fort Donelson it was different. For three days the land and naval forces carried on a siege. Then the commander of the Confederates asked Grant what terms would be allowed if the fort were given up. Grant replied, "No terms except an unconditional and immediate surrender can be accepted."

THE UNION GUNBOATS ATTACKING FORT DONELSON.

This was characteristic of General Grant. He was the kindest of men to a conquered enemy, but he was firm and would not budge an inch before he had gained a victory. After the siege of Fort Donelson people said that Grant's initials stood for "unconditional surrender."

The surrender of Nashville soon followed the capture of Fort Donelson, and General Grant with his victorious soldiers marched along the Tennessee River to Shiloh. Here they were attacked and driven back. But the next day, more Union troops having come, Grant again won a great victory.

Another post of vast importance held by the South was Vicksburg, and in the spring of 1863 Grant laid siege to that city. Never was a city more nobly defended than was Vicksburg. Week after week Grant and Sherman kept up their attack by day and by night. Within the besieged city the food became so scarce that a soldier had only one cracker and a small piece of pork for a days rations. During the last days the Confederates were compelled to use cats and rats for food.

In some places the Union and Confederate lines were so close that the Confederates would call across, "Well, Yank, when are you coming into town?"

"We propose to celebrate the Fourth of July there," the Union men would call back.

"The Yankee soldiers say they are going to take dinner in Vicksburg on the Fourth," said the Vicksburg paper. "The best receipt for cooking a rabbit is, 'First catch your rabbit.'" The last issue of the newspaper was printed on the back of wall paper on the Fourth of July and admitted that the Yankees had "caught their rabbit." Vicksburg had fallen.

When the Yankee soldiers entered the city, all hard feelings between the two armies were at an end. "I myself," said General Grant, "saw our men taking bread from their haversacks and giving it to the enemy they had been so recently engaged in starving out." When the Confederate soldiers passed out of the works they had defended so bravely, not a cheer nor an insulting word was uttered by the Union soldiers.

After the battle of Chattanooga in the following November, President Lincoln saw that the one man who ought to be at the head of the whole army was General Grant. So he made him Lieutenant General, with the power to manage the rest of the war according to his own ideas.

LIEUTENANT GENERAL AND PRESIDENT

When Ulysses S. Grant took command of the Union forces, there were two Confederate armies in the field,—one under General Johnston in Georgia, the other under General Robert F. Lee, in Virginia. General Grant decided that he himself would lead the Army of the Potomac and march against Lee. Sherman was to conquer Johnston, and then push his way through Georgia to the sea. They were to hammer away at the two Confederate armies at the same time.

INTERIOR OF A CONFEDERATE FORT ON THE COAST.

One of the first things that General Grant did was to look around for the man most fit to take charge of the cavalry of the Army of the Potomac. He chose General Philip Sheridan.

General Sheridan made it his business to torment Lee's army as much as possible. He captured its supplies in the Shenandoah Valley. He destroyed miles of railroad and telegraph lines. He defeated Lee's cavalry in several battles. In fact he made the United States cavalry seem like a swarm of hornets, buzzing around the Confederate army. He burned so many barns, and mills stored with grain that some one said, "If a crow wants to fly down the Valley, he must carry his provisions with him."

In the meantime General Grant and General Sherman were "hammering away" at the enemy. Sherman went first to Atlanta, conquering the troops that he met on the way. Then, having taken Atlanta and destroyed everything that might be of use to the Southern army, he began his famous

THE WAR IN THE EAST.

march to the sea. On the 22nd of December, 1864, Sherman telegraphed to President Lincoln, "I beg to present you as a Christmas gift the city of Savannah."

His army had mowed down everything in the way and had reached the coast. He now turned northward to march through the Carolinas and advance upon Lee from the south.

But General Grant did not need Sherman's help. He had met the Confederates in several fierce battles in the "Wilderness," the desolate woody region south of the Rapidan River. His losses had been great; but in spite of everything he would not turn back. "I propose to fight it out on this line if it takes all summer," he insisted. Then he turned his attention to Petersburg, south of Richmond; and the city was captured on April 2nd, 1865.

On the fall of Petersburg, Lee withdrew his army along the Appomattox River. The next day, April 3rd, the Union army marched into Richmond; and for the first time in four years the stars and stripes floated over the capital of the Confederacy.

It was at Appomattox Court House, about seventy-five miles west of Richmond, that General Lee, Commander-in-chief of the Confederate army, finally surrendered to General Grant. This was a few days after the fall of Richmond. General Lee was tall, handsome, and noble looking. Dressed in a beautiful new Confederate uniform he looked most splendid beside the plain, round-shouldered, quiet man, in rough soldier's dress, with nothing but the straps on his shoulders to tell that he was Lieutenant General of the Union army.

In the terms of surrender Grant's usual kindness showed itself. He would not take the officers' swords and allowed the soldiers to keep their horses, as they would need them for the spring plowing. The men in the Union lines, hearing that Lee's army had surrendered, were about to fire a salute of one hundred guns in honor of the victory. But Grant would not allow his men to rejoice over a fallen foe, and forbade the firing.

When the news of Lee's surrender reached Sherman's army, the men went nearly wild with joy. They shouted, threw up their caps and turned somersaults. Indeed the whole country rejoiced that the long, hard war was ended. But into the midst of all the joy came the appalling tidings of President Lincoln's assassination. When a new President was to be elected in 1868, there was but one man great enough for the place. That was the Ohio plowboy, the quiet modest soldier, the Commander-in-chief of the Army of the United States.

"Let us have peace," he said in accepting his nomination. And during the eight years of his presidency Grant fought as hard for peace as ever he had fought in war. The Southern States were once more received into the Union; and, in 1871, for the first time in more than ten years, there was a representation of all the states in Congress.

Honors and Death

At the end of his second term, General and Mrs. Grant took a trip around the world. Great men gathered to see them off. Crowds lined the shore, greeting them with cheers. Bells rang and whistles sounded.

When the steamer arrived in Liverpool, it was welcomed with even greater display. In France, Germany, on the Mediterranean—everywhere, it was the same. Grant was entertained by kings and emperors and received many beautiful and costly gifts. At last, after traveling through Asia, he sailed eastward across the Pacific to San Francisco, and was received home at the west gate of the country.

But General Grant's fighting days were not over. One more hard struggle lay before him after his trip around the world. Going into business in New York City with a faithless friend, he lost all his property, and found himself penniless and obliged to live on borrowed money. The hand of the last great silent conqueror was already upon him; but he did not falter. Courageously he went to work writing the two

THE TOMB OF GENERAL GRANT.

big volumes of "Memoirs," the sale of which he hoped would support his family after he was gone.

On General Grant's last Memorial Day, the old soldiers of the Grand Army of the Republic in New York City rose early. They unfurled their old battle flags, and formed their lines in the streets. At home, upon his bed, lay the great commander. Suddenly the sound of the drum and the slow heavy tread of many marching feet came to his ears. He could not lie there motionless with the music of Vicksburg and the Wilderness ringing in his ears. With all his strength he dragged himself to the window. He saw the tattered, blood-stained, bullet-pierced battle flags dipped to him in salute. Once more as of old he raised his hand to his brow. It was his last salute to the soldiers and the flag he loved so well.

On July 23, 1885, General Grant died. During the hour of the funeral, services were held over the entire country. Thousands followed his body to the vault where it was laid.

April 27th was the anniversary of Grant's birth, and on that day in the year 1897 his casket was removed from the vault and carried to a splendid mausoleum raised by his countrymen on Riverside Drive in New York. Over the portico are his words, "Let us have peace."

XXV

Robert E. Lee

Through the Mexican War

While reading of the courage and wisdom of the men who fought for the Union, one must not forget that there were two sides. Among the men who fought for the South were some of the bravest soldiers and truest men in all history. Numbers of them believed that slavery was right; that the negroes were created to be slaves, and that only as slaves could they be taken care of. Others knew in their hearts that slavery was wrong. But they thought that it could not be blotted out in a single day. They felt that the negro slaves could not be turned loose as free men without homes or means to care for themselves. One of the men who believed in this way was Robert E. Lee, and it is his story that I am going to tell.

Between the Rappahannock and the Potomac rivers in Virginia lies the county of Westmoreland. Here, in the midst of broad lawns and mighty trees stood stately Stratford, the home of "Light-Horse Harry Lee," a brave cavalry commander of Washington's, during the Revolution. And here, in 1807, "Light-Horse Harry Lee's" son, Robert E. Lee, was born.

A few years later the father died. The elder sons were

away, and it was Robert who took the tenderest care of his delicate mother. As he grew older, Robert decided, like his father, to be a soldier. He obtained an appointment to West Point and entered in 1825. At West Point he stood high in his class. Hard study, perfect drill, good conduct, all helped to make his cadet life a success. He was graduated second in his class and was assigned to the engineer corps of the army.

On the Virginia bank of the Potomac near Washington stands Arlington, a beautiful old house with broad porticoes. In Lee's youth this was the home of George Washington Parke Custis, the adopted son of George Washington.

One June evening, two years after Robert Lee had left West Point, Mr. Custis's great house was aglow with a hundred lights, and strains of wedding music floated out across the lawn. Before the altar stood the bride and groom, Mary Custis and Robert E. Lee. It was through this marriage that Lee later came into possession of Arlington.

From the time of his marriage until the outbreak of the Mexican War, Lee remained an army engineer. In 1847 he was with the American soldiers encamped before the City of Vera Cruz, Mexico. After one of the battles of this war he wrote to Custis, the eldest of his little sons, "I thought of you, my dear Custis, in the battle and wondered, when the musket balls and grape were whistling over my head in a perfect shower, where I could put you, if with me, to be safe....You have no idea of what a horrible sight a battlefield is."

During the Mexican War Lee did gallant service. The war over, he continued his work as engineer by fortifying the vicinity of Baltimore. The year 1852 saw him made superintendent of the military academy at West Point, from which he had been graduated twenty-three years before. In 1855 Congress formed two new regiments of cavalry. As Lieutenant Colonel of one of these regiments, Lee was sent to Texas, where he was stationed until that state seceded from the Union.

When home on a short vacation in 1859, Lee received orders from Washington to go to Harper's Ferry and capture John Brown and his band of men. There happened to be visiting at Arlington, on the day when Lee received the order, a young cavalry lieutenant named J. E. B. Stuart. Ever bold and ready for adventure, he begged Lee to take him along to Harper's Ferry. This dashing youth a few years later became Lee's trusted cavalry commander, "Jeb" Stuart, celebrated for his big plumed hat and his brave spirit.

COMMANDER OF THE CONFEDERATE FORCES

In the lives of many men there comes a time when they must choose between two things, both of which they dearly love. That time had now come to Robert E. Lee. During the beautiful days at Arlington, in the spring of 1861, his soul struggled with the choice between loyalty to the Government under which he had fought and loyalty to the South.

In April, President Lincoln offered him the command of the Union army that was being prepared to invade the South—to invade his own state, his father's state, his home. Lee refused the offer and two days later sent in his resignation from the United States army.

To his sister in Baltimore he wrote, "I have not been able to make up my mind to raise my hand against my relatives, my children, my home." Having taken his stand, Lee went from Washington to Richmond, leaving his beautiful Arlington to fall into the hands of the Northern army. In Richmond he was made Commander-in-chief of the Virginia forces.

Before long Mr. Jefferson Davis, President of the Confederacy, came to Richmond; and that city was made the capital of the Southern Government. All was bustle in the new capital. The South was busy collecting guns and ammunition. Nothing was ready for war. Everything had to be done. Even the soldiers had to be made from raw recruits. General Lee knew that Virginia would be the great battlefield for the two armies. There were two moves to be made: to defend Richmond, and to try to make a counter attack upon Washington.

On July 21st, the Union troops attacked General Beauregard at Manassas, or Bull Run. Beauregard's men were beginning to fall back when General Jackson advanced upon the center of the Union line and drove the troops back to Washington.

In this case defeat really helped the North more than victory helped the South. The North saw that war was on in deadly earnest and that serious preparations must be made. The South, however, grew over confident through its first victory.

In 1862 General Lee was made Commander-in-chief,

under Jefferson Davis, of all the armies of the Confederacy; and in June he took command of the troops defending Richmond. Already the invading army under General McClellan had crept so close that the roar of its cannon could be heard in the city. Lee planned to attack McClellan's army and drive it away.

Looking about for a man who would have the courage and quickness to go out and explore the enemy's right, he chose "Jeb" Stuart, the dashing young cavalryman who lead helped him at Harper's Ferry. Lee made no mistake in his choice. Within forty-eight hours Stuart had ridden entirely around McClellan's army and was back in Richmond, besides leaving torn up railroads and destroyed provisions in the enemy's rear.

From June 25th to July 1st, Lee and McClellan fought what are known as the "Seven Days' Battles." By these battles Lee succeeded in forcing McClellan to retreat, though in the last, at Malvern Hill, thousands of the brave Confederates lost their lives.

About two months later the Northern general, Pope, led his army against Richmond. Lee and Jackson advanced to meet him and won the second battle of Manassas, or Bull

Run. Pope fell back to Washington, defeated, and gave up his command.

Then followed Lee's advance across the Potomac and his retreat after the terrible battle of Antietam.

Late in 1862 General Burnside took charge of the Northern army and pushed toward the Rappahannock. No sooner had Lee discovered Burnside's move than he and his army took possession of the Heights near Fredericksburg, through which Burnside would pass on his way to Richmond. At dawn one December morning, when Burnside's men tried to throw their pontoon bridges across the river, Confederate guns boomed out the signal which called Lee's men to arms. Instantly the riflemen began to pick off the bridge builders. The Union army was delayed on the river bank for many hours; and when finally they did cross, they found Lee well prepared and the Confederates stationed in the best positions.

The battle was begun on the morning of the 13th. All day long the Confederate soldiers, many of them barefoot, stood in the December snow and created havoc among the enemy. Only once did General Meade, later the victor of Gettysburg, break through a gap in Jackson's lines; and then he was quickly driven back. By nighttime Burnside's army had been beaten, and Burnside, with the men that were left, recrossed the river.

In the spring of 1863 "fighting Joe Hooker" was in command of the Union forces in Virginia. At the head of a splendid army of one hundred and thirty thousand men, he felt sure of defeating Lee, who had less than half that number. For this purpose he marched toward Chancellorsville, to the west of Fredericksburg, where Lee's army was still encamped.

A PONTOON BRIDGE.

But Lee did not wait for Hooker to carry out his plan. With Stonewall Jackson, Lee moved promptly forward and confronted Hooker's main body in a tangled forest, only a few miles from Chancellorsville. Here a two-days' battle took place. The Confederates won the fight, but their victory cost the life of Stonewall Jackson.

In June, 1863, came Lee's daring ivasion of Pennsylvania. And in July the South received the double blow of Gettysburg and Vicksburg. Lee's army was compelled to retreat to Virginia, and from this time on Lee was constantly worried about his ragged, hungry men. At Richmond his wife and daughters with flying needles were knitting socks for the soldiers. The General wrote to Mrs. Lee, "Tell the girls to send all they can. I wish they could make some shoes too. We have thousands of barefooted men."

SURRENDER

You remember that in the spring of 1864 General Grant was put at the head of the Union army and led the Army of the Potomac into Virginia. Then followed the terrible Wilderness campaign in which the ranks of the Confederates grew steadily thinner, and the men grew steadily weaker from lack of food and clothing.

Yet even in the Wilderness there were victories for the Confederates. At Cold Harbor they held back the Union lines with frightful slaughter. It was here that a hungry soldier had his only cracker shot from his hand. "The next time I'll put my cracker in a safe place down by the breastworks where it won't get hurt, poor thing," he said.

In spite of much hard fighting, "On to Richmond!" was still Grant's cry. He knew that if he could take Petersburg to the south of Richmond, it would be an easy matter to capture Richmond at last. For over nine long months Lee bravely defended Petersburg, his men ever growing fewer and weaker, and arms and ammunition becoming scarcer. Between Grant and Sherman the workshops had been destroyed, and there was no way of getting new supplies.

On the first Sunday morning in April, 1865, a boy came into the church where Jefferson Davis was listening to the sermon and handed him a telegram. It was from Lee. "I can no longer defend Petersburg," it said. "You must give up hope of saving Richmond."

The next day, as Grant rode through the deserted streets of Petersburg, Lee was leading his army along the banks of the Appomattox. Grant pursued Lee to Appomattox Court House. Though General Lee felt that he must save the remainder of his men for their wives and children at home, he declared, "I would rather die a thousand deaths than surrender."

There were five houses at the place called Appomattox Court House. The largest was a square brick house; and here, on April 9, 1865, General Grant and General Lee met to arrange the terms of the surrender.

After the meeting Lee rode up to break the news of his surrender to his brave troops. They crowded about him

RICHMOND IN FLAMES—THE END OF THE WAR.

eager to shake his hand, to touch his horse; and tears ran down their cheeks as they looked upon their beloved leader. "Men," he said, "we have fought through the war together. I have done my best for you. My heart is too full to say more."

The war over, the trustees of Washington College in Virginia begged Lee to become its President. For five years he directed the affairs of the College, beloved by the students as he had been by his soldiers. On a September day in 1870, after attending a meeting of the vestrymen of his church, he was stricken with an illness from which two weeks later he died.

From far and near the old Confederate soldiers gathered to escort their leader to his last resting place. Behind the hearse walked Lee's riderless horse, Traveler, his trappings all in black.

In Richmond there now stands a statue of Lee mounted on Traveler. It is a tribute to a great soldier and a true gentleman.

XXVI

David Glasgow Farragut

MIDSHIPMAN

One day a man in a splendid uniform paid a visit to David Farragut's father at his home near New Orleans. He was Commander Porter of the United States Navy. He asked that he be allowed to adopt one of the motherless Farragut boys and train him for a career in the navy. The chance was offered to eight-year-old David. David wanted to go, and he said good-by to his father whom he was never to see again.

Commander Porter returned to Washington, and David went with him. There he met the Secretary of the Navy, and was promised a Midshipman's warrant as soon as he should be ten years old. The promise was not forgotten.

Not long after he had passed this tenth birthday, his foster father was given the command of the frigate *Essex* and took the little midshipman into his service. During the War of 1813 the *Essex* under Porter, with Midshipman Farragut on board, started on a cruise around Cape Horn to destroy the British whale-fishing in the Pacific. Having captured several British vessels along the western coast of South America, the *Essex* entered the harbor of Valparaiso. Here she was over-taken by two British warships, the *Phoebe* and the *Cherub*.

CAPTAIN PORTER BRINGING
MIDSHIPMAN FARRAGUT
TO THE "ESSEX".

According to the laws of nations, ships belonging to countries at war with each other may not fight in a neutral harbor. So the English vessels waited for the *Essex* just outside.

During a great windstorm a cable of Porter's ship gave way. She drifted out to sea, and the British began their attack. The English guns could shoot much farther than most of those on the *Essex;* so, staying out of reach of the short-range guns of the American ship, the English poured one broadside after another into the helpless frigate. Captain Porter tried every means in his power to close with the *Phoebe*, but owing to the disabled condition of his ship, he could do little. After a fight which lasted two hours and a half, the *Essex* was forced to surrender.

Farragut had found that whatever no one else had time to do was a midshipman's work during a fight. He had carried messages for the Captain, brought powder for the gunners, and had done his duty so well that when Captain Porter sent home his dispatches to the United States, David Farragut was one of those mentioned for bravery. He was twelve years old at this time and stood exceedingly straight because, as he said, "I cannot afford to lose one fraction of my scanty inches."

After the surrender of the *Essex* David, with the crew, went aboard one of the British ships, where he was included in an invitation to breakfast in the captain's cabin. His grief at the loss of the *Essex* was so great that the captain noticed it and said kindly, "Never mind, my little fellow; it will be your turn next, perhaps." David replied that he hoped so indeed and hurriedly left the cabin that the men might not see how badly he felt.

Having made the officers and crew of the *Essex* promise not to take up arms against England until they had been exchanged, the British sent them back to the United States.

Officer in the Navy

It was not long before young Farragut was exchanged and was again free to enter the service of his country. For the next few years after the close of the War of 1812, he was on several different ships sailing the Mediterranean and fighting the pirates of the West Indies. Much of his success in late life was due to the fact that during these years he formed the habit of always doing his level best, not thinking, as do many, that the present does not matter.

In 1825, Farragut was promoted to the rank of lieutenant on the *Brandywine,* a beautiful new ship. One of his first duties was to carry General Lafayette back in safety to his home in France. In the following years Farragut had various duties to perform. In 1854, he was sent to the Pacific coast, where a navy yard was to be built on Mare Island near San Francisco. To plan and construct this yard was an important task, and Farragut was just the man to do it well.

Four years were given to the work, and then he returned to the East. He was now a captain and was given command of

DAVID G. FARRAGUT.

the *Brooklyn*, one of the first steam warships in our navy. After a two years' cruise on the *Brooklyn*, Farragut left the ship and went to Norfolk, Virginia.

A few months later the war between the North and the South broke out, and our captain had a new query to settle. Farragnt was born in the South; his home at this time was in Norfolk, and most of his friends were Southerners. Now came the question. Should he side with the South, his old home, or should he follow the flag for which he had worked and fought for fifty years?

Farragut and his Norfolk neighbors met daily and discussed the great questions before the country. He expressed his opinions fearlessly, but he soon saw that his friends did not agree with him. One day one of them said, "A person of your sentiments cannot live in Norfolk." "Very well," he replied, "I will go where I can live with such sentiments."

Going home Farragut told his wife that she, too, would have to decide whether to stay with the South or to go with him. Together they left Norfolk and went to a little village on the Hudson River, called Hastings. The people here looked askance at them, however. The Government, too, hesitated to trust a Southerner with a great responsibility, in spite of the fact that he had shown his loyalty again and again.

But the time was not far away when the North needed just such a man as Farragut.

NEW ORLEANS

The South held possession of New Orleans and the mouth of the Mississippi, both of which the North wanted to control; and in 1862 Farragut was ordered to go and take them from the South. He was delighted with the plan for capturing New Orleans, and was sure it could be done. So with a large Union fleet he sailed for the mouth of the Mississippi.

Once there, it took him two weeks to get the ships across a bar formed at the mouth of the river by its mud deposits. This was only the first obstacle that lay in the path. Beyond the bar, the Confederates had stretched across the river two great cables on hulks. Beyond the cables were two forts, one on each side of the river; and still beyond was a Confederate fleet.

Farragut's operations were begun by storming the two forts for six days and nights, but with no success. Then he decided to run his ships past the two forts and on to New Orleans. This was easier said than done. First a passageway for the ships must somehow be made through the cables. To break these the brave commander of the steamer *Itasca* ran her under the fire of both forts straight up against the chain. It snapped. The hulks drifted apart and made a breach large enough for the warships to pass through. In preparing the fleet for the run past the forts, hammocks, bags of sand, and ashes were piled around the boilers and engines to protect them from the shot of the enemy's guns. Some of the ships were daubed on the outside with Mississippi mud, so that they could not be seen in the dark.

FARRAGUT'S SHIPS PASSING THE FORTS.

One night the signal was given to weigh anchor and move up the river. In single file the vessels set out to run the gantlet of fire, which was sure to greet them from the forts. The *Cayuga* ran through the breach unharmed; but, as the second boat passed the barrier, the guns of the two forts blazed forth. The ships' broadsides answered, and flying shells filled the air.

Down the river came a flaming fire ship straight for the flagship *Hartford*. Farragut was helpless to get away. The flames from the fire ship leaped up, and soon the *Hartford* was ablaze. Men were detailed to fight the flames while all the time the gunners loaded, fired, and reloaded their guns. At length the flames were put out, and the flagship once more started upstream.

On went the Union boats. They had passed the bar, the cables, and the forts. Ahead of them now lay the Confederate fleet. Fiercely did Farragut's ships rush to the attack, and in short order they overcame this last obstacle to their advance.

When the people of New Orleans saw the Union fleet coming, they became desperate. They sent rafts of burning

cotton bales down-
stream. They set
fire to cotton-laden
ships, smashed
hogsheads of molas-
ses and sugar, and
destroyed property
right and left to pre-
vent it from falling

THE LAST OF THE "ALABAMA".

into the hands of the Union men. In the last week of April, 1862, Captain Farragut sent men ashore at New Orleans to haul down the Confederate flag from the public buildings and to run up the stars and stripes instead.

After the city was taken, the forts were soon captured, and the North had control of the mouth of the Mississippi. Captain Farragut's capture of New Orleans was the second great naval success to cheer the North. Coming, as it did, so soon after the repulse of the dreaded *Merrimac* by Lieutenant Worden in his little ironclad *Monitor*, it put new hope into every Northern soldier.

About two years later another great naval battle was fought, this time on the other side of the ocean, near the coast of France. During the war the Confederates had fitted out ships which coasted about and harassed Northern merchantmen. For a long time the Union warships could not check these doings. One of these Southern warships was the *Alabama*. At last the *Kearsarge*, commanded by Captain Winslow, discovered the *Alabama* in a French harbor. This was a neutral port, so the *Kearsarge* waited for the *Alabama* outside, just as the English ships had waited for the *Essex* at Valparaiso. The Confederate vessel suddenly sailed forth and attacked the *Kearsarge*. A terrific battle ensued; but the men of the *Kearsarge* were better marksmen, and after an hour's fight the *Alabama* sank, and the victory was won.

Another Confederate war vessel was the *Albemarle*—an enormous ironclad ram. She, too, had attacked Northern ships, and Lieutenant Cushing determined to put a stop to her marauding. So, one dark night in October, he took a boat and, making his way to the *Albemarle*, where she lay-off Plymouth, North Carolina, exploded a torpedo under her. Then he jumped into the water to escape capture and returned unharmed to the Union fleet.

Meanwhile Farragut was kept busy for over a year, silencing batteries along the Mississippi. On July 4, 1863, came Grant's victory at Vicksburg; and, satisfied at last that he could do no more on the river, Farragut soon after turned his command over to another officer, and with three of his ships sailed for New York.

Mobile Bay

After the fall of New Orleans the next fort on the Gulf to be considered was Mobile Bay, and in 1864 Farragut undertook to conquer this port. Two forts near the entrance to the bay protected the city of Mobile, and these had to be passed by Farragut's ships before they could encounter the Confederate fleet which lay inside the bays. In this fleet was an ironclad ram—the *Tennessee.*

The Confederates had made great preparations against the attack. A triple line of torpedoes had been laid in the channel, and the forts had been strengthened in every way possible.

Farragut had four ironclad monitors, besides twenty-one wooden vessels. He ordered his wooden ships lashed together in pairs, a larger with a smaller. Then, with the stars and stripes floating from every peak and masthead, early on the morning of August 5, 1864, the entrance into Mobile Bay was begun. Farragut wanted to lead the column in his flagship, the *Hartford*; but his officers begged him not to do it. They felt that the commanding officer ought not to be exposed to the greatest danger. So, to please his men, Farragut gave in, and the *Hartford*, with her running mate, took second place in the column of wooden ships.

In order to see things more clearly, and to be able to direct the movements of the fleet to better advantage, Farragut climbed into the rigging; and, as the smoke of the guns became more dense, he went higher and higher until he was close under the maintop. Here he had a good view of the whole field of battle, and, by bracing himself against the shrouds, could use his spyglass.

The four ironclads were in single file, a little ahead of the wooden vessels. The *Tecumseh* was leading the line. Suddenly she ran into a torpedo; and Farragut, from the rigging of the *Hartford*, saw her plunge below the water and disappear. The *Brooklyn*, in the first rank of the wooden ships just behind, began to back, and thereby caused confusion in the line of ships in the rear.

This was the supreme moment of Farragut's life. To go on meant the raking fire of the forts, the torpedoes, the Confederate fleet, and possible victory. To turn back meant a crushing and humiliating defeat.

"Full speed ahead!" he shouted down. And passing by the *Brooklyn*, the *Hartford* dashed straight at the line of torpedoes. As the flagship passed over them, they could be heard

ONE OF FARRAGUT'S WOODEN SHIPS ATTACKNG THE
CONFEDERATE IRONCLAD, "TENNESSEE".

knocking against the bottom of the ship; but none exploded. With the flagship safe beyond this danger, the other ships followed; and the attack on the Confederate fleet began.

One Confederate gunboat was destroyed by fire, one was captured, and one ran away. Then, coming down from the *Hartford*'s rigging, Farnigut was just telling his signal officer to order his fleet to drop anchor when a shout arose. The ironclad *Tennessee*, which had withdrawn from the battle and had been lying under the protection of one of the forts, was boldly approaching to fight the entire Northern fleet.

Farragut ordered each of his monitors to attack the monster. The wooden vessels also were ordered to charge the *Tennessee* at full speed. Down they rushed upon the ironclad, striking her with all their force, although their bows were crushed by the blow. The monitors did their part by keeping up a ceaseless fire until the *Tennessee*'s steering chains were shot away, her smokestack destroyed, and her commander wounded. She had made a bold fight and lost. To surrender was all that was left for her, and she surrendered.

Thus ended the battle of Mobile Bay. "One of the hardest earned victories of my life, and the most desperate battle I ever fought since the days of the old *Essex*," said Farragut.

Soon after the surrender of the *Tennessee*, the forts were captured, and the victory was complete.

Farragut's work in the Gulf was now done, and he sailed for the North. Great was the reception given him when the reached New York! The citizens formally invited him to make his home among them and gave him fifty thousand dollars to enable him to do so. And for his faithful, loyal, continued service to his country, Congress, at the close of the war, created a new and higher rank in our navy and named David Glasgow Farragut the first American Admiral.

XXVII

Cyrus McCormick

In the first quarter of the nineteenth century there lived on a Virginia farm a little fellow by the name of Cyrus McCormick. During seed and harvest time he was expected to be in the fields each morning by five o'clock.

Those were the days when harvesting was hard, because it was all done by hand. First the grain had to be cut down with a scythe. Next it was gathered into bundles and tied together with a cord. Then it was carried to the barn and laid on the floor, while the men beat the grain free with flails.

As he helped in the fields, Cyrus McCormick kept thinking that perhaps he could make a machine which would lighten his work. And when he was only fifteen years old he made a harvesting cradle by which he himself could do in a day as much work as an able-bodied man could do.

Cyrus's father had attempted to invent a machine that would cut the grain. Though he had not

CYRUS MCCORMICK.

ONE OF THE GREAT HARVESTING MACHINES ON A WESTERN GRAIN FIELD.

succeeded, his failure inspired his son to try. Cyrus McCormick's idea was even greater than his father's. He believed that he could make one machine that would cut the wheat, gather it into sheaves, and bind it. This was not an easy task—far from it. But after working and working, Cyrus McCormick completed, in 1831, a reaping machine that was to prove a lasting success. What is more, every bit of the machine was made by his own hands.

The essentials of this reaper were those of the great reapers used to-day. There was a divider to separate the grain to be cut from that to be left standing; there was a cutting blade, a reel to bring the grain within reach of the blade, and a platform to receive the falling grain. This machine was patented in 1834.

Success had come at last, and Cyrus McCormick began to manufacture reaping machines in a little workshop on his father's farm at Walnut Grove, Virginia. He worked under great difficulties because there were few railroads in those days, and much of the material for the reapers had to be carried across the country by horses. He could make hardly fifty machines during the whole year.

Then came the question of carrying the finished machines to the immense plains and wide grain fields of the West, where they would be of far greater use than in the East. While this proved difficult, the Western market offered large inducements; so Mr. McCormick decided to move to the West and there set up his factories.

First he went to Cincinnati, but a few years later he settled in Chicago, where he built a large manufacturing plant. This now turns out yearly more than 150,000 machines. It is said that each one of these machines saves the labor of six men in the field.

Before his death, in 1884, Cyrus McCormick had received many honors, and had been elected a member of the Institute of France, because he had "done more for the cause of agriculture than any other living man."

XXVIII

Clara Barton

Fort Sumter had been fired upon; and in response to Lincoln's call for troops, Massachusetts had sent a regiment to Washington. As the soldiers were passing through Baltimore they were attacked by a mob. Some were killed, and forty were wounded.

Among the anxious crowd waiting about the Washington station for the arrival of the wounded men was Miss Clara Barton. Her heart was full of sympathy when she

CLARA BARTON.

saw the suffering soldiers. She followed to where they were carried, and gave up her time to nursing them. Hard as the work was, she liked it. And seeing how much she could do to help and comfort the sick soldiers, she nobly offered her services for as long as they might be needed.

The women of the North responded to Lincoln's call

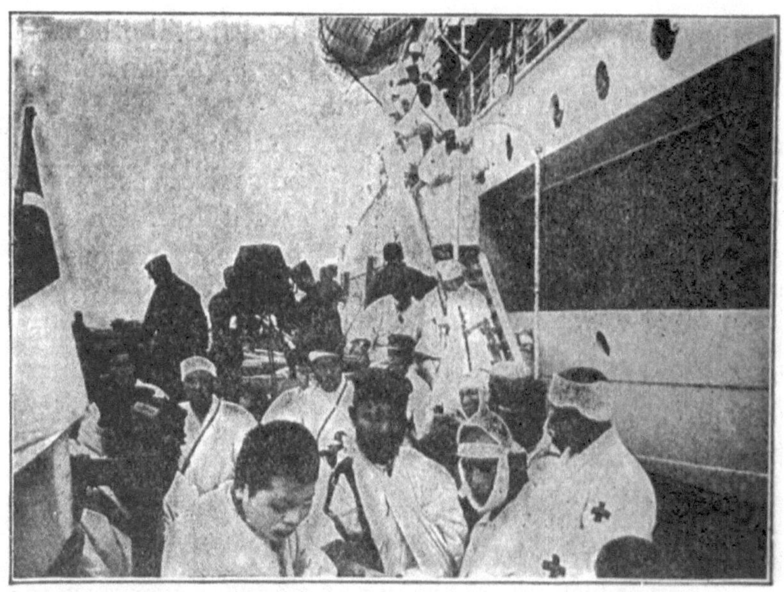

THE WORK OF THE RED CROSS IN THE RUSSO-JAPANESE WAR.

as promptly as the men. While the troops were gathering to defend the Union, the Northern women were rolling bandages, making delicacies, and collecting comforts to be sent to the front—a work which they kept up throughout the war.

That all these supplies might be handled wisely, the United States appointed the Sanitary Commission. With the money and necessities sent from the different Northern States and, above all, with the help of such women as Mary Livermore, Dorothy Dix, and Clara Barton, this Sanitary Commission did a wonderful work. Many a soldier, wounded in the battles of the West, was carried north on the Mississippi ambulance boat. Still others—and these in thousands—were cared for by nurses on the battlefield or in the camp hospital.

When the war was over, and Miss Barton was no longer needed to attend the country's injured soldiers, she went abroad. She was worn out and needed rest. In the course of her travels she learned that the chief nations of Europe had organized the Red Cross Society, and had pledged themselves to uphold it. The object of this society was to care for all sick or wounded soldiers needing help, whether friend or foe. It had adopted a flag—a red cross on a white ground—the reverse of the flag of Switzerland, where the society had been organized; and it was agreed that even on the battlefield this flag should be respected by both sides alike.

What possibilities lay before such a society! Miss Barton, after her Civil War experience, easily saw what it could do; so she became a member of the Red Cross, and served under its flag on European battlefields.

When at last she returned to America, it was with the determination to induce her country to sign the international agreement regarding the Red Cross Society. At this time the United States was at peace, and it was hard to interest people in a society to care for injured soldiers. But after five years of constant effort on Miss Barton's part, the Association of the American Red Cross was formed, with Clara Barton as its president. Not only did the American Red Cross Society pledge itself to the care of wounded soldiers in the time of war; it also agreed to render relief to the victims of any great national calamity.

Great calamities have, in one year and another, befallen the American nation since; and time and again the Red Cross Society has worked to relieve the results of flood, fire, or pestilence. In May, 1889, the breaking of a dam in western Pennsylvania was followed by a flood which nearly swept Johnstown out of existence. Houses were carried away, thousands of people were killed, and those who survived were homeless and without food. To this scene of desolation Miss Barton and her fellow Red Cross members went. And for five months they stayed, sometimes in tents, sometimes shelterless, distributing the money, food, and other supplies sent to the afflicted city.

Nor was this all. Six "Red Cross Hotels" were put up as quickly as possible, and here the homeless people were sheltered and fed. Three thousand houses were built by a general committee, and the Red Cross Society supplied each and every one of them with furniture and made them ready for use. When she went home, Miss Barton left behind her the beginnings of a new and grateful Johnstown.

Nine years later came our war with Spain. Spain owned several of the West Indian Islands, Cuba among them; and the cruel treatment of the Spanish Government had driven Cuba to revolt. For a while America watched the unequal struggle, and then our country ordered Spain to give the Cubans their freedom. She refused, and American soldiers and sailors were sent to win for the Cubans what they could not win for themselves.

Even before our country took a hand in Cuba's war, Clara Barton had visited the island and tried to relieve the terrible misery and starvation caused by Spanish brutality. Then, during the war, while the Red Cross flag waved over the army hospitals, the plucky nurses fed and nursed the wounded soldiers, helped the surgeons at their work, and comforted the dying.

Thirty-seven years lay between the opening of our Civil War and our war with Spain. These thirty-seven years had changed Miss Barton from a young woman to a woman of nearly seventy. Yet she served as energetically, as loyally and unselfishly in Cuba as she had served the boys in blue and gray so many years before.

Through her efforts the Red Cross Society is now firmly planted in America, its members always ready to share the hardships and lessen the sufferings of the victims of future disasters. In years to come, as in years gone by, Americans will richly bless the name of Clara Barton.

XXIX

George Dewey

"The Hero of Manila"

The splendid battleship *Maine* rode peacefully at anchor in Havana Harbor. Over her floated the stars and stripes. Cuba was in revolt against Spain, and the little island was suffering tortures from Spanish cruelties; but the United States battleship was there to take no part in the war. She was a neutral vessel, merely paying a visit to the harbor.

It was the 15th of February, 1898, and the officers and sailors aboard the *Maine* were performing their daily duties. Suddenly there was a tremendous explosion, and two hundred and sixty-six American seamen were killed. The *Maine* had been blown to pieces, and all that was left of the splendid battleship was a mass of wreckage.

What caused this frightful disaster? Who was responsible for the dastardly deed? Was the explosion an accident, or was it a piece of Spanish treachery? Americans north, south, east, and west clamored for an explanation. A Court of Inquiry was appointed to sift the matter to the bottom and find the cause. And after many days came the report, "The *Maine* was destroyed by the explosion of a submarine mine."

It was late in March when the Court of Inquiry made its

HOW BATTLESHIPS HAVE CHANGED IN HALF A CENTURY:
THE "MAINE" AND THE OLD "CONSTITUTION".

report. In April, Congress resolved to recognize the independence of Cuba, and demanded that Spain give the Cubans their liberty.

Spain refused. Then the United States resolved to take up arms in Cuba's behalf. Troops were called out. Ships were sent to blockade the Cuban ports. President McKinley telegraphed Commodore George Dewey, in command of our Asiatic squadron at Hong Kong, China, to go at once to Manila and to capture or destroy the Spanish fleet guarding that port.

With all dispatch Dewey started for the Philippine Islands, and the last night of April saw his six war vessels outlined in the moonlight off Manila Bay.

Before them opened the harbor, planted with submarine mines and protected by Spanish batteries. In the harbor lay the fleet Dewey had come to "capture or destroy." And he meant to do it, cost what it might. Through the darkness of the night, the moonlight having waned, his flag-

DEWEY ON THE BRIDGE
OF THE "OLYMPIA".

ship, the *Olympia*, led the way. By daylight the ships were off Manila and were fired upon by five batteries and the Spanish fleet. Two mines exploded ahead of Dewey's flagship, but failed to harm it.

In line, one behind another, our ships advanced to battle. Commodore Dewey was on the flagship's bridge. At last the moment of attack came, and Captain Gridley heard him say, "You may fire when ready, Gridley."

Our squadron opened fire at 5:41 that morning. About 7:30 the signal went up to stop firing and to withdraw from action. What had happened? The Commodore had tried to find out how many rounds of ammunition were left on his ship, and by mistake had been told that only fifteen remained. That could not be! But to make sure, the ships were ordered to withdraw from the battle. While the crews had breakfast, the officers consulted and learned that all was right with the ammunition.

Then back to the battle went the American ships, and in an hour and a half the Spaniards ceased firing. Their ships had been sunk, burned, or riddled; and Dewey's work was done. Throughout May and June the war went on. Then in

July an American fleet destroyed another Spanish fleet in the harbor of Santiago. And a few days later the city of Santiago was surrendered to an American army. The Spaniards had now had enough and sought terms of peace. The treaty which closed the war gave the Cubans their freedom and ceded to the United States Porto Rico and the Philippine Islands, for which we agreed to pay $20,000,000.

In the rough and tumble of a village school, the stricter discipline of a military preparatory school, and the still more severe training of the united States Naval Academy at Annapolis, George Dewey received his education.

He was graduated from Annapolis in 1858. Three years later came the Civil War. And under Farragut, Lieutenant Dewey was assigned to the warship *Mississippi* and had a share in the attack on New Orleans.

One year after the battle of New Orleans, eight American vessels made their way up the Mississippi River and tried to weather the deadly fire of nearly four miles of Southern batteries. It was the attack upon Port Hudson. The flagship and another passed the batteries safely. At last the *Mississippi* was almost by. She put on steam and shot ahead a little faster. But amidst the smoke of battle she lost her bearings and ran aground. There was no chance to set her free. She must be burned and abandoned, so the torch was applied. Almost the last to leave the ill-fated ship was Lieutenant Dewey.

In Annapolis Dewey was carefully taught the duties of a naval officer. In the Civil War he learned to put this knowledge to the test. And these two schools—the one of studies, the other of experience—successfully prepared him to become "The Hero of Manila" and Admiral of the American Navy.

XXX

Edison and Hoe

Newsboy and Telegraph Operator

The flaming pine knot used long ago burned well, and pine was easy to get. But it smoked and dripped tar in the cabins of the early housewives, so candles came to take its place.

Candles give a mellow light. But they were expensive to buy, and it was tedious to dip, dip the twisted wicks in the melted tallow, so whale-oil lamps were introduced.

Then some fifty-odd years ago whale oil was pushed aside for kerosene, which supplies to-day the customary light of the farmers' houses. Many people in towns and cities as well still use the kerosene lamp, but unlike the isolated farmer they do so from choice. The city houses of the present may be lighted by the soft light of gas or the steady glow of Thomas Edison's electric bulb.

Thomas Edison's father was not well to do, and very early Thomas had to begin to earn money. He was twelve years old when he became newsboy on the Grand Trunk Railroad, and a pretty shrewd newsboy he was, too. He soon learned that exciting news sold better than dry items, and he would run over a paper's headlines and judge how many he could sell before deciding how many he would buy. What is more, he printed the only newspaper ever printed on a train—a little paper full of railroad gossip.

One thing that especially fascinated the newsboy was the click, click of the telegraph. Endless questions were put to the operators along the road. Then came a day when the little child of a station agent was playing on the track all unnoticed. Down upon it came a freight train nearer and nearer. When it was almost too late, Edison spied the child. Like a flash he made a dive, grabbed, the baby, and cleared the track without a moment to spare. The grateful father could hardly do less than teach Edison how to telegraph. Night lessons began, and in a few months the newsboy had become an excellent telegraph operator.

To the train boy this had seemed a fair ambition, but now that Edison knew how to run the machine he wanted to perfect it. So he studied his work, spent his money for books, and made experiment after experiment, which have resulted in more than one priceless improvement.

EDISON LISTENING TO THE PHONOGRAPH.

He was engrossed in his work and disliked interruption. The manager of his circuit had found from experience that operators were not always on hand, and he insisted that each operator should signal to him over the wire each half hour. This was a decided nuisance to Edison, so he managed to connect his clock to his machine in such a way that the signal was promptly turned in at headquarters every thirty minutes, whether the young operator was in the office or not.

He had another device, too, which gave the impression that he could receive a long message very rapidly, when such was not the case. In both of these little frauds he was found out, and he had the good sense to be ashamed of his deception rather than proud of his invention. The chagrin over the discovery of his real lack of speed in taking a message led him to work, work, work in this line, until there was no one who could equal him. At least he would be all he claimed to be.

The Inventor

After drifting from place to place in the West, Thomas Edison went to Boston and then to New York. When he reached New York he had little but debts to call his own. Man after man refused him work, until, by chance, he reached a large broker's office just at the time all was in confusion because the recording machine had broken down. Edison offered his services and soon made it right.

Such a man was too good to lose. He was promptly appointed superintendent at two hundred dollars a month, and from that hour his fortune was made. At once he set to work to make improvements on the machines used in this and similar offices. These improvements he offered for sale,

EDISON'S LABORATORY AT MENLO PARK IN 1879.

hoping to get a few thousand dollars out of them. Imagine his surprise at being offered forty thousand!

With the forty thousand Mr. Edison established his first large laboratory and engaged a force of men to work with him. Now had come the longed-for opportunity to perfect the ideas with which his brain was teeming.

From his first laboratory grew a second and then, in 1876, he founded one at Menlo Park, a small village in New Jersey. Here, by his marvelous inventions, Mr. Edison earned the name, the "Wizard of Menlo Park." His latest laboratory, where he is still working, is at Orange, New Jersey.

In the days when he was a fifteen-year-old telegraph operator, a telegraph wire could carry only one message at a time. Edison determined to find a way to send two messages at once over one wire. Effort followed effort until the desired result was reached. But still the inventor was not content. He would make one wire do the work of four. He did this, too. Then once again he began to work to make a single wire carry six messages, and he has succeeded!

Asked a few years ago to name his principal inventions he said, "The first and foremost, the idea of the electric lighting station; then—let me see—what have I invented? Well, there was the mimeograph and the electric pen, and the carbon telephone, and the incandescent lamp and its accessories, and the quadruple telegraph and the automatic telegraph, and the phonograph, and the kinetoscope and—I don't know a whole lot of other things."

This is a modest answer surely, when one considers that the number of Mr. Edison's inventions reaches high into the hundreds.

Many men would be content with the honor of having invented the phonograph alone. Think of inventing a machine that will make a record of sound and will reproduce that sound any number of times afterwards! Let one or more persons talk, sing, or whistle; let a band play, or a medley of sounds be poured into a phonograph arranged to receive it, and later each note received will be repeated over and over as often as the record is adjusted in the machine.

What Edison's phonograph does for sound, his kinetoscope does for sight. Who has not seen the wonderful "moving pictures" so full of life and action that it is hard to believe they are pictures at all?

But perhaps the greatest gift Mr. Edison has given the world so far is the incandescent light. The principal of this light is simple, but to apply it to practical use was an undertaking that for some time taxed even Mr. Edison's great genius. The trouble was to find the right material for the little coil which runs inside the air-tight glass bulb. He tried a piece of cotton thread that had been carbonized. He tried paper, manila hemp, and an endless variety of bamboo fibers. At last he adopted the platinum wire and gained success. Compare the bright, clear glow of these little bulbs with the smoky light of a whale-oil lamp and the feeble gleam of a candle, and you will realize what a marvelous invention is this of Thomas Edison's. It was in 1879 that Mr. Edison showed the world a complete system of lighting by electricity.

Will the wonderful inventor go on and do more? Here is his answer: "The achievement of the past is merely a point of departure, and you know that in our art, 'impossible' is an impossible word."

Richard M. Hoe

Printing was performed slowly and laboriously in colonial times. The press of Benjamin Franklin was a simple wooden affair. The type, held in form by wooden frames, was placed on a wooden bed and inked by hand. Then a sheet of paper was spread over it and a flat wooden plate, called a platen, was screwed down on the paper to press it against the type and make "an impression." The platen had to be screwed up again with a bar after each impression. It was tedious work at best.

Soon after Franklin's day, however, improvements in printing presses were made. By the time Richard M. Hoe, of New York, was twenty-one and had become the head of his father's printing-press factory, the cylinder press had been invented.

There were two kinds of cylinder presses, single and double cylinder machines. In the single cylinder press, the flat bed containing the type moved back and forth beneath a revolving cylinder about which was rolled the sheet to be printed. A press of this sort could turn out 2,000 impressions an hour. In the double cylinder press, the type traveled back and forth beneath two cylinders, turning out impressions twice as fast as the single cylinder press. On both these presses, however, printing was done only on one side of the sheet at a time.

The growing demand for news could not long be supplied even by these machines. In 1847, Richard M. Hoe made a press with the type form ingeniously fastened to a large revolving central cylinder about which were grouped from 4 to 10 cylinders carrying the paper to be printed. This greatly increased the output of a single press and did much to make cheap newspapers possible.

For some time, flat metal plates had been cast from the type forms and used in printing. Later, an invention was perfected whereby curved castings from the type forms were make to fit the revolving cylinders. Hoe used this invention in a new printing press, called the web-perfecting machine. This press printed a continuous roll on both sides, cut, folded, and delivered perfect papers at a rate of from 15,000 to 60,000 copies an hour depending on the size of the sheet.

To-day, still another press, made by Richard Hoe's son Robert, does more. In one hour it can print, paste, fold, and count 300,000 eight-page papers. The Hoe machine of to-day is made of 50,000 pieces of metal. Compare that with Franklin's simple wooden hand press. The age is different, the demand is different, and the output of the two presses differs as widely as either. Whereas, Franklin printed one page at a time and carefully laid it aside to dry while he re-inked his type, the Hoe printing press of to-day prints a strip of paper three feet wide on both sides at the rate of 120 miles an hour.

XXXI

Andrew Carnegie

On the 25th of November, 1837, Andrew Carnegie was born in Dunfermline, Scotland.

His father earned a modest living by making hand-woven linen and selling it to merchants. As time went on, the father became poorer and poorer because factories were being built, where steam was used to run the looms. This put an end to hand work, and ruined many a small weaver. Consequently the Carnegies turned their eyes to the New World.

It was a great sacrifice to the parents to leave their old home and friends; but they said, "It will be better for the boys." It was when their son Andrew was ten, that they embarked in a sailing vessel bound for America.

They settled in Allegheny City, Pennsylvania. Andrew was soon given work as a bobbin boy in a cotton mill, at one dollar and twenty cents a week. The father also was employed in the same place. The mother took in washing, besides working for a shoemaker.

The next year Andrew was promoted to the position of engine boy at a dollar and eighty cents a week. And after another year he secured work as a district messenger boy at three dollars a week.

In later years Mr. Carnegie thus describes this change in

his life: "My entrance into the telegraph office was a transition from darkness to light, from firing a small engine in a dark and dirty cellar to a clean office with bright windows and a literary atmosphere; with books, newspapers, pens and pencils all around me, I was the happiest boy alive."

ANDREW CARNEGIE.

While sitting on a bench waiting for orders he was not idle. He was constantly listening to the telegraph instruments, and before long learned how to translate the sounds made by the ticker. One morning before the operator arrived, there came a message over the wire. Andrew rushed to the receiver and took the message accurately. The messenger boys were not allowed to take messages, but he was forgiven and promoted to the position of operator with a salary of three hundred dollars a year. As he was supporting his mother and younger brother at this time, the increase in salary was very welcome to the lad of sixteen.

Carnegie was so ambitious and quick that he attracted the attention of Colonel Scott, the superintendent of the Pennsylvania Railroad, who made him the telegraph operator in his office. One day an accident occurred which threatened to block traffic for some time. Colonel Scott was away; so his operator took matters into his own hands, sent orders to all the trains, telling them what to do, and signed Scott's name to the orders. Although Carnegie had no authority to do this, the superintendent was pleased. The young man had done the right thing at the right moment. Later, when Carnegie had devised a plan for managing the train schedule by telegraph, Colonel Scott appointed him his private secretary. When he was twenty-eight he was made superintendent of the Western Division of the Pennsylvania Railroad.

It was to Carnegie that the inventor of the sleeping car brought his plans. Carnegie saw at a glance what a valuable idea it was, and secured the introduction of these cars into his division.

At about this time the Pennsylvania Railroad began to use iron bridges instead of wooden ones. Carnegie organized the Keystone Bridge Works and built the first iron bridge over the Ohio River. Then he saw the need of producing his own iron, so he erected furnaces and rolling mills. This business was not very profitable at first.

Carnegie's readiness to seize the right opportunity, however, and his ability to judge men made his business prosperous. One plant after another was added, until he had the largest steel and iron business in the country.

At Homestead, Pennsylvania, there are several immense establishments in which Carnegie has much money invested, although in 1901 he retired from active business. Here are made armor plates for the United States navy and building material of many kinds. Every working day over three thousand tons of steel ingots are turned out; and these are manufactured into a great variety of forms, from the steel rim of a bicycle to the armor plate of two hundred tons. These different articles are shipped all over the world. In six days, from one department, can be turned out all the material necessary for the great steel frame of a "skyscraper."

At the time of his retirement, Carnegie's company, which had been called The Carnegie Steel Company, and was valued at five hundred millions, was changed to The United States Steel Company. This was the fortune that Mr. Carnegie had built in the fifty years since, as a bobbin boy, he earned a dollar and twenty cents a week.

Mr. Carnegie has said that "the man who dies possessing millions, free and ready to be distributed, dies disgraced." He believes that "surplus wealth is a sacred trust to be administered for the highest good of the people." He is attempting to live up to that trust by distributing his own wealth, and by doing so wisely. He feels that if he gives his money without considering the needs and worth of those who receive it, he may be doing more mischief than good. So he has made it a rule to give only to those who help themselves. He has given many libraries and other public buildings, and in each case he obliges the town or city that receives the building and its endowment to pledge a certain amount each year to keep it in repair and pay the running expenses.

It was through an incident in his early life that Carnegie came to give libraries. While engaged in hard labor in Allegheny City, he was given the opportunity of browsing among the books of a small library. The owner had announced that on every Saturday he would be ready to lend books to working boys and men. Carnegie, remembering the pleasure given in this way, determined to use a good share of his millions in establishing libraries where he found the people willing to help.

Not only has he given libraries. Hospitals, public halls, baths, parks, churches, schools, and colleges are being built or helped through his kindness. His greatest single gift is Carnegie Institute at Pittsburg.

XXXII

The United States of America

Before the middle of the eighteenth century, thirteen colonies, all owing allegiance to England, were scattered along the Atlantic coast of North America. The settlers were Old World folks tempted across the seas either by fabled wealth, love of adventure, or an unconquerable desire to worship God as they saw fit.

There was little temptation to journey far from home. Great lumbering coaches, the saddled back of a horse, or small sailing boats offered the only means of travel. So for the most part the colonist was a stay-at-home.

Then came the cruel French and Indian War. A common danger threatened the thirteen colonies. For the first time the colonies united to fight a common foe. And they conquered!

But even while they still rejoiced in their victory England's king tried to tax the colonists unjustly. The colonists resisted. The king's grasp tightened, and Old England seemed about to crush her American children.

Then from colony after colony rose the cry for freedom. The struggle was long and bitter. At last the victory was won. The power of England, mighty England was broken. Her king had lost his grasp on his American colonies. And by their united courage, perseverance and pluck these colonies had gained their freedom and the world a new nation—the United States of America.

From the time the thirteen separate English colonies became the United States of America our country has grown and prospered. It is true we have fought a civil war in which the very unity of the Nation itself was at stake. But, terrible as it was, that very war established our union as "one and inseparable," and removed from us the stigma of being a slave-holding nation.

From the eastern shore of our land pioneers early began to work their way west. At first they rode on horseback, gun on shoulder, beside the lumbering canvas covered wagons that held their families and household goods. Some sought rich land for farming, others went in search of gold. But west, ever west they have pushed until those wildernesses, where herded the buffalo of old, have been turned into flourishing cities or widespread fields for the vast grain crops of America.

To-day railroads cross our country from the Atlantic to the Pacific. The old-time farming tools are being laid aside and great steam-driven machines plow the ground, sow the seeds and reap the harvests. Coal, silver, gold, and copper are mined. Factories of every sort are at work throughout the land. American-made locomotives, American steel bridges, American automobiles, sewing machines, type-writers, and many other products of American labor are known the whole world over. To-day America leads the nations of the world in the magnitude of her foreign trade.

Nor are we content with all this. Through annexation, purchase, and conquest we are still extending our dominion. Alaska, the Philippines, Porto Rico, and Hawaii have all become ours. Then, too, we have bought from the Republic of Panama the right to open a canal across that isthmus that our great merchant vessels and splendid battleships may pass easily and quickly from our eastern to our western coasts.

Growth and improvement have been the history of our land since the days of the Nation's birth. On that flag which floated over the plucky little states which won our independence were thirteen stars and thirteen stripes. To-day the American flag shows nearly fifty stars, each one representing a state in our union. The stripes still number thirteen. The number of our states may increase and our Nation's flag proudly boast the fact. But with even greater pride does it constantly proclaim that, do what they will, the Americans to come can never make to America as great a gift as did those men of the thirteen original states. We rejoice in America's greatness, her wide possessions, her immense achievements, but our glory, our great and lasting glory, is first and always America's freedom.

And America's freedom does not mean merely our independence of England's king. It means much more. It means that every citizen of our land, rich or poor, has a voice in the government of America; has a right to protest against oppression; has a claim to justice for himself or for his neighbor; has a chance to make of himself the best of which he is capable.

Prizing this freedom and glorying in it as we do, America has done a deed unprecedented in the history of the world. She has lent her strength to help the Cubans throw off the rule of a tyrannical power. She has then taught that people the lesson of self-government and left them free to rule their land.

In the harbor of New York stands a towering statue of Liberty holding high in her hand a flaming torch. And every night its light shines far out to sea, a beacon to all incoming ships, a welcoming guide to the land of the free—America.

Review Questions

I. Patrick Henry

1. Who governed the colonies at the close of the French and Indian War? At that time what was the feeling of the colonies toward that government?
2. What change did the war make in the feeling of the colonies toward one another? Why?
3. Why did King George III wish to tax the colonies? How did he try to do it?
4. Why did the colonists object to paying the tax? Who was the first American publicly to speak against it? Where and when was this speech made?
5. What were the resolutions adopted by the House of Burgesses?
6. What other laws that England was trying to enforce were unfair to the colonies? Why?

II. Samuel Adams

1. Who was Samuel Adams? Name four occasions on which he guided the Massachusetts colony.
2. Why did England repeal the Stamp Act? What did she substitute in its place? With what result?
3. Why were British regulars in Boston?
4. What was the effect of the Boston Massacre?
5. What were Committees of Correspondence, and why were they needed?
6. Describe the Boston Tea Party. What did England do to punish the colony for this? Why was it a severe punishment? How did the colony retaliate?

7.　What was the first battle of the American Revolution? What caused it? What were the soldiers of the colonists called? Why?

8.　What were the results of the fighting at Lexington and on Bunker Hill?

III. George Washington

1.　Tell what you can of Washington's family and of his boyhood in Virginia.

2.　What training had Washington had to make him a fit messenger for Governor Dinwiddie to send to the French commander?

3.　What was the object of his first journey to the Ohio? Describe his route.

4.　What was the object of General Braddock's campaign? Why was he not successful?

5.　Tell of four things that Washington did during his expeditions that showed him to be a good soldier.

IV. Washington, Commander and President

1.　Describe plantation life in Virginia.

2.　What was the First Continental Congress? Why did it meet? When and where?

3.　What important step was taken by the Second Continental Congress? Why?

4.　Compare Washington's army with England's forces in America.

5.　Describe briefly three campaigns during 1776, when Washington outwitted the English.

6.　What was the most important event of 1776? Why?

7.　Name three friends of Washington, and tell what each did to help the Revolution.

8.　How did Washington plan for the surrender at Yorktown? When did the war end?

9.　What did Washington do for his country after the war?

V. Philip Schuyler

1. At the beginning of 1777, what plan did England have for ending the war?
2. At the outset how did General Schuyler prove himself an able commander?
3. What three patriots greatly assisted Ceneral Schuyler, and how?
4. When, where, and to whom did General Burgoyne surrender? How is this explained? What were the effects of this victory?
5. Tell what you can of the story of our first American flag.

VI. NATHANAEL GREENE

1. In what colony was Nathanael Greene's native home? How was he honored there?
2. How did he come to have a command in Washington's army?
3. Why did Cornwallis undertake a southern campaign? Who opposed him before Nathanael Greene? Why was Greene appointed to the southern command?
4. What officer assisted General Greene in the South? What was Greene's plan of campaign?
5. Describe the flight of Greene's army.
6. How did Georgia reward General Greene?

VII. JOHN PAUL JONES

1. How was it that John Paul of Scotland became John Paul Jones of Virginia?
2. What was his first achievement in the American navy?
3. What were the exploits of the Ranger?
4. What was Paul Jones's greatest victory?
5. How did it happen that Paul Jones had funeral honors in 1905?

VIII. LAFAYETTE

1. In what year, and where, was the last battle of the Revolution?
2. What did Lafayette do for the American cause?
3. What kind of man was he as shown by his behavior at Monmouth?

4.   When did he last visit America? How did this country show its appreciation of his aid?

IX. ALEXANDER HAMILTON

1.   With what city is Alexander Hamilton most closely associated? In what ways? Describe some scene there in which he took part before the Revolution.

2.   What were "Liberty poles"? What name was given to the British sympathizers at this time?

3.   How did Alexander Hamilton win recognition as a soldier?

4.   At the close of the Revolution what difficulties proved the need of a National Constitution?

5.   Explain what is meant by "depreciated money."

6.   What did Hamilton do toward the adoption of the new Constitution?

7.   Who was the first President of the United States? When and where was he inaugurated?

8.   What position did Hamilton occupy during this administration? What did he accomplish?

9.   Recount the circumstances of Hamilton's death.

X. THOMAS JEFFERSON

1.   When did Jefferson enter upon public life? What training had he had for it?

2.   What was his greatest work? To whom was it submitted, and by whom adopted? Give the date of its adoption. What did the occasion mean to the American people? Why do we celebrate the 4th of July?

3.   What did Jefferson do for Virginia?

4.   Who were his predecessors in the Presidency? How did he differ from them in his ways of living?

5.   What was the territory of the United States at the beginning of Jefferson's administration? at the end? Account for this.

6.   Who were Lewis and Clark, and why are they famous?

XI. Daniel Boone

1. Why are the pioneer woodsmen to be counted important characters in our history?
2. What territory did Daniel Boone explore?
3. What was his route into the West?
4. Describe the fort at Boonesborough, and explain why it was built as it was.
5. How much farther west did Boone explore?

XII. Whitney and Howe

1. Where did Eli Whitney spend his youth?
2. How did he become interested in Georgia cotton?
3. Describe Whitney's cotton gin.
4. What difference did the cotton gin make to the planter? to the merchant? to the purchasers of retail goods?
5. How did it affect foreign commerce? the growth of the whole country?
6. How were clothes made in early colonial times?
7. Who invented the sewing machine? When? How did he come to do this? Tell what you can about his efforts.
8. How was the sewing machine received by tailors and those who sewed for a living? Why? What do we think of it to-day?

XIII. Robert Fulton

1. How did the early colonists travel from one settlement to another? In what kind of vessels did they cross the ocean? About how long did it take?
2. How long does it take now to go from this country to England?
3. What has brought about the change?
4. What were some of Robert Fulton's first inventions?
5. Where was Fulton's native home? In what city did he make his fame? Who was his friend and helper?
6. Describe the first trip of the *Clermont*.

7.   What scheme of Fulton's, discarded in his day, is now of great use to all the navies of the world?

xiv. George Stephenson

1.   Describe methods of land travel in colonial times.
2.   How quickly can a California senator to-day travel from his home to the National Capital?
3.   When was the first line of railroad across our country completed? When was our first railroad opened? Where?
4.   Had there been steam engines before Stephenson's Rocket? For what were they used? Give the story of Stephenson's boyhood and early work.
5.   In what ways have railroads helped this country?

xv. Oliver Hazard Perry

1.   Why did America have war with England in 1812?
2.   What work did this Government have for Perry to do? What were his forces? How did he prepare to defend his position?
3.   What training had fitted Perry for such work?
4.   What famous command was on Perry's flag? By whom was it spoken first?
5.   Quote Perry's message which has become famous in our naval history. What did it mean?
6.   Why was the battle of Lake Erie a very important one?

xvi. Thomas Macdonough

1.   What was the combined attack planned by the British in 1814?
2.   Describe the battle of Lake Champlain.
3.   Where else had Thomas Macdonough fought for his country? Under whom?
4.   How did the Barbary pirates exact tribute?

XVII. Andrew Jackson

1. During what events of our history was Andrew Jackson born? Where was he born?
2. What part did he take in the different wars of our country during his lifetime? What great victory did he win?
3. Where did he spend most of his manhood? What were his occupations there?
4. What Government positions did he hold? When did he go to the White House?
5. Explain one of the great National disputes during Jackson's administration. What two men led the great debate in the Senate? What were Jackson's views?

XVIII. Henry Clay

1. How did Henry Clay fit himself to be a lawyer?
2. What state did he represent in Congress? In what position?
3. What topics were interesting Congress during Clay's first two terms? during his later years in Congress?
4. Why did one half of our country hold to slavery and the other half not?
5. What conditions led Clay to offer the Missouri compromise? For what did it provide? When was it adopted?
6. What conditions led to another compromise in 1850? What were the terms of this? What name was given to this compromise? Why?
7. What name has been given to Clay, and why?

XIX. Daniel Webster

1. Tell the story of Daniel Webster's love for the Constitution. Where and how was Webster educated?
2. Who were some of Webster's associates in Congress?
3. What was the great question of debate argued by Webster and Clay between 1813 and 1828?
4. What was the question of 1830? Who opposed Webster in this?

5.　For what principle does Webster stand in the history of our country?

6.　Describe Daniel Webster as an orator.

7.　What stand did Webster take which injured his chances for the Presidency?

xx. De Witt Clinton

1.　Why was it desirable to have a canal across New York State? What are the terminal points of the Erie Canal?

2.　After the canal was completed, what changes did it make in the growth of commerce? in the cost of goods? in the growth of New York State?

3.　To whom chiefly was the building of the canal due? How was the cost of building it defrayed? Did the building of it prove a financial gain or loss to the State, and why?

4.　Describe the opening of the Erie Canal. When was this?

xxi. Samuel F. B. Morse

1.　What were the different ways of sending messages before the invention of the telegraph?

2.　Why could not the sealed letter be sent by telegraph?

3.　Who was the inventor of the telegraph? What was the first message sent?

4.　What was the great work of Cyrus W. Field? What was the Great Eastern? How many attempts were made to lay a cable across the Atlantic, and between what years? How does the cable differ from our land telegraph lines?

5.　When was the telephone first exhibited? Who was its inventor?

6.　What is the chief feature of Marconi's telegraph system?

xxii. Abraham Lincoln

1.　Taking the Lincoln family as a type, describe the life of a Kentucky settler before 1820.

2. What were the happenings of most importance to Lincoln in his boyhood?

3. In what places in the West did Lincoln live? What circumstances decided his going to each?

4. In what war did Lincoln serve as Captain? What public offices did he hold before 1860?

5. What qualities of Lincoln made him both beloved by his neighbors and a worthy candidate for public office?

6. Who was Lincoln's chief opponent in politics? What bill did he offer in Congress? In what year?

7. What was the result of Douglas's bill? Give the story of John Brown.

8. What was the famous court decision of 1857?

XXIII. Lincoln and the Civil War

1. When was Lincoln inaugurated President?

2. Which were the first states to secede? How did they govern themselves after they left the Union? What other states soon joined them? Was slavery or secession the immediate cause of the war?

3. When and where did the Civil War begin? What was Lincoln's attitude on the question of slavery?

4. What was the objective point of attack of the North for the first year of the war? of the South? Why?

5. What were some of the great battles between 1861 and 1863? At the end of that time what had been gained by each side?

6. What change in the condition of the South was made at the beginning of 1863? What great battles hastened the war to a close? When did it end?

7. What were the circumstances of Lincoln's death?

XXIV. Ulysses S. Grant

1. Where was the home of Grant's boyhood?

2. What military training and experience did Grant have before the Civil War?

3.   What was the cause of the Mexican War?

4.   Describe General Grant. Tell what made him a good commander.

5.   Give an account of his great campaign in the West.

6.   What were his plans in 1864 for ending the war? What two generals greatly assisted him?

7.   Quote three famous sentences spoken by Grant, and give the circumstances in which each was said.

XXV. ROBERT E. LEE

1.   Tell what you know of the home life and family of Robert E. Lee.

2.   What was Lee's military training and experience before 1861?

3.   Who was President of the Confederacy? What advantage did the North have over the South at the opening of the war? What was the effect on each side of the first battle of Bull Run?

4.   Who were the successive Union commanders in the East, and in what important battles did they command? Why was so much of the war fought in Virginia and Maryland?

5.   What was General Lee doing from the summer of 1864 to April, 1865? What was the importance of this? Give the events of April, 1865.

6.   What kind of man was General Lee? Give incidents and quotations to illustrate what you say.

XXVI. DAVID GLASGOW FARRAGUT

1.   What war was going on while Farragut was a boy, and what part did he take in it?

2.   On what occasion did Farragut escort a Revolutionary commander?

3.   What kind of ships were most of our war vessels before 1854?

4.   How did Farragut differ from Lee in deciding his part in the Civil War?

5.   What were Farragut's two greatest naval battles? When? Why were these two points important for the North to take?

6.   Describe the action of Farragut's fleet on the Mississippi.

7. Describe the kinds of vessels used in the Battle of Mobile Bay? Tell what you know of Farragut himself in this battle.

8. Name three other famous vessels and three naval commanders of the Civil War, telling what part each took.

XXVII. Cyrus McCormick

1. What year marked the great change in grain farming? How had grain been harvested before this?

2. What can McCormick's one harvesting machine do? How much labor does it save?

3. From what you have read and, if possible, from your own observations, describe the parts of one of these machines.

4. What was McCormick's home state? Why did he go west? Where did he build his factories? What great characteristic had Cyrus McCormick besides inventive power?

XXVIII. Clara Barton

1. For what was the Red Cross Society organized, and what are some of the things it does?

2. When and by whom was it organized in this country? What took the place of such a body during the Civil War? Name two other women who helped this commission.

3. Where did the Red Cross Society originate? What is the American Red Cross Society? Name some disasters in times of peace, in which it has worked.

4. Where and when has this American Society done work outside of our own land?

5. What influence do you think that this whole Society has had on the spirit of modern warfare?

XXIX. George Dewey

1. What reason did the United States have for fighting Spain in 1898? What was the immediate cause of the declaration of war?

2.   Who was President of the United States at that time? What were the two important moves to be made by the American forces?

3.   What squadron was ordered to attack the Spanish fleet in the Philippines? Why? Who commanded it?

4.   What had been Commodore Dewey's career before this battle? What promotion did he receive afterwards?

Xxx. Edison and Hoe

1.   How were houses lighted before the use of gas and electricity?

2.   When and by whom was lighting by electricity accomplished?

3.   What had been Edison's chief work before he went to Menlo Park? What improvements has he made in telegraphy?

4.   Name and describe as well as you can two other inventions of his.

5.   Describe Benjamin Franklin's printing press. How was a cylinder press an improvement over the press of Franklin's day? Why were not the single and double cylinder presses perfectly satisfactory?

6.   What kind of printing press did Richard M. Hoe invent in 1847? What did it accomplish?

7.   What other kind of press did Hoe make? How did it differ from his earlier one?

8.   Tell about the printing press of to-day and what it can do.

Xxxi. Andrew Carnegie

1.   To what does Mr. Carnegie owe his success in life?

2.   What is the name of the great business that he has built? What does this business supply to the world? Where are its headquarters?

3.   How did Mr. Carnegie work up to the founding of such a business?

4.   In what ways has Mr. Carnegie used his millions to help the world?

5.   Where was Mr. Carnegie born?

Chronology

1765.	Parliament passes the Stamp Act.
1766.	Stamp Act repealed and Declaratory Act passed.
1767.	Duties placed on glass, paper, paints, and tea.
1768.	English troops land in Boston.
1770.	Boston Massacre, *March 3rd.*
1773.	All duties repealed but that on tea.
	Boston Tea Party.
1774.	Boston port closed.
	First Continental Congress.
1775.	Second Continental Congress.
	Battles of Lexington and Concord, *April 19th.*
	Washington appointed Commander-in-chief.
	Battle of Bunker Hill, *June 17th.*
1776.	British evacuate Boston, *March 17th.*
	Declaration of Independence signed, *July 4th.*
	Battle of Long Island, *August 22nd.*
	Washington's retreat across New Jersey.
	Battle of Trenton, *December 26th.*
1777.	Battle of Princeton, *January 3rd.*
	Washington's army at Morristown.
	Battle of Beoniogton, *August 16th.*
	Battle of Brandywine, *September 11th.*
	Battle of Bemis Heights, *September 19th.*
	Howe enters Philadelphia.
	Battle of Germantown, *October 4th.*
	Battle of Stillwater, *October 7th.*
	Burgoyne's surrender, *October 11th.*
	Washington's arrival at Valley Forge.

1778.	France acknowledges America's independence.
	British leave Philadelphia.
	Battle of Monmouth, *June 28th.*
	Savannah captured, *December 29th.*
1779.	Paul Jones captures the *Serapis, September 23rd.*
1780.	Fall of Charleston, *May 12th.*
	Battle of Camden, *August 16th.*
	Arnold's treason.
	Battle of King's Mountain, *October 7th.*
1781.	Battle of Cowpens, *January 17th.*
	Greene's retreat north through the Carolinas.
	Battle of Guilford Court House, *March 16th.*
	Cornwallis in Virginia.
	British surrender at Yorktown, *October 19th.*
1783.	Treaty of peace with England.
1787.	Federal convention frames the Constitution.
1789-1797.	Washington, President.
1791.	United States Bank established.
1792.	United States Mint established.
1793.	Whitney invents the cotton gin.
1797-1801.	John Adams, President.
1800.	City of Washington becomes the National Capital.
1801-1809.	Jefferson, President.
1801-1805.	War with Tripoli.
1803.	Purchase of Louisiana.
1804.	Lewis and Clarke Expedition.
1807.	Fulton launches the Clermont.
1812.	War declared against England.

1813. Battle of Lake Erie, *September 10th.*

1814. Battle of Plattsburg, *September 11th.*
Treaty of Ghent.

1815. Battle of New Orleans, *January 8th.*

1819. First Steamship crosses the Atlantic.

1820. Missouri compromise.

1824. Lafayette visits America.

1825. Opening of the Erie Canal.

1830. Opening of the first steam railway.

1834. McCormick invents the reaper.

1844. Morse sends the first telegraph message.

1845. Texas annexed.

1846. Elias Howe patents the sewing machine.
War declared against Mexico.
Battle of Monterey, *September 24th.*

1847. Fall of the City of Mexico, *September 14th.*
Richard M. Hoe invents a type-revolving rotary-printing press.

1848. Treaty of peace with Mexico.

1850. Omnibus Bill.

1854. The Kansas-Nebraska bill.

1857. Dred Scott decision.

1858. First Atlantic cable laid.

1859. John Brown's raid on Harper's Ferry, *October 16th.*

1860. Secession of South Carolina.

1861. Confederacy formed.

1861-1865. Civil War.

1861-1865. Lincoln, President.

1861. Fort Sumter fired upon, *April 12th.*

Norfolk Navy Yard seized, *April 20th.*
Battle of Bull Run, *July 21st.*

1862.   Attack on Fort Henry, *February 6th.*
Attack on Fort Donelson, *February 16th.*
Battle between the *Monitor* and the *Merrimac,*
March 9th.
Battle of Shiloh, *April 6th-7th.*
Farragut takes New Orleans, *April 25th.*
Lee takes command of the Confederate army.
Seven Days' battles, *June 26th - July 1st.*
Pope's campaign in Virginia, *August.*
Second battle of Bull Run, *August 30th.*
Battle of Antietam, *September 17th.*
Battle of Fredericksburg, *December 13th.*

1863.   Lincoln's Emancipation Proclamation, *January*
1st.
Battle of Cliancellorsville, *May 2rd-3rd.*
Battle of Gettysburg, *July 1st-3rd.*
Fall of Vicksburg, *July 4th.*
Capture of Port Hudson, *July 9th.*
Siege of Chattanooga, *October-November.*

1864.   Grant made Lieutenant, General.
Campaign in the Wilderness.
Battle of Cold Harbor, *June 3rd.*
Battle between the *Kearsarge* and the *Alabama,*
June 19th.
Destruction of the *Albemarle,* October.
Battle of Mobile Bay, *August 5th.*
Sherman takes Atlanta, *September 2nd.*
Sherman takes Savannah, *December 22nd.*

1865.   Capture of Petersburg, *April 2nd.*

Grant takes Richmond, *April 3rd.*

Lee's surrender, *April 9th.*

Assassination of Lincoln, *April 14th.*

1866. Second Atlantic cable laid.

1869-1877. Grant, President.

1869. Pacific Railroad completed, *May 10th.*

1871. All states again represented in Congress.

1889. Johnstown flood.

1898. Destruction of the *Maine, Febmary 15th.*

War with Spain declared.

Battle of Manila Bay, *May 1st.*

1899. Treaty of peace with Spain.